Three of a KIND

THREE OF A KIND
With Friends Like These,
Who Needs Enemies?
Home's a Nice Place to Visit,
But I Wouldn't Want to Live There
Will the Real Becka Morgan Please Stand Up?

SISTERS
Phoebe
Cassie
Daphne
Lydia

A Friend Like Phoebe

Two's Company, Four's a Crowd

Cat Morgan, Working Girl

101 Ways to Win Beauty Queen

Marilyn Kaye

This edition published 1994 by Diamond Books
77–85 Fulham Palace Road
Hammersmith, London W6 8JB

Printed and bound in Great Britain

ISBN 0 261 66448 4

Two's Company,
Four's a Crowd

For Polly Winograd

One

At noon on the first Friday in November, the cafeteria at Green Falls Junior High was in its usual state of noisy commotion. Cat Morgan picked up her lunch tray and started towards her table. Along the way, she was greeted by several classmates at other tables, and she paused to chat briefly with a few. Finally she reached the table where she'd been having lunch every weekday for the past two months.

"Hi, guys," she hailed her lunchmates.

"Hi," they chorused as Cat sat down.

"Your hair's different," Marla Eastman noticed. "What did you do, get a perm?"

"No," Cat replied, fingering a glossy black ringlet. "I just used hot curlers."

"How come?" Trisha Heller asked.

"I don't know. I felt like doing something different." She moved her head from side to side. "What do you think?"

5

Marla, Trisha, Sharon, Karen, and Britt all stopped eating and gave Cat's hair their full attention. Cat waited for them to pass judgment.

"It's cute," Britt stated.

"I like it," Sharon and Karen said simultaneously.

Marla wasn't so quick to approve. "It's okay, but I like it better straight."

Cat wasn't disturbed by her comment. Since Marla was her closest friend, Cat felt she was entitled to criticise. "You just want to be the only one with curly hair," she told Marla in a teasing voice. Marla ran a hand through her mass of dark curls and grinned.

"I wish I could change *my* hair," Trisha said. "Sometimes I'm sorry I had it cut so short. It always looks the same."

"Short hair suits you," Cat assured her.

"But don't you think it's kind of boring?" Trisha asked anxiously.

This set off one of their typical lunchtime discussions, arguing the merits of short hair versus long hair. As the conversation took its usual course, Cat's attention wandered and she began looking around the cafeteria.

Everything looked so familiar, as if she'd been coming here for all of her thirteen years. It was weird to think that only three months ago she'd been a total stranger, not just to this school, but to Green Falls, Vermont. Before that, she'd been Cat O'Grady of Willoughby Hall, an orphan. Then Annie and Ben Morgan came into her life and everything changed. Now, here she was, adopted, with a new home, new parents, and a new name.

To top it all off, she'd become a recognised person at school, with very cool friends and a boyfriend who was co-captain of the football team. She had everything she'd ever wanted.

Unfortunately, there was something else that came with adoption. Sisters. Not content with getting one daughter, Annie and Ben had adopted two other thirteen-year-old girls, Cat's Willoughby Hall roommates. A sigh escaped her lips as she spotted one of them.

"What are you moaning about?" Marla demanded.

Cat responded simply, "Look at Josie."

Heads turned in the direction Cat indicated. Sharon, who was supposed to wear glasses but wouldn't because she was so vain, squinted. "Is she sitting with *boys*?"

Cat nodded sadly. It was an unwritten law at Green Falls Junior High that boys sat with boys in the cafeteria and girls sat with girls. Cat had figured that out the first week of school. It was okay to stop by a boy's table and talk, and the boys could do the same with the girls. But you never sat down with the opposite sex. Cat wasn't sure why, but that didn't matter. It was the way

7

things were. Either Josie was so dense that she hadn't picked up on it, or she was intentionally disregarding the rules.

"Who are they?" Sharon asked. Her eyes became narrow slits as she tried to make out Josie's lunch companions.

Cat couldn't get a good look at the faces, but the boys were taller than the average junior high student. "Basketball players," she decided.

"That makes sense," Marla said. "She's on the team."

"The only girl on the boys' basketball team," Britt mused. "Doesn't that make her feel weird?"

"Are you kidding?" Cat snorted. "Sometimes Josie thinks she *is* a boy."

Karen giggled. "You know, from a distance she almost looks like one, with her short hair and those beat-up jeans."

"Not to mention the fact that she has no figure whatsoever," Cat added. "And she doesn't even care."

"Hi, Becka," Marla called out.

Cat turned to see her other sister coming towards their table.

"You want to join us?" Marla asked.

"No, thanks," the short, fair-haired girl replied. "I have to go to a newspaper staff meeting. Cat, did Mademoiselle Casalls hand back the French quizzes this morning?"

Cat nodded. "I got a B plus."

"Do you have her for French, too?" Trisha asked Becka.

Becka nodded. "Fifth period." She started chewing on a fingernail.

"Stop that," Cat scolded her. "And don't tell me you're worried about getting the quiz back." She turned to the others. "Becka's made As on every French quiz this term. You can imagine how that makes *me* look."

"You could be making As if you really wanted to," Becka pointed out.

Cat sniffed. "Yeah, if I had my very own private bedroom to study in." The fact that Becka had gotten the newly renovated bedroom at home still rankled her. Especially when *she* was still sharing a room with Josie, and there was no telling when Ben would get another bedroom done.

"That wouldn't help," Britt said. "I've got my own room and I'm still making Bs."

"Hey, Cat, don't faint, but look who's coming," Becka said.

Cat looked up to see Todd Murphy and two other boys heading up the aisle. Becka batted her eyes and pretended to swoon. Cat made a face at her. Becka giggled and took off.

Cat rearranged her features and formed her special smile as Todd drew nearer. He responded with his appealing lopsided grin and paused at the table. "How ya doing?"

"Fine," Cat said. "How are you?" She tossed

9

her head so the new curls bobbed around her shoulders. Todd didn't seem to notice the new hairdo. Of course, she wasn't surprised. He never noticed things like that.

"Great," he said, shifting his weight from one foot to the other. One of the boys with him snickered.

"Uh, so I'll see ya later," Todd said hastily, and moved on with the boys.

Cat shook her head wearily as she gazed after his retreating figure. "What a great conversationalist."

"He doesn't need to be a good talker with eyes like that," Karen said. "Cat, you're so lucky."

Cat had to admit she was probably right. Todd was considered a great catch.

"What are you and Todd going to do this weekend?" Trisha asked.

Cat considered the question. "Well, it's Friday, right? That means there's a football game after school. First, I'll watch Todd play, then we'll go over to my house for dinner. After that, we'll probably sit around and watch TV. On Saturday night we'll go to Luigi's for pizza, then to the movies. If we've already seen the movie, we'll go bowling. And then we'll go to Brownies for ice cream.

Marla raised her eyebrows. "Isn't that exactly what you did last weekend?"

Cat nodded. "And the weekend before that,

and the weekend before that." She looked up at the clock. "I better get going. I have to stop at my locker. See you guys at the game."

She picked up her tray and headed to the conveyor belt. Just as she was putting her tray down, she felt someone come up alongside her. She turned her head and met two eyes not quite as green as her own.

Her lips automatically formed a stiff, even smile. "Hello, Heather."

Heather Beaumont's face bore an identical expression. "Hello, Cat."

That was the extent of their conversation. Cat watched thoughtfully as Heather sauntered away, her long blonde hair cascading down her shoulders. No one would ever in a million years call them friends, but at least now they were acting civilly to each other.

Which was a definite improvement, considering their past relationship. It had started on registration day, when Heather had conned Cat into choosing the strictest teacher in school for English. Cat retaliated by flirting with Todd, who was Heather's numero uno back then. Heather tried to get back at her by setting up a public humiliation for Becka and arranging to keep Josie off the basketball team. Cat not only managed to rescue her sisters, she also got the ultimate revenge – snaring Todd.

By now, Heather must have realised that Cat

Morgan was not to be pushed around. She was off the warpath. It was hard for Cat to believe Heather had actually given up, but if she'd wanted to get back at Cat, she would have pulled something by now. All had been peaceful between them lately.

Too peaceful. In the strangest way, Cat sort of missed the excitement of wondering when, where, and how Heather would strike next.

That's crazy, Cat told herself sternly. *Everything's perfect. You're pretty and popular, and you haven't a care in the world.*

Then why did she feel so . . . so *blah*?

Becka tried very hard not to daydream in French class. She couldn't afford to, since Mademoiselle Casalls always seemed to know when someone's attention was drifting away. Besides, Becka was enchanted by the teacher's voice, with its beautiful, exotic accent.

She was fun to watch, too. Her face was expressive, and as she talked she used her hands a lot, making dramatic gestures to emphasise what she was saying. And her clothes were very stylish. Cat was always talking about how chic Mademoiselle Casalls was. It was one of the few subjects she and Becka agreed on.

Gazing at the teacher now, Becka admired her look. Maybe someday *she'd* wear a short black skirt and a white silk blouse, with a bright red scarf at the neck and huge gold hoop earrings. She tired to envision herself looking as sophisticated as her teacher, with long red nails and lips the exact same colour. But try as she might, all she saw in her mind was a short, frizzy-haired, slightly chunky thirteen-year-old with chewed fingernails.

"Becka!"

Becka's vision cleared. "*Oui*, mademoiselle?"

"Please, *s'il vous plâit*, I must have your full attention!"

She spoke kindly, with a smile, but Becka flushed. From the seat in front of her, her friend Patty turned and winked in sympathy.

"Now, class," the teacher continued, "I shall distribute your examinations. Some of you did very well, and I am pleased." Then the corners of her mouth turned down. "But most of you . . . *ooh la la*, you must begin to study!"

She began passing out the papers. Becka automatically began chewing on her thumbnail. At this rate, she'd never have nails like Mademoiselle Casalls.

The teacher stood before her. Her blue eyes warmed as she presented the paper to Becka. "*Très bien*, Becka! Very good." To the class, she announced, "Becka had the only score which was perfect!"

Once again, Becka flushed, but this time

with pleasure. She sensed, rather than saw, the admiring glances from some of her classmates. Of course, there was probably a hostile look from one or two, but that didn't bother her. Her friend Patty turned again and gave her a thumbs-up sign.

The bell rang, and everyone began gathering up their books. "What a relief," Patty told Becka. "I only missed two."

"I can't believe I got all those conjugations," Becka said. "Are you going to the game after school?"

"Yeah," Patty replied. "Meet me and Lisa at my locker, and we'll sit together, okay?" They headed for the door. A boy stood there, looking at his paper with a rueful expression. He was blocking their way.

"Excuse me," Becka murmured.

He looked up. "Sorry," he said and stepped inside. He indicated his test paper. "I really blew this one."

"I gotta run," Patty said. She took off down the hall. But there was something about the boy's deep brown eyes that held Becka there in the doorway.

"It was harder than usual," she said.

He grinned. "But not for you, right?" Pulling her paper out from between her notebooks, he whistled. "You must really study this stuff."

He's cute, Becka thought. *But he probably*

14

thinks I'm some boring brainy type who buries herself in books. "Not *that* much," she said.

He grinned. "Okay, I guess maybe you're just a natural genius. Check this out." He held up his own paper and hung his head in mock shame.

Trying not to appear shocked by the big red D on the paper, Becka said, "Gee, I'm sorry."

He shrugged. "It's not your fault. I'm just a lazy bum." His eyes were dancing.

"I'm sure that's not true," Becka said quickly. "I mean, some subjects come easier to some people than to others."

"Right," he said. "That's life."

Becka repeated his words in French. *"C'est la vie."*

He laughed. "See? You *are* a genius!" With a wave, he took off.

Becka's skin was tingling and her heart was pounding as she walked in the opposite direction. Her mind raced through the roll call until she reached his name. Keith Doyle.

He had the nicest smile. . . .

The entire crowd in the bleachers stood up, and a deafening roar filled the air. Cat rose with the others and assumed the noise meant that Green Falls had won the game. She'd spent the past half hour filing her nails.

Out on the field, the players were slapping

each other on the back and heading over to the door leading to the gym. The cheerleaders, led by Heather, went into a final chorus of "Green Falls Forever," and people began moving out of the bleachers.

"How did Todd do?" Cat asked Britt.

Britt looked at her in surprise. "Didn't you see? He scored two touchdowns!"

"Isn't that what he scored last week?" Cat asked. "I think he's in a rut."

When they reached the bottom of the bleachers, Cat turned to her friends. "Where are you guys going?"

"Back to my house," Marla said. "My sister said maybe she'd take us all to Dream Burger."

Cat eyed them enviously. She'd always wanted to go to Dream Burger. It was the major high school hangout in Green Falls, and no junior high student dared go there without being accompanied by a high school student. "Lucky you," she said.

"Lucky *us*?" Trisha's eyebrows shot up. "*You're* the one with a real live date!"

"Yeah, I guess," Cat said. She waved good-bye to her friends and pulled her jacket tighter against the brisk autumn wind.

"Great game, huh?" Josie stood there, her hands deep in the pockets of her windbreaker.

"Was it?" Cat asked vaguely.

"Weren't you watching?"

16

"Yeah, sure."

Josie looked at her reprovingly. "Your boyfriend's co-captain, Cat. The least you could do is try to understand the game."

Cat made a "who cares?" gesture. "Josie, if you knew anything about boys, you'd realise that it doesn't matter if you understand football or not."

Becka joined them. "You guys going home?"

"I have to wait for Todd," Cat said. "He's coming over for dinner."

"So's Red," Josie said.

"That's nice," Becka said, but something in her face caught Cat's eye.

"What's your problem?"

"Nothing . . . it's just that, well, you've got Todd, and Josie's got Red—"

"Wait a minute," Josie interrupted. "There's a big difference. Red's a friend, not a date. I mean, he lives next door, for crying out loud."

"The boy next door," Becka repeated. "That's the name of a romance book I read." Her eyes shifted away from Josie's face and seemed to focus on something beyond her.

"Well, there's nothing romantic about me and Red MacPherson," Josie retorted. "So don't start drumming up one of your usual fantasies. I better go find him. See you at home."

"She's always saying that about Red," Cat noted. "Personally, I think it's bull. I mean, why would she hang around with him all the time if she wasn't feeling at least a tiny bit romantic about him?"

Becka didn't respond. She was distracted by a group of passing boys. One of them wore a baseball cap, and he tipped it as he passed. "*Bonjour*, mademoiselle!"

Becka giggled. "It's too late for *bonjour*," she called after him. "*Bonsoir*, monsieur!"

"How do you know Keith Doyle?" Cat asked.

"He's in my French class. Don't you think he's cute?"

"Very. Well, I guess I ought to go meet Todd."

"Mmm." Becka was still staring after Keith Doyle.

As she walked over to the gym entrance, Cat wondered if she had time to run into the building and fix her hair and make-up. She decided it wasn't worth the effort. Todd wouldn't even notice.

Behind her, she heard two people talking in French. She turned and saw Mademoiselle Casalls with a man. "*Bonjour*, mademoiselle," she said, and then remembered Becka's words to Keith Doyle "I mean, *bonsoir*."

"*Bonsoir*, Catherine," the French teacher replied. She introduced Cat to the man by her side. "This is my very good friend Monsieur Christophe Durand, who is visiting from Paris."

18

He murmured something that sounded like "enchanted."

"How do you do?" Cat said politely. Meanwhile, she was thinking that this Monsieur Durand had to be the handsomest man she'd ever seen. He looked like a movie star. And he wasn't just good-looking. Even in casual jeans, he had style. She loved the way he had a sweater tied around his shoulders.

"My, it is getting cold," Mademoiselle Casalls murmured. Her friend whipped off his sweater and placed it around her shoulders. *"Merci, mon cheri,"* she murmured. *"Au revoir,* Catherine."

"Au revoir," Cat echoed. With appreciation, she watched the couple walk away. It was so romantic how he had his hand lightly on her arm, like a real escort.

"Hiya, babe." Todd stood there, his freshly washed hair hanging over his forehead in wet clumps.

Cat tore her eyes away from the French couple and smiled at Todd. "Hi. Congratulations. That was a great game."

Todd nodded. "Yeah, wild, huh? Did you see Erickson make that pass in the third quarter?"

They started off towards the Morgan home, and Todd began a blow-by-blow description of the game. As he talked, Cat smiled and nodded and occasionally gasped. Every once in a while she said, "Really?" and "Oh, wow," and "You're kidding!" In the past few weeks, it had become a routine. Todd talked sports, and Cat pretended to listen. She used the time to mentally put together her outfits for the next school week.

Finally, they reached the big old farmhouse the Morgans called home. Every time she walked up the driveway, Cat recalled her dismay the first time she saw the place. It had looked like a rundown dump to her. But a month ago, Ben had finally fixed the lopsided shutters and the sagging porch. Now, it looked like – well, still a little rundown, but it looked like home.

Todd was still rambling on about the game as they climbed the steps, automatically avoiding the one that creaked. Annie appeared at the door. "Hi, we were wondering about you guys! Come on in, dinner's on the table."

"Great," Todd said. "I'm starving. I think I could eat a horse."

Cat grimaced. That was what he *always* said.

But the sight of the dinner table cheered her. Josie had been giving Annie cooking lessons, and they were beginning to pay off. Plus, she had to admit there was something nice about seeing the whole family gathered around the table in the cosy dining room. The setting sun peeking through the windows bathed the room in a golden light. Remembering her years sitting with a bunch of screeching orphans at long tables in a huge, ugly dining hall, Cat found herself smiling happily as she kissed Ben on the cheek and took her seat.

The platters of chicken, roast potatoes, and green beans began making the rounds. "How was the game?" Ben asked Todd.

Cat closed her eyes and stifled a groan. That was the wrong question. Now she'd have to listen – or not listen – to the whole story all over again. And with Ben, Annie, Red, and Josie urging Todd on and showing actual interest, Todd went into even more detail.

Tuning him out, Cat concentrated on her food. As she ate, her eyes roamed the table. Annie and Ben . . . even though they'd been married for at least fifteen years, they still seemed to love each other. Cat wondered how they were able to make a relationship last so long. Probably because they had so much in common, she decided. Like fixing up this old house, the health-food store across the street, their daughters.

She looked at Josie and Red, both of whom were bombarding Todd with questions about the game. They had a lot in common, too. Red hair, for one thing. Also they were practical, they didn't care about clothes or social things, and they were both seriously into sports and horses.

Her eyes shifted to Becka. Becka's head was down as she ate, and Cat suspected there was a book on her lap, hidden by the tablecloth. Someday, Cat mused, Becka would meet a boy she had stuff in common with, and . . . they'd read to each other or something.

Then she looked at Todd. His face was animated as he described how he'd tackled some guy on the other team. His true-blue eyes were gleaming like sapphires, and his hair, now dry, hung like silk down his forehead. He was awfully good-looking.

The girls at school were right, Cat assured herself. She *was* lucky.

She poked at her green beans and considered Mademoiselle Casalls and her French boyfriend. What were they doing right now? Probably sitting in some fancy restaurant, the kind with candles and flowers on the table and soft music in the background. Maybe, right now, they were gazing deeply into each other's eyes and clinking their glasses of champagne.

What would they be talking about? Cat didn't have the faintest idea. But she had a pretty good feeling it wasn't football.

Two

Saturday mornings were the only really busy times in Morgan's Country Foods, and this week was no exception. For three hours, Cat had been behind the checkout counter ringing up purchases. Annie ran from one customer to another, while Ben hastily scrawled prices on cards to put up in front of the fruit bins. Becka was scurrying around, gathering items in a basket for a phone-in order.

"Becka, please put this by the apples," Ben called, waving a price sign in the air.

At the same time, Annie's voice rang out. "Becka, could you check in the back for strawberry jam?"

Becka plunked the basket down on the checkout counter. "I've only got two hands," she muttered before heading to the back of the store.

Cat had to grin. Back when they'd first arrived at the Morgans', Becka had been Little Miss Perfect, working like a maniac and never

23

complaining. Now that she was comfortable and secure in her new home, she could whine like a normal teenager.

"That will be four seventy-five," Cat told the waiting customer. She took the woman's money, gave her some change, and handed over a bag of purchases.

There was a momentary lull in activity at the checkout counter. Cat had just plunked her elbows on the counter and rested her chin in her hands when the telephone rang. With a weary sigh, she reached for it. "Morgan's Country Foods."

"Cat, hi, it's Marla."

Cat brightened. The girls weren't supposed to use the store phone for social calls, but both Annie and Ben were occupied, so she relaxed. "Hi. What's up? Did you guys go to Dream Burger last night?"

"No, my sister had a last-minute date and finked out on us. But that's why I'm calling. She says she'll take me there for lunch in about fifteen minutes. Want to come?"

"I'd love to!" Cat exclaimed. She lowered her voice as two more customers walked in. "I don't know how I'm going to get out of here, though. But I'll think of something."

"Great. Meet us in front of Dream Burger at one."

Hanging up the phone, Cat looked around.

Josie was still at basketball practice. It had gotten fairly quiet in the store, but that probably wouldn't last. She knew it wouldn't be very nice to leave them all in the lurch, but how many chances did she get to go to Dream Burger? She resumed her position of elbows on counter, her chin in her hands.

Annie joined her at the counter. "Whew, what a morning. What time is it?"

"Quarter to one," Cat replied automatically.

Annie eyed her curiously. "Why so glum?"

Cat searched her mind for a good reason to leave the store. For once, her mental bag of excuses was empty. She couldn't think of even one acceptable story.

She gave up. "Marla's invited me to go to Dream Burger with her and her sister. In fifteen minutes."

Annie nodded. "Well, Josie should be back from practice in a few minutes, and you've been working awfully hard. I think you deserve a break."

Cat gazed at her in disbelief. "You mean, I can go?"

"Of course. Have a good time."

Amazing, Cat thought as she raced out of the store. Sometimes honesty really *was* the best policy.

There was just enough time to go home, pull a brush through her hair, apply some lipstick, and grab her purse before heading down the road to Main Street.

She'd just arrived when she spotted Marla and her sister coming from the opposite direction. She'd met Chris before, briefly, at Marla's house. If Marla was pretty, Chris was gorgeous, with an incredible figure and masses of lustrous black curls streaming down her back.

Marla's eyes were sparkling with anticipation, and Cat tried not to show she was just as excited. "It's nice of you to take us here," she told Chris.

"No problem," Chris said easily. "Though why you two get such a kick out of going to a dive like this is beyond me." Behind her back, Cat and Marla rolled their eyes at each other. Maybe to *her* it was a dive. She could come here anytime she wanted.

Once inside, however, Cat had to admit that the place did look like – well, maybe not a dive, but not like anything special. It could be any burger joint in the world. There was a long counter with stools, and the rest of the small room was taken up with tiny, not-very-clean tables and beat-up chairs with cracked vinyl seats.

But the occupants of the seats made the place special – tall, good-looking guys, girls with great hair and an air of confidence. For a split second, Cat experienced a sensation totally unfamiliar to her – insecurity.

26

Marla read her mind. "We look just as good as these girls," she whispered staunchly. Trying to be objective, Cat scrutinised some of the girls. She decided Marla was right. They both looked older than thirteen, and they were just as pretty.

They followed Chris to a table. Once they sat down, Cat reached for the plastic-coated menu, but a look from Chris froze her hand in midair. "Don't bother with that," the older girl instructed her. "Just order a cheeseburger and fries. That's what everyone gets. They're always out of everything else anyway."

Cat was grateful for the tip. What if she had ordered a BLT and made a total fool of herself?

"Check out those guys," Marla hissed, cocking her head to the left.

Cat peered out of the corner of her eye. There were four of them, all blond, all big, and all with football jackets slung over their chairs. They had something else in common, too.

"They're all gorgeous," Cat breathed.

Chris waved to a girl who had just walked in. "Debbie! Over here."

"Hi, Chris." The girl slid into the fourth seat at their table. Chris introduced her to Marla and Cat, and the two of them started talking, pretty much ignoring the younger girls. Cat and Marla didn't care. It was enough just to be there and get a taste of what life would offer them in a couple of years. They gave their orders to a waitress and settled back to look around.

"I think we could pass for high school girls," Marla mused.

"It's the boys who are really different," Cat said. "They look so mature."

"Not like the guys we know." Marla sighed.

Cat agreed. She visualised the scene at Green Falls Junior High. Suddenly, every boy she knew seemed scrawny and awkward.

"Doesn't that guy over there look exactly like Tom Cruise?" Marla asked.

Cat took a look. For a moment she could have sworn he smiled at her. Wishful thinking, probably.

Beside them, Chris's voice rose slightly. "Are you serious? You're going to Escapade?"

"Shh," Debbie admonished her. "I said maybe."

"What's Escapade?" Cat asked.

"Nothing you need know about," Debbie said shortly.

Chris was more forthcoming. "It's a new dance club, on Green Street."

"I've heard of it," Marla said. She looked at Debbie oddly. "Don't you have to be twenty-one to get into a place like that?"

"Well, there are rumours going around that they let anyone in," Chris explained.

"Oh, Marla," Cat said suddenly. "Turn very

slowly to your right, and look at the boy sitting at the counter. Third stool from the end."

Marla turned. "Wow."

That was an understatement. The tall, slender boy had fashionably longish black hair and one pierced ear. He wore a black turtleneck sweater and black jeans, and he looked like he could be a rock star.

He turned his head in their direction. Both girls quickly averted their eyes.

"He was looking at you," Marla said excitedly.

"No, at you," Cat returned. But she thought Marla was probably right.

Their food came and they all started eating. Cat thought the hamburger was tasteless and the french fries were greasy, but she didn't mind. Who cared about food when there were all these wonderful boys around?

Marla was barely touching her food, too, and her thoughts were obviously running along the same lines. "So many cute guys," she murmured.

"Don't get any bright ideas," her sister warned. "High school boys don't go out with junior high girls."

Cat nodded sadly. "We'll just have to wait," she told Marla.

"But we still have another year after this one," Marla mourned.

All too soon they finished, and Chris announced

it was time to leave. At the door, Marla turned and gave the place one last, longing look. "Someday . . ."

"Yeah," Cat said. But someday seemed so far away. They opened the door and walked out. Just as Cat emerged, she saw Heather Beaumont and one of her awful friends, Blair Chase, crossing the pavement in front of them.

"What a nice day," Cat said loudly.

At the sound of her voice, Heather turned. She didn't say anything, but her eyes widened. Then she moved on.

Marla nudged Cat. "Perfect!"

Cat beamed. It was like frosting on a cake, having Heather see her come out of Dream Burger. Maybe she'd think Cat had been meeting a boy there. If only that were true . . .

Late that afternoon, Becka and her friend Lisa Simon left Jason Wister's house together.

"Honestly," Lisa grumbled, shaking her head. "Can you believe we had to have a newspaper staff meeting on *Saturday*? Couldn't we have waited until Monday after school?"

Becka smiled, but privately she didn't mind giving up a Saturday for the newspaper. Being on the staff was a lot of fun. She remembered how lonely she'd been two months ago, how hard it had been to make friends at school.

"Well, you know how Jason is," she reminded

Lisa. "Being editor, he thinks everything's an emergency. He wanted to get that editorial in the next issue, which meant he had to have our approval today."

"Yeah, but why was he in such a rush?" Lisa asked. "I mean, what's the big deal about having an honour code?"

Becka felt she had to defend Jason. "He's afraid people are cheating, so he thinks all the students should sign an honour code, like the one they have at the high school."

Lisa sniffed. "No one *I* know cheats. And if people really did want to cheat, signing an honour code wouldn't stop them."

She had a point. There was something else about Jason's honour code idea that bothered Becka. "What did you think of that part about having to turn people in if you see them cheating?"

Lisa wrinkled her nose. "I didn't like it. It's none of my business if someone cheats. Besides, I'd hate being a tattletale."

"Me, too," Becka agreed. "But I guess Jason thinks we have to protect the reputation of the school." She changed the subject. "Lisa, are you going to the dance?"

Lisa nodded. "You know Bobby Raines in our homeroom? He asked me."

"You're kidding! I've never even seen you two talking to each other."

31

"We never have," Lisa said. "I guess he's been admiring me from afar." She made a dramatic gesture, and Becka started giggling. Lisa was one of her favourite people. She sat next to Becka in homeroom, but it had taken Becka two weeks to get up the nerve to speak to her. Then it was no time at all before they became pals.

They were passing a playground where some boys were playing basketball. Becka stopped abruptly. "Isn't that Keith Doyle?"

Lisa looked. "Yeah. Why?"

Becka hesitated. Lisa was a good friend, though, and she was dying to confess. "I think he's so cute."

Lisa grinned. "Ah-ha! Well, you're absolutely right. He's very cute."

They watched the boys play. Keith had the ball, while another boy guarded him, trying to prevent him from throwing it to the guy standing by the hoop. Keith shot the ball over the guard's head. It was high, and the boy by the hoop ran backwards to catch it. It happened so fast, Becka didn't have time to jump out of the way before the boy slammed into her. And suddenly, she was sitting on the ground.

"Hey, I'm sorry!" the boy said.

Too stunned to move, Becka just sat there. Then Keith appeared. "You okay?"

I must look like an idiot, Becka thought in

32

dismay. She started pulling herself up. Keith grabbed her hand and helped her.

"I'm fine," Becka said.

Keith dazzled her with his smile. "Are you sure?"

"Really, I'm okay," Becka insisted. *"Très bien, merci."*

Keith laughed. "It's Saturday. You can speak English."

"Hey, where's the ball?" called one of the boys still on the court. With a wink and a wave, Keith ran back to join them.

Becka looked at the hand Keith had held when he helped her up.

"I bet you're never going to wash that hand again," Lisa teased.

Becka laughed. "Very funny." Even so, she could almost feel his hand still there.

Josie sat cross-legged on her bed and studied the diagram Coach Meadows had passed out during practice that afternoon. It was a new play, a tricky one, but if the team could pull it off it would be brilliant. And she had a key part to play.

It was scary but exciting. Being the first girl on what had been an all-boys team was such a responsibility. The guys seemed to have accepted her, but she still felt like she had to prove herself worthy. By the time the first game rolled around next month, she wanted to be able to hold her own, to show them she was every bit as good as they were.

Staring at the diagram, she tried to commit it to memory. But she was distracted by a cry of distress coming from the direction of the closet.

"What's the matter?" Josie asked Cat.

Cat whirled around to face her. Her face was a picture of tragedy. "I don't have anything to wear tonight."

"Go naked," Josie suggested.

"Ha ha." Cat pointed a finger at the closet. "There's absolutely nothing in there."

"Gee, that's strange," Josie commented. "From here, I can see skirts and dresses and shirts. . . . I must be having hallucinations."

Cat threw up her hands in disgust. "What would you know? You haven't been out of those jeans in three months."

"That's not true," Josie objected. "I take them off every night before I go to bed."

Cat took one more look into the closet. "There's not one thing in here that Todd hasn't already seen."

"What does that matter?" Josie asked. "You're always saying he never notices what you wear anyway."

Cat crossed the room to her bed and flopped down. "That's the truth."

Josie glanced at her curiously. Ever since she'd returned from Dream Burger, Cat had been in the strangest mood, grumpy and sullen. That was the way she used to act all the time back at Willoughby Hall. But in the past few months, Josie had become accustomed to a slightly less obnoxious Cat. She hoped Cat wasn't returning to her old ways.

Becka walked in. "Hi."

"Who invited you in here?" Cat asked.

Becka appeared somewhat taken aback by her tone.

"Don't mind her," Josie said. "She's been growling all evening."

"How come?" Becka asked. "Did you have a fight with Todd?"

Cat got up and moved around the room restlessly. "No." She frowned as Becka sat down on her bed. "What do you think you're doing?"

"Sitting on your bed," Becka replied.

"What's the matter with yours?"

Becka gave her an abashed smile. "It gets lonely in there sometimes."

Cat brightened slightly. "Want to trade?"

"No." Turning to Josie, Becka asked, "Are you doing anything tonight?"

"Red's coming over. He's having some trouble with the algebra homework, and I'm going to help him."

"Oh my, that's so romantic," Cat sneered.

Josie and Becka exchanged puzzled looks. After years of living together, they were accustomed to Cat's moods. But she was usually cheerful on Saturday nights, especially since she'd started dating Todd.

"Cat, do you know Keith Doyle very well?" Becka asked.

"Not really. I've seen him at some parties. Why?"

"I was just wondering . . ."

"Keith Doyle," Josie said. "I've seen that name somewhere."

Cat was staring at Becka. Then comprehension filled her eyes. "Oh, I get it. You've got a crush on Keith Doyle."

Becka squirmed. "It's not a crush, exactly."

"Don't give me that," Cat said. "It's written all over your face. Is he interested in you?"

"I don't know. How can you tell if someone's interested in you?"

"Oh, you can tell," Cat said wisely. "The first time I met Todd, I knew. Of course, that's not enough. You have to work on a guy for a while to make him realise he likes you."

"Why?" Josie asked.

"Because these boys are very immature. They don't know what they want."

"You think Todd's immature?" Becka asked. "He's the same age you are."

"Girls mature faster than boys, everyone knows that," Cat told her. "We should really be going out with boys two or three years older than us."

"You're nuts," Josie stated. "What sixteen-year-old boy would want to go out with a thirteen-year-old girl?"

An expression of overwhelming sadness crossed Cat's face. "I know."

"I'll never understand it," Becka sighed. "I'm going downstairs." She pulled herself off the bed and left the room.

"What time is Red coming?" Cat asked Josie.

"About an hour," Josie replied. She became aware that Cat was looking at her strangely. "What are you staring at?"

"Your hair. Have you ever thought about cutting your fringe?"

"Oh, sure," Josie said. "Sometimes I can't sleep at night thinking about it."

"Seriously," Cat went on, "let me see what I can do with your hair."

Josie clutched her head protectively. "No way you're coming near me with scissors."

"I won't cut it," Cat said. "I just want to try some of these hot curlers on it. Really, Josie, it'll be fun. I'll give you a whole new look."

"But I'm perfectly happy with my old look," Josie protested.

"Come on," Cat wheedled. "Don't you want to look special for Red?"

Josie groaned in exasperation. "How many times do I have to tell you, I'm not interested in Red that way."

"Okay, okay," Cat said hastily. "Let me do it anyway. Please? It'll be fun to do something different."

Josie was totally bewildered by her pleading tone. For the first time that evening, Cat wasn't pouting or whining. Josie took pity on her.

"Okay," she relented. "But nothing too drastic."

For the next twenty minutes, Josie sat there obediently while Cat fussed over her. In horror, she gaped at the array of cosmetics Cat spread out on the dresser. She flinched as Cat tugged at her hair and wound her red locks around the hot curlers. But she kept her mouth shut. Cat was humming and looking almost excited as she applied some greasy slime to Josie's face.

When she finished, Josie felt like she'd been covered with plaster. "Cover your eyes," Cat commanded. Then she sprayed what felt like a quart of hair spray on Josie's hair. "Now, look at yourself!"

In shock, Josie stood before the mirror. Somehow, she forced her lips into something like a smile. "Nice," she lied. Actually, she thought she bore a close resemblance to a circus clown.

"Red's going to flip!" Cat exclaimed.

He sure will. But not in the way you think. Cat can be so thick, Josie thought. "We're just studying together, not going to a ball."

Cat disregarded that. "It doesn't matter. Come on, let's go show Annie and Ben."

With a silent sigh, Josie allowed herself to be dragged from their room and down the stairs. In the living room, Annie, Ben, and Becka were setting up a game of Scrabble. "Recognise this person?" Cat asked, thrusting Josie forward.

Josie wasn't surprised when they all stared at her, speechless.

"Josie, what did you do to yourself?" Ben asked.

Josie gave them a thin smile. With all the junk on her lips, she couldn't manage any more than that. "Ask Cat."

"Doesn't she look good?" Cat asked.

Annie was the first to recover. "Very nice. It's certainly a new look for you, Josie."

"And a major improvement," Cat added.

"I don't know about that," Ben said. "None of you girls need all that make-up to be beautiful."

"Oh, Ben," Cat teased. "You're a guy. You don't understand these things." She eyed Josie. "I think she looks fantastic."

39

She seemed so proud of her work that Josie had to say something. "Yeah, I feel really . . ." She struggled for an appropriate word. "Really beautiful. Thanks, Cat."

Cat beamed. Annie's eyes darted back and forth between Josie and Cat in amusement. Ben still looked totally bewildered.

"I never thought you were interested in that sort of stuff," he finally said.

"Well, everyone likes a change now and then," Josie said lamely. "But this is just for today," she added hastily, before Cat could get any ideas.

Becka spoke up tentatively. "Isn't that a lot of green eye shadow?"

"I think it could be toned down a bit," Annie suggested gently.

Josie nodded. "Absolutely. I'll go take some of it off right now."

"No, no," Cat said. "It just needs some blending. And then we'll pick out something for you to wear."

This was going too far. "Uh-uh. I'm not getting dressed up to do algebra problems."

"Algebra," Annie echoed, and smiled. She turned to Ben. "Remember that?"

"Do I ever," Ben sighed. "My worst subject in high school," he told the girls.

"It had its benefits, though," Annie said, still smiling at him. Ben smiled back.

"You're right. It certainly did."

"What do you mean?" Becka asked.

"That's how Ben and I met," Annie explained. "I put an ad in the school newspaper offering to tutor people in algebra. Ben was my first customer."

Cat poked Josie in the ribs. Josie groaned and fell back on the sofa. Once Cat got a notion in her head, it took nothing short of dynamite to blast it out.

"When is Todd coming for you?" Ben asked Cat.

Cat looked at the clock on the mantel. "Fifteen minutes. Guess I'd better get ready." She left the room.

"That's strange," Annie said. "Doesn't Cat usually spend at least an hour getting ready for a date with Todd?"

"Closer to two," Ben replied.

"I just hope he's on time and gets her out of the house fast," Josie said.

"Why?" Annie asked.

Josie grinned. "So I can get this stuff off my face before Red gets here."

Three

On Wednesday afternoon, Cat left her last class of the day and headed to her locker. Along the way, she stopped to watch Larry Jacobs, the student body president, tack a poster on the wall. A small crowd gathered around him.

"SAVE THE ENVIRONMENT," someone read out loud from the sign.

Those weren't the words that had caught Cat's eye. She focused on the next line: BENEFIT DANCE.

"What's this all about?" a girl asked Larry.

"The student council wants to start a re-cycling programme here at school," he explained. "We're having the dance to raise money."

Cat had only the vaguest notion what a re-cycling programme was, but if it was an excuse for a dance, it had to be something good.

Marla came up beside her. "The first dance of the school year," she noted. "I hope I can drum up a date with someone halfway decent."

"What about Bobby Kent?" Cat asked. "Hasn't he been hanging around you a lot lately?"

"I'm keeping my fingers crossed," Marla replied. "At least *you* know you don't have to worry about a date."

"Yeah," Cat said. Marla didn't pick up on the lack of enthusiasm in that word.

"It must be such a good feeling to know you've got a guy you can count on," Marla continued.

"Yeah," Cat said again. This time Marla noticed her tone.

"What's the matter?" Marla asked. "You sound like you're really down."

Cat shook her head. How could she describe these strange feelings of dissatisfaction? "It's nothing." She nodded towards the books in her arms. "Just tons of homework. Annie and Ben have been on at me lately to get my grades up. I better go home and get started."

Clearly Marla wasn't entirely satisfied with that explanation. "Is everything okay between you and Todd?"

"Sure," Cat replied. "Nothing's changed." *Nothing ever changes,* she added silently.

Walking home, she thought about the forthcoming dance. Maybe she could talk Ben and Annie into a new dress. It was a pretty good possibility. Why didn't the thought excite her more?

Her thoughts went back to a movie she'd seen recently. It was about a senior prom at a high school. The girls had worn long gowns and corsages, the boys dinner jackets. The boys had been such gentlemen, too, helping the girls take their coats off and pulling out chairs for them. She knew the Green Falls Junior High dance wouldn't be like that. She couldn't even picture Todd in a dinner jacket. As for manners, Todd was more likely to pull a chair out from *under* her.

That's not fair, she scolded herself. Todd had never done anything like that to her. But he could be so juvenile sometimes. She recalled the scene at Brownies on Saturday night. A bunch of kids from school had been there. The boys had started blowing the wrappers off their straws, trying to see who could shoot their paper the farthest. Todd had really gotten into it. She couldn't imagine anything like that going on at Dream Burger.

By the time she got home, she'd worked herself into a thoroughly bad mood. The silence of the empty house didn't do much to improve her spirits. She dropped her books on the little table in the foyer where the mail was piled and went into the kitchen. Nothing in there interested her. Through the window, she saw that the door was open in the old shed. That meant Annie was painting. She went outside and walked across the yard.

"Hi," she said, entering the shed.

Annie stood before an easel. "Hi, honey." Her greeting was warm but preoccupied.

Cat moved around to look at the canvas on the easel. "That looks nice."

"I can't get the colour right," Annie murmured.

When Annie was absorbed in a painting, she didn't see or hear anything around her. Of course, Cat knew that all she had to do was tell Annie she felt down, and she'd get all the attention she could handle. But nobody could help her with the way she was feeling. So why bother?

"I guess I'll go do my homework," Cat said.

Even that extraordinary suggestion didn't distract Annie. But as Cat was walking out, Annie did look up. "Cat, there's a letter for you. On the table by the door."

"A letter? For me?"

"Mmm." Annie was dabbing paint on the canvas and frowning. Cat left and walked quickly back to the house. Who could be writing to her? She never got letters.

She went to the foyer and flipped through the mail on the little table. There it was, a plain white envelope with her name and address typed on it. There was no return address. She tore the envelope open and pulled out a white sheet of paper.

She read the letter quickly. Then she read it again. She was aware that her pulse had quickened.

The front door opened. "Hi," Becka said. "What's up?"

"Nothing." Cat stuffed the letter in her pocket, gathered her books, and ran upstairs where she could read it again in privacy. Once in her room, she smoothed the letter out on her bed. Then she re-read it, slowly this time, savouring each and every word.

Dear Cat,

You don't know me, and I may never know you. But I saw you at Dream Burger on Saturday, and I can't get you out of my mind.

Do you believe in love at first sight? I didn't, until I saw you. Then I knew you were the girl I'd been waiting for. Where have you been all my life?

I know there's a difference in our ages. That doesn't matter to me. But I know it would matter to your parents. So perhaps we will never meet, and I will have to live with that sorrow. But I had to let you know my feelings, because my heart has told me you are my one and only, now and forever love.

There was no signature at the bottom. Cat's mind was racing as she visualised the boys she'd seen at Dream Burger. Was he one of the blond football players? The Tom Cruise look-alike? The long-haired one in the black jeans? And whoever he was, how had he learned her name?

She snapped her fingers. Marla's sister Chris. Maybe he was a friend of hers. Clutching the letter, she ran into Annie and Ben's bedroom where there was a phone extension. Her hand trembled as she punched in Marla's number.

Please, Marla, be home, she pleaded silently. She must have let it ring a hundred times. Finally, she gave up and went back to her room. She couldn't resist reading the letter again. This was the most romantic thing that had ever happened to her. She actually had a secret admirer! If she didn't tell someone about this, she'd explode.

At the sound of footsteps on the stairs, she ran to the door. Well, Becka was better than nobody. "Becka, come here. I've got something to show you."

Becka came in, and Cat handed her the letter. "Read this," she commanded.

She enjoyed watching Becka's expression as she read. Her eyes grew huge, and her mouth dropped open. "Cat! This is incredible! Who is he?"

"I don't know. There were so many guys at Dream Burger that day. High school boys, Becka! He could be sixteen, maybe seventeen years old!" She fell back on her bed. "And he's in love with me!"

"Wow," Becka breathed. "This is like something out of a book, or a movie. A secret love."

"I'm his 'one and only, now and forever love,'" Cat quoted from the letter. She'd already committed those words to memory.

"You have to find out who he is," Becka said excitedly. "You could go back to Dream Burger. Or hang around in front of the high school when classes get out."

Cat considered this. Then she shook her head. "No, that's childish. I don't want him to think I'm that anxious to find out who he is."

"Why not?" Becka asked.

Cat smiled at her kindly. Becka knew nothing about boys. "Never let a guy know you're available, Becka. Playing hard to get is always the best policy. Guys want what they think they can't get."

"Then what are you going to do?"

"I'll just have to be patient and wait until he comes after me." She shivered with delight. "If he's as much in love with me as he says he is, he won't give up."

"I wish I could be like you," Becka said. "I

want to know how to make a boy like me."

"Anyone in particular?" Cat asked. Then she remembered. "Oh, yeah, Keith Doyle."

Becka struggled with her words. "Do you think . . . I know this sounds silly, but . . . could you teach me how to act with boys?" She looked up at Cat with that wistful, pathetic expression that usually got on Cat's nerves. But Cat was feeling so good, she found herself actually wanting to help.

"Sure. It's all a question of attitude, you know. If it doesn't come naturally to you, you can always fake it. Now, let me think . . ."

Josie came out of the girls' locker room, her knapsack slung over her shoulder. Todd and another player, Alex, were coming out of the boys' locker room at the same time. "That was a good practice," Josie told them.

"Yeah," Todd said. "I could have sworn I saw Coach Meadows smile."

"Are you crazy?" Alex hooted. "You must be seeing things, buddy."

Josie grinned. Coach Meadows was famous for his grim expression. "You think it's going to be a good team?" she asked the boys.

"Yeah," Todd said. "But we sure could use someone with a good hook shot." He shook his head in regret. "Too bad we lost Keith Doyle."

The name rang a bell, but Josie couldn't think

why. "How come he's not on the team anymore?"

"Grades," Alex told her. "He dropped to a C average last spring."

"There was that other business, too," Todd noted.

"What other business?" Josie asked.

Both boys looked uncomfortable. Alex grimaced. "There was a rumour going around that he copied from someone else's test paper and turned it in as his own."

"But nobody could prove it," Todd added. "The girl he copied from had a crush on him and wouldn't turn him in." He eyed Josie suspiciously. "How come you're so interested in Keith Doyle?"

"No reason," Josie said. "I'm just curious."

"Are you sure?" Alex asked. "He's got a reputation, you know."

"What kind of reputation?"

Now both boys were grinning, and they exchanged looks. "He's, you know, kind of a playboy," Todd told her. "He's always getting girls to fall for him."

"You don't want to get involved with him," Alex advised.

"I have no intention of getting involved with him," Josie said indignantly. "But thanks for the warning."

"Try it again," Cat ordered Becka.

Becka cocked her head at an angle, slightly dropped her eyelids, looked to the side, and formed a small smile.

Cat shook her head. "You still look like you've got a stiff neck."

Becka eyed her reflection in the mirror. Cat was right. "It doesn't look natural." She flopped down on the bed beside Cat. "I don't think acting like you is going to work."

"You don't have to act like me," Cat objected. "You can flirt in your own style."

"But I don't have a flirting style," Becka said. "I really want Keith to ask me to that dance. But I want him to ask me because he likes *me*. Not because I'm pretending to be you." She sighed. *"C'est difficile."*

"Huh?"

"I said 'it's difficult' in French. Did Mademoiselle Casalls tell you guys there's going to be another quiz next week?"

"Yeah." Cat pulled her feet up onto her bed and wrapped her arms around her knees. "I don't know how I'm going to study. I can't think about anything but my secret love."

"I don't blame you," Becka sighed.

"Listen," Cat said suddenly. "Don't tell anyone about my letter, okay?"

"Not even Josie?"

"Especially not Josie. She'll just tease me and make jokes about it."

"You're right," Becka agreed. "Josie wouldn't understand. I don't think she knows anything about romance."

"But she could," Cat mused. "You know, all she and Red need is a little push."

"Are you thinking about giving them the push?"

Cat grinned. "Why not? If Josie fell in love, she'd be a lot more feminine. And a lot easier to live with."

They heard Ben's call to dinner from downstairs.

"Now remember what I said," Cat cautioned as they ran down the stairs. "Not a word about you-know-what."

"Not a word," Becka promised. Having Cat's confidence gave her a warm glow. It wasn't too long ago that they couldn't bear to be in the same room. Becka and Cat joined Annie, Ben, and Josie at the table. Becka cast an appreciative eye on the main course.

"Mmm, chicken pie."

"Annie made it all by herself," Josie announced with the air of a proud parent.

"I think I got it right this time," Annie said as she began dishing it out.

"How was your day, girls?" Ben asked.

"We had a great basketball practice," Josie reported. "Oh, Cat, Todd said to tell you he'd call tonight."

"Okay," Cat said.

"Cat, don't you like your chicken pie?" Annie asked anxiously.

"What? Oh, sure, it's great. I guess I'm just not very hungry."

"Uh-oh," Ben said. "Isn't loss of appetite a sign of being in love?"

"Not for me," Annie said cheerfully. "Every time I fell in love, I ate like a pig. When I first met Ben I gained five pounds."

"Maybe Becka's in love, then," Josie remarked.

Becka looked at her plate and flushed when she realised she'd already devoured her dinner. Annie and Ben were looking at her with interest.

"Well, there is a boy I kind of like," she confessed.

"Who is he?" Ben asked.

"Now, Ben, don't pry," Annie chided him. "When Becka wants to tell us about him, she will."

"It'll be interesting to see how Josie reacts to being in love," Ben said in a teasing voice.

"I'll be sick to my stomach," Josie replied promptly.

"Josie!" Cat exclaimed. "Not at the table, *please!*"

"Don't worry. It's not going to happen any time soon. If ever."

Cat turned her head and gave Becka a significant wink.

"What's going on at school?" Annie asked.

"There's going to be a dance," Cat said.

Annie clapped her hands. "Your first dance! Oh, we have to go shopping."

"For what?" Ben asked.

"Ben! We've got three daughters going to their first dance! Three daughters means three new outfits."

"Not three," Josie said. "I'm not going."

"How do you know?" Cat said. "Maybe Red will ask you."

Josie made a face. "I'm sure Red isn't any more interested in going to a dance than I am."

"Are you going, Becka?" Annie asked.

"If somebody asks me."

"You mean, you have to have a date?" Ben asked.

"You don't have to," Cat told him. "But everybody does."

Annie shook her head. "Kids grow up so fast nowadays."

"Too fast, in my opinion," Ben said. He turned to Annie. "Did you hear about that place on Green Street? The one that's letting in underage kids? What's it called?"

"Escapade," Cat answered.

Ben frowned. "How do you know about it?"

"I haven't been there," Cat said hastily. "I

54

just heard some older kids talking about it."

"Something should be done about that place," Annie commented.

"Nobody's caught them letting the kids in," Ben said. "And I doubt that any kids will be going to the police to confess."

After dinner, the girls cleared the table. Once they were alone in the kitchen, Josie turned to Becka. "Who's this boy you kind of like?"

Cat answered for her. "Keith Doyle."

"Keith Doyle! Gross!"

"What's gross about him?" Becka asked indignantly.

"I heard some of the guys talking about him. They said he plays around, he flirts with everyone. He gets girls to fall madly in love with him."

"Oh, *please*," Cat snorted. "All boys do that." Her eyes grew misty. "Until they get older. Then, one day, they find their one and only, now and forever love."

Josie brushed that aside. "I heard worse about Keith Doyle. There's a rumour that he cheats."

"I don't believe that," Becka said stoutly. "If he cheated, he wouldn't be making Ds in French."

"What's the big deal, anyway?" Cat challenged Josie. "Okay, maybe he cheats a little. So what? He's cute, and he's popular, and Becka likes him. So mind your own business!"

"I'm just warning her," Josie countered. "You've got to watch out for guys like that. If you ask me, he sounds kind of sleazy."

"Nobody asked you," Cat shot back.

"Come on, you guys, stop it," Becka pleaded. "Look, he hasn't even asked me out."

"*Yet,*" Cat added.

Josie threw up her hands and went back out to the dining room. Becka stared after her thoughtfully. "You know, Cat, I think you're right about Josie."

"Right about what?"

"She *does* need to fall in love."

Four

Becka was in a rush to get to French class. She'd noticed that Keith's locker was right by the door and that he usually stopped there just before class. Surely she wouldn't look peculiar hanging out in front of her own classroom. She'd be in a perfect position to strike up a conversation.

But about what? She was mentally exploring various topics as she ran down the stairs. Then she heard her name being called.

She turned to see a small, thin girl with an uneven fringe and glasses slipping down her nose hurrying down the stairs to catch up with her. "Hi, Louise."

Lousie was in Becka's homeroom and had been one of the first friends Becka had made at her new school. Louise waved the latest issue of the *Green Gazette*, which had just come out that day. "Becka, I just wanted to tell you how much I liked this editorial."

Becka edged down another step. "Thanks," she said hurriedly, "but I didn't have anything to do with it. Jason was the one who wrote it."

"I think the idea of an honour code is excellent," Louise went on. She started talking about how it would cut down on cheating and make students think twice if they were tempted. Becka kept glancing down the stairs, but Louise didn't take the hint, and Becka didn't want to be rude.

When Becka finally got away, she dashed down the remainder of the stairs. But she was too late. Just as she tore around the corner, she saw Keith slamming his locker door and going into the room.

Becka slid into her seat just as the bell rang. There was only time for a brief hi to Patty before Mademoiselle Casalls started talking. Becka gazed at the back of Keith's head, but she couldn't afford to daydream about him. They were doing irregular verb conjugations that day, which required a lot of concentration.

"For tomorrow, Friday, you will answer the questions on page sixty," the teacher announced at the end of class. "And do not forget about the test on Monday."

The bell rang. Becka watched wistfully as Keith ran out of the room. Patty turned around and read her expression. "You've got it bad."

Becka didn't even attempt to deny it. She gathered her books and left the room with Patty. "Cat tried to give me flirting lessons," she confessed.

Patty laughed. "I'll bet she's a good teacher. She's an authority on that subject."

"But I was a crummy student. It just didn't feel right to me. If I tried to fake it, I'd look goofy. Patty, how can I get him to notice me?"

Patty twisted a strand of her short, fair hair, which meant she was thinking. Then she clutched Becka's arm and pulled her out of the flow of moving students. "I've got it! You're a whiz in French, right?"

"I do okay," Becka said modestly.

"Keith stinks in French, right?"

Becka drew back. "Well, I wouldn't put it like *that*."

"Oh, come on, I've seen the way Mademoiselle Casalls looks at him when she hands back the quizzes. Why don't you offer to help him?"

Becka stared at her. "You mean, be a tutor?" She gasped. "That's brilliant! I don't know why I didn't think of that. You know, that's how my parents met. Annie tutored Ben in algebra when they were in school."

"And look how they turned out," Patty said. She gave Becka a light punch on the shoulder. "Go for it!"

For the rest of the day, Becka gave only

half her attention to her classes. The rest she devoted to imagining her approach to Keith. She would accidentally-on-purpose run into him at his locker after the last bell. She'd casually make a comment about the forthcoming quiz. With any luck, he'd say something about dreading it. Then, acting like the idea had just occurred to her, she'd hit him with her offer.

Throughout her last class, she kept her eye on the clock. She was poised to move as soon as class was over. When the bell rang, she shot out of the room like a marathon runner who'd just heard the gun.

She turned the last corner, expecting to see Keith at the end of the hall. But he wasn't there. Becka strolled down the hall very slowly, her eyes glued to his locker. The corridor was so crowded with kids pulling books and coats out of their lockers, she was able to go back and forth, up and down the hall, without attracting attention. But after a few minutes, the hall began to clear as students left. Soon only a handful were still hanging around. And at least one of them was beginning to eye her curiously.

Becka was passing the room where her French class was held when she happened to glance through the door's window. Her heart leaped. There was Keith, at Mademoiselle Casalls' desk. The teacher wasn't there. He was probably waiting to have a meeting with her.

Becka thought quickly. She could say she left a book in her desk. Before she could lose her nerve, she put her hand on the knob and walked in.

Keith jumped back from the desk with a stricken expression. But when he saw who had come in, relief crossed his face and he grinned.

A rush of excitement filled Becka. *He's glad to see me*, she thought.

"Whew," he said. "For a second, I thought you were Mademoiselle Casalls."

"Isn't that who you're waiting for?" Becka asked.

He laughed as if she'd just said something funny. It was then that Becka realised the teacher's desk drawer was open. "What are you doing?"

He hesitated for a moment, then winked at Becka. "I was just looking for a copy of Monday's French quiz," he replied.

Now it was Becka's turn to laugh. "Very funny." But then, as Keith continued to rifle through the papers in the desk, a cold chill shot through her. It dawned on her that maybe he wasn't joking.

"Keith! You – you're not serious, are you?"

He glanced up and gave her a disarming smile. "You may be a genius, but some of us need a little advantage when it comes to quizzes."

Becka was dumbstruck. But even in her

shock, she knew how Cat would react in a situation like this. She'd laugh it off. She might even offer to help search the drawer! But there was no way Becka couldn't let her feelings show. "Keith, that's cheating!" she blurted out.

"Oh, I'm not going to steal it," he assured her. "I just want to peek at some of the questions."

"It's still wrong," Becka insisted.

His smile faded slightly. "Wait a minute. Are you going to tell on me? I didn't think you were a goody-goody."

"I'm not," Becka protested. "And I didn't say I was going to tell anyone." She saw a copy of the school newspaper lying on the desk. "If we had an honour code, I'd *have* to turn you in."

"But we don't have an honour code, right?"

Becka nodded slowly. "Right. Not yet, at least. But that doesn't mean it's okay to cheat."

She jumped as Keith slammed the drawer shut. "It's not in there anyway," he muttered.

Becka gazed at him sorrowfully. Then she turned away and started towards the door. "Wait a minute," Keith said. Becka paused and looked back.

Keith was smiling again. "I guess you think I'm some kind of criminal, huh?"

Becka didn't know what to say. She stared down at the floor. Keith came closer, touched her chin, and lifted her face so she had to look right up into his eyes.

62

"Listen, I got tossed off the basketball team because of my grades. But Coach Meadows says he'll let me back on before the season starts if my grades improve this month. Becka, playing basketball means a lot to me."

Becka swallowed. He sounded so sincere, so anxious. And his eyes . . . she could have sworn they were misting over.

"So you see, I've got to do well on this test."

Becka's insides were turning to mush. He was pleading for her to understand. Who was she to pass judgment on him? He'd been driven to this act out of desperation, like someone who robs a bank to feed his hungry children.

Still, she couldn't let him think she approved of this sort of behaviour. "There . . . there are other ways to get your grades up."

Keith hung his head. "You wouldn't believe how hard I study. But this French stuff just doesn't sink in. I guess I'm not the smartest guy in the world."

Becka caught her breath. Here it was, the perfect opportunity. "Maybe I could help you."

He looked at her with hope in his eyes. "Yeah?"

Becka nodded. "I could tutor you. We could get together, um, this weekend . . ." Her voice trailed off. Was she imagining it, or had the hope faded?

63

But then he smiled. "Yeah, okay. What about tomorrow night?"

"Tomorrow night?" Becka repeated.

"What's the matter? You got a date?"

"A date?" Becka wanted to kick herself. She was making it sound like the possibility of having a date was nonexistent. "No, I don't have a date *Friday* night," she said, emphasising the Friday. "You could come over to my house."

"Great," he said. "You can try to pound some knowledge into my head, and then we'll go to Luigi's. How about if I come by around five?"

"Okay."

"It's a date," he said.

A date. The words were ringing in her ears long after he walked out of the room. She had a date with Keith Doyle. Okay, maybe it wasn't a *real* date. But it was close. Closer than she'd ever been to a date before.

Sitting across from Marla in Brownies, Cat waited to see her friend's reaction to her story. She wasn't disappointed.

Marla put a hand to her heart and moaned in rapture. "Cat! That's so amazing! Honestly, I've never heard of anything so incredibly romantic before!"

"Will you find out from Chris if anyone asked her my name?"

64

"Absolutely. But I think she would have told me if anyone had."

"How else could he have found out my name?"

Marla thought about it. "Let's see . . . he couldn't have looked you up in the yearbook, because you weren't in last year's. Maybe he knows someone in junior high." Her eyes widened. "Maybe he hired a private investigator."

The idea had never occurred to Cat. "Do you think any guy would go to that much trouble to find out a girl's name?"

"Why not? A man would go to the ends of the earth to find the woman he loves."

Cat stirred her ice cream soda. "I wonder if I'll ever meet him. Even if I did, Annie and Ben would never let me go out with a high school boy."

"How tragic," Marla said. "Destined never to meet, never to share your love. Star-crossed lovers."

Cat experienced a feeling of melancholy that wasn't exactly unpleasant. She felt like a heroine in a sad but beautiful love story. "Star-crossed lovers," she echoed. "Like Romeo and Juliet."

"At least you still have Todd," Marla said.

That brought Cat back to earth. "Todd . . . can you imagine him calling me his one and only, now and forever love? All he ever calls me is 'babe.' " She shuddered.

"Come on, he's not so bad," Marla argued. "He's one of the cutest boys at school, he's a jock, and he's got a nice personality."

"Yeah, I know. I just wish I could get him to be more romantic."

"I'm sure you can if you try," Marla said.

"Hi, Marla, Cat."

The girls looked up. Heather stood there, with Blair Chase and Eve Dedham.

"Hi," Cat and Marla replied.

"What's new?" Heather asked pleasantly. Behind her, Blair muffled a giggle. Eve just looked uncomfortable.

"Not much," Cat replied, her eyes darting among the girls.

"Well, see you around."

As soon as they were out of earshot, Cat leaned across the table. "What was *that* all about? Why is she so friendly all of a sudden?"

"I don't know," Marla said. "But there's something I don't like about it. I still can't believe she's given up on getting Todd back."

"You think she's got some sort of rotten scheme cooking?" Cat asked.

Marla shrugged. "Maybe it's just my suspicious mind. But I think you should keep an eye on Todd."

Cat got up. "You know, Todd's working at his father's store right now. Maybe I'll go by there and see if he wants to take a break."

Marla nodded in approval. "Good idea. Don't let this secret admirer distract you. After all, *he* can't take you to the dance."

The girls separated, and Cat walked down the street to Sports Stuff. The store was quiet. Todd was standing by the counter, looking bored. He brightened when Cat came in.

"Hi, babe," he greeted her.

Cat winced, but she forced a bright smile. "Can you get away for a little while?"

"I'll ask my dad." He left the counter and went to the back of the store. Cat idly picked up a card lying on the counter.

In fancy, curly script, it read: You are cordially invited to enjoy a complimentary dinner for two at La Petite Maison.

La Petite Maison. Cat had absorbed enough French to know this meant "the little house." But she also knew what La Petite Maison was and it definitely wasn't any little house. It was the only really elegant, fancy French restaurant in Green Falls. Annie had told Cat that Ben had taken her there for their anniversary last year.

"Hello, Cat," Mr Murphy boomed. The heavy-set, balding man beamed at her jovially. Cat wondered if this was what Todd would look like someday.

"Hi, Mr Murphy," she said. "I was just wondering if Todd could take a break."

"Sure," he said. "And you kids could do me a favour while you're out." He took out his wallet and turned to Todd. "I need you to pick up a birthday gift for me to give your mother. She likes perfume called Everlasting. I think you can get it at Harrison's."

"Okay," Todd said, pocketing the money.

Cat pointed to the card on the counter. "Are you taking her to La Petite Maison for her birthday?"

He shook his head in regret. "No, Mrs Murphy and I are both on diets." He picked up the card. "Todd, why don't you and Cat use this? It would be a shame to waste it." The tinkle of a bell indicated the arrival of a customer, and Mr Murphy left to wait on him.

Cat clapped her hands in glee. "Oh, Todd, I'd love to go to La Petite Maison."

Todd looked at the card. "Is this one of those places where a guy has to wear a coat and tie?"

"Uh, yes . . . but you'd look great in a coat and tie! And it will be so nice to get really dressed up for a change."

Todd frowned. "French food? That's stuff like snails and frogs' legs."

"I'm sure they have other things, too," Cat said.

Todd still didn't look very happy about the idea. "This isn't my kind of place."

"How do you know? You've never been there!"

Todd sighed. "Well, if you really want to go . . ."

"I do! How about tomorrow night? There's no football game."

He shoved the card in his pocket. "Yeah, okay."

Cat rewarded him with her very best killer smile. They left the store and walked around the corner to Harrison's Department Store. Just inside, there were mannequins displaying men's suits from Italy. Even without faces, the mannequins looked suave and debonair. "Todd, how do you like this?" she asked.

Todd glanced at the suit and snorted. "Looks like something a sissy would wear."

She should have known. "Come on, Todd, let's go find the perfume."

He hesitated as they neared the perfume counter. "Hey, Cat, could you ask for the stuff?" He fumbled in his pocket for the money. "I feel stupid buying perfume."

Cat rolled her eyes. "Todd, guys buy perfume for women all the time."

"*I* don't. Look, just do it for me, okay?"

Taking the money, Cat went to the counter. "I'd like a bottle of Everlasting, please." While the saleswoman went to get it, Cat examined the sample bottles of perfume. She selected one and sprayed a little on her wrist. Then she breathed the scent in deeply.

It was glorious, flowery and feminine. She could see herself walking into a place like La Petite Maison, trailing clouds of this heavenly scent behind her. Men would look up, attracted by the fragrance. Maybe she could save her allowance and buy some. Or maybe she could get it as a gift. This scent could become her signature. Every time people smelled it, they'd know Cat Morgan was around.

"Here you are, dear," the saleswoman said. Cat paid for the perfume and joined Todd, who was leaning against a pillar.

He sniffed. "You smell funny."

Cat closed her eyes and counted to ten. Turning Todd into a romantic was going to be even harder than she thought.

Five

It was a few minutes after five on Friday when Josie burst into Morgan's Country Foods. "Sorry I'm late," she said breathlessly.

"That's okay," Annie said. "It's been quiet. Do you want to unpack that box of preserves on the counter?"

Cat wrinkled her nose as Josie came closer. "Ick, you smell like a horse."

"That's not surprising," Josie replied. "Considering the fact that I've been on one for the past hour."

Annie laughed. "Just don't get too close to any customers, if we have any. How was your ride?"

"Great. With all the basketball practices, I haven't been on a horse in . . . well, it feels like ages."

"That's not true," Cat said. "You ride Maybelline all the time."

"That doesn't count," Josie replied.

"Poor old Maybelline," Annie sighed. "Ben and I didn't know anything about horses when we bought her. We couldn't understand why the farmer was selling her so cheap. Now we know."

"Sometimes I wonder if she's really a horse," Josie said. "Maybe she's a cow in disguise. Anyway, that's how she moves."

Cat eyed Josie in distaste. "How did you get that sweaty riding her?"

"I wasn't riding Maybelline," Josie said. "Red let me take Dusty, and I got him up to a real gallop."

"A gallop?" Worry lines appeared on Annie's forehead. "Josie, you haven't been riding that long. I don't like the idea of your racing around on a horse by yourself."

"I wasn't by myself," Josie assured her. "Red was with me. He took their new horse, Belinda."

"Well, that's better," Annie said, turning back to the pickle jars she was labelling.

"Much better," Cat echoed. She gave Josie a sly smile, which Josie responded to by sticking out her tongue.

"Cat, what time is Todd coming for you?" Annie asked.

"Six-thirty. Can I go now? I want to take a long bubble bath and French braid my hair."

Josie raised her eyebrows. "For Todd? The last time you went out with him you spent five minutes getting ready."

"This is different," Cat said. "Tonight is going to be special, not the usual Friday night."

"I think you'll enjoy La Petite Maison," Annie commented. "It's very elegant."

Josie chuckled. "Todd Murphy at La Petite Maison."

"What's so funny about that?" Cat demanded.

"I just can't picture Todd eating in a place whose name he can't pronounce."

Cat glared at her in annoyance. "I'm going to get ready." She flounced out of the store, practically colliding with Ben, who was on his way in. "Sorry," she called as she passed him.

"Why is she in such a rush?" he asked Annie.

"Big date tonight with Todd," she replied.

He shook his head sadly. "Seems like we just got our daughters, and already the boys are standing in line to take them away from us."

Annie smiled. "Did you meet Becka's friend?"

"Yeah, he just arrived. He seems like a nice enough boy."

Josie's head jerked up. "What's his name?"

"Keith something," Ben replied. "Becka's tutoring him in French." He winked at his wife. "And we all know what that can lead to."

"Do you know him, Josie?" Annie asked.

"Not really. I know *about* him," Josie tried to keep her voice even, but something in her expression must have betrayed her thoughts.

"Is there something about him we should know?" Annie asked.

Josie bit her lip. She could tell Annie and Ben what she'd heard about Keith Doyle, and they could discourage Becka's interest. But Becka would *kill* her. No, she'd better handle this herself.

"Oh, it's nothing. I'm just thinking about all this homework I've got. There should be a law against assigning homework on weekends."

"Why don't you go get started on it now?" Ben suggested. "Then you'll get it over with and have the weekend free."

That was exactly what Josie wanted to hear. "Thanks," she said and ran out. When she walked into the house, she could hear the murmur of voices coming from the dining room. She paused, uncertain about what to do.

Why was she so worried anyway? If it had been Cat in there with a boy, she wouldn't be the least bit concerned. But Becka – she was so gullible. It would be just like her to be swept off her feet by some phony Romeo.

But Josie couldn't exactly burst in and order Keith out of the house. She had to play it cool. She'd scope out the situation and then decide what needed to be done.

Shoving her hands in her pockets and whistling, she ambled into the dining room. Everything looked pretty innocent so far. Keith was slumped

74

in a chair, his elbows on the table and his eyes glazed over. Becka, sitting next to him, was reading out loud from the French textbook propped in front of her. Both of them looked up as Josie entered.

"Hi," Becka said. "Josie, do you know Keith?"

Josie was about to say "only by reputation," but she held it back. "Hi, Keith."

He smiled. "So you're the famous Josie Morgan."

"Famous?" Josie asked, momentarily put off by his tone and his killer smile. The guy was dripping with charm.

"Well, you're the first girl ever on the basketball team. You must be some athlete."

Flattery will get you nowhere with me, Josie thought. But being perfectly objective, she could see how he'd earned his reputation. "What are you guys doing?"

"Studying French," Becka said. "We've got a quiz on Monday."

"Becka's trying to drum some irregular verbs through my thick skull," Keith added.

"Oh, Keith," Becka remonstrated. "Don't put yourself down like that."

Josie didn't like the way Becka was looking at him, like a lovesick calf. She pulled out a chair and plunked herself down. "Maybe I can help."

"But you're taking Spanish," Becka protested.

"Spanish, French, what's the difference? They're both foreign."

Keith tossed back his head and laughed. Josie fixed steely eyes on him. "It wasn't *that* funny," she muttered.

Becka consulted her book. "Okay, let's conjugate the verb *aller*." To Josie, she said. "That means 'to go.' "

Keith pretended to pout. "Do we have to?"

Becka nodded. "Come on, Keith. I know this will be on the quiz."

"Haven't we already worked enough for today?" Keith asked plaintively.

Becka frowned. "You've only been here fifteen minutes!"

"Okay," Keith said with a sigh. "We'll work for an hour. And then we'll go to Luigi's, okay?"

Becka nodded happily. Josie drummed her fingers on the table. So this wasn't just a tutoring session. They were going to Luigi's, where Green Falls Junior High boys took girls for dates on Friday nights.

Becka sniffed. "I smell something funny."

"It's me," Josie said. "I've been riding." She stood up. "I'm going to take a shower."

"I think Cat's in the bathroom," Becka told her.

"I'll chase her out. Excuse me."

She took the stairs two at a time. Sounds of splashing and singing came from behind

76

the bathroom door, but Josie ignored them. She went directly into Ben and Annie's room, picked up the phone, and dialled.

"Hi, Red, it's Josie."

"Hi, what's up?"

"You want to go to Luigi's?"

There was a silence on the other end. "Luigi's? Now?"

Josie knew why he sounded puzzled, and she couldn't blame him. She and Red had been to Luigi's a zillion times, but not on a Friday night. Not on a date night. "Look, I can't explain now, but it's important."

"Well, okay."

"Come on over in an hour." She hung up the phone and smiled grimly. At least she'd be there to keep an eye on that slimy charmer.

"What are you smiling about?" Cat stood in the doorway, her hair wrapped in a towel.

"Just thinking about something."

"Did you see Becka downstairs with Keith?"

"Yeah."

The corners of Cat's lips turned up. "Better get your act together, Josie, or you'll be the only unattached Morgan girl."

"You mean, I'll be the only *sane* Morgan girl," Josie retorted. They both turned as Becka came running up the stairs.

"Did Keith leave already?" Cat asked in dismay.

"No," Becka said. "I just have to get my French dictionary."

"Well, don't leave him alone too long," Cat scolded. "How's it going down there?"

"Okay, I guess. I don't know if I'm helping him all that much. I think he's got a mental block when it comes to French."

"I'm not asking about *that*," Cat said impatiently. "I mean, how's it going with you and Keith?"

Becka smiled shyly. "He's taking me to Luigi's."

"Excellent!" Cat exclaimed.

"Is it okay if Red and I go with you?" Josie asked.

"Sure," Becka said. "That'll be fun." She was getting that dreamy look in her eyes that Josie found so irritating. "Just think, Josie, all those years when we were roommates at the orphanage . . . who would have thought one day we'd be double-dating?" She sailed off into her room.

Josie scowled. When she turned to Cat, her frown deepened. "What are you smirking at me like that for?"

"You and Red," Cat replied promptly. "Going to Luigi's on a Friday night, huh?" As she turned to go into her room, she sang out, "I told you so!"

For once, Cat's fantasies had become a reality. La Petite Maison was everything she'd imagined it to be and more. It was a small restaurant, with dim lighting and candles that cast a pale glow on each lace-covered table. Soft violin music blended with the low murmur of conversation and the tinkling of glasses. A man in a black suit with a bow tie had seated them, and he'd pulled Cat's chair out for her. Cat hoped Todd had noticed this, but she doubted it.

There was a gold-framed mirror on the wall by her table, and Cat caught her reflection. In all modesty, she had to say she'd never looked better. The dark green dress made her eyes shine like emeralds, and the French braid made her look at least sixteen, she thought.

Across from her, Todd was tugging at his collar and shifting around in his chair.

"What's the matter?" she asked.

"I hate ties," he muttered. "And these chairs are too hard." He opened the menu. "It's so dark in here I can't even read this." He grabbed the candle and pulled it closer. "Hey, this is in French!"

"It's a French restaurant," Cat said.

"Yeah, well, I'm American. Jeez, look at these prices."

Was he going to complain all evening? "Todd, you don't have to pay, remember?" She opened her own menu. Once, Mademoiselle Casalls had

79

brought a menu from a French restaurant to class, and she'd explained what all the different words meant. Too bad Cat hadn't paid much attention.

She was distracted by a young couple who were being seated at the table next to them. They couldn't be that much older than she and Todd were, she thought. Maybe five years. But five years certainly made a big difference. The guy was gazing intently at his date, as if he were hypnotised. Cat strained to hear what he was saying.

"You're looking very beautiful tonight," he said.

"Thank you, darling," she replied.

Cat sighed, "Todd . . ."

He was still staring at the menu. "Yeah?"

"Do you like my hair this way?"

"Yeah, sure." His eyes hadn't even left the menu.

"Should I wear it like this for the dance at school?"

"Sure, if you want to."

He was *impossible*. A waiter appeared by their table. "May I take your order?"

Cat looked at the menu again. She could say she wasn't ready, but then, she could study this menu for an hour and still not be ready.

"May I explain some of our dishes to you?" the waiter asked kindly.

"Oh, no, that won't be necessary," Cat replied. "I'll have, um, the *escargots* and the *canard*."

She didn't know if she'd pronounced the words properly, and the waiter gave no indication whether or not she had. "And for you, sir?"

"Uh, I guess I'll have the same thing."

As soon as the waiter left them, Todd asked, "What are we getting?"

Cat didn't want to tell him she didn't have the slightest idea. "Let it be a surprise."

Todd tugged at his collar again. "Why can't they have decent music in here?"

Cat glanced at the couple next to them again. Now their hands were touching across the table. Cat let her own hand sneak across the table. Todd didn't notice. He was counting the silver by his plate. "What do we need so many forks for?"

"Todd . . ."

"Huh?"

"How's the basketball team coming along?"

Answering that question kept him occupied until the waiter returned. Ceremoniously, he placed silver dishes in front of them.

Cat stared at the little shells. In each was nestled a glob of something that looked pretty disgusting. She hoped her face didn't reveal her reaction.

Todd didn't even try to hide his feelings. "What's that?"

"*Escargots*, sir," the waiter replied. Then he translated. "Snails."

Todd's face turned a rather interesting shade of green.

Luigi's was packed and noisy. Kids were hopping from one table to another. Becka sat in the corner of a booth and picked a cold piece of pepperoni off the remnants of a pizza. Across from her, Josie and Red were engaged in a lively argument over some football game they'd seen on TV. Keith had wandered off to talk to a guy at another table.

"There're Cat and Todd," Josie said suddenly.

Becka turned. Todd was in the process of pulling off his tie as he strode towards them. He had a broad, relaxed grin on his face, as if he'd been lost in the woods and finally discovered his campsite. Cat walked behind him, an expression of resignation on her face.

"Hi guys," Todd said when he reached their booth. "Can we squeeze in?"

Red and Josie moved over to make room for him, and Cat slipped in next to Becka. "Where's Keith?" she asked.

"Around," Becka replied. "What are you doing here? I thought you were going to that French restaurant."

"We went," Cat said. "But Todd's still hungry."

Todd snorted and turned to Red. "You

wouldn't believe what they call a meal in that joint. It's not enough to feed a baby. Can I have a slice of that pizza?"

"It's cold," Josie warned him.

Todd didn't care. He took a slice and practically crammed the whole thing in his mouth.

"Hiya, buddy!" Keith had reappeared. Todd was obviously surprised to see him.

"How'd you get out of the house? I thought you were grounded for life after your last report card!"

Cat hopped out of the booth and let Keith get in next to Becka. Becka shot her a grateful look. Cat was becoming remarkably sensitive.

Keith tossed an arm loosely around Becka's shoulder. If there was such a thing as heaven on earth, Becka had just found it.

"Becka here rescued me," Keith told Todd. "When I told my father I was being tutored, he let me out." He gave Becka an endearing smile. "Thanks, Becka."

"You're welcome," Becka said. "I'm happy to tutor you anytime you want."

"You mean it?" Keith gave her a little squeeze. "This is great. Whenever I want to get out of the house, Becka will provide me with an excuse."

Becka laughed uncertainly.

"You going to be playing basketball this season?" Red asked.

"If I can get the grades up," Keith said.

Todd shook a finger at Becka and pretended to be stern. "You better do a good job. The whole team's counting on you."

"I'm willing if Keith is," Becka said. She liked the way Keith gazed at her appreciatively.

"I'm going to hold you to that," he said. "Hey, there's Alex." Todd and Red joined Keith and headed across the room.

Becka didn't miss the way Josie's eyes followed Keith and the way they narrowed. "Why don't you like him?"

"I just don't think he's all that serious about learning French," Josie replied. "It seems to me he wasn't paying much attention when you were working at home."

"That's okay," Cat said. "It just means his mind was on Becka."

"You really think so?" Becka asked eagerly.

"Absolutely."

"How was dinner at La Petite Maison?" Josie asked. "I guess Todd wasn't too crazy about it."

Cat's smile disappeared. "I don't think Todd's mature enough to appreciate a place like that. Not like—" She stopped suddenly.

"Not like who?" Josie asked.

"No one."

But Becka caught the glint in Cat's eye and knew she was thinking about her mysterious admirer. She gave Cat a knowing, sympathetic look.

Red returned and started to sit down. "Wait," Josie said. "Let me get out first. I have to go to the bathroom." She climbed out of the booth. "Too many sodas."

A look of agony crossed Cat's face and she closed her eyes. "I can't believe she said that in front of a boy," she whispered to Becka.

Becka nodded fervently. She herself might not have had much experience with boys, but even she knew you *never* told a boy what you were going to the bathroom for.

Red sat down, and Cat smiled brightly at him. "I'm glad to see you and Josie out together."

Red looked at her blankly. "We're together a lot. You know that."

Cat uttered a tinkling laugh. "Oh, come on, you know what I mean. Out on a *date*."

Red just stared at her.

"And it's about time," Cat went on. "She's been waiting ages for this."

Becka watched Red's freckles begin to merge. "She . . . she has?" he stammered.

"Shh," Becka hissed. Josie was returning. Red got out of the booth. "Uh, I'll be right back."

Josie looked after him curiously. "Why is his face so pink?"

"Maybe because he was thinking about you,"

Cat said. "Really, Josie, you should be more aware of his feelings."

"You're nuts," Josie said succinctly.

Before long, it was time to go. They all left together and started up Main Street. Cat lagged behind the crowd.

"Cat, come on," Josie called.

Becka turned and saw Cat staring across the street. She followed the direction of her eyes and realised they were focused on Dream Burger. There was an oddly wistful smile on her face. Becka was the only one who knew what she was thinking.

Six

As Becka took her seat in French on Monday, Patty turned around. "I bet I know how you're feeling right now."

"I studied pretty hard," Becka said.

Patty grinned. "I'm not talking about the test. I heard you went out with Keith on Friday night."

It was amazing how fast stories spread. "It was no big deal," Becka said in an offhand way. "I was tutoring him. Then we went to Luigi's."

"That's still a date," Patty insisted. "Do you think he's going to ask you to the dance?"

Becka dropped her mask of nonchalance. "I don't know. Keep your fingers crossed for me."

Patty's voice dropped to a whisper. "Here he comes now."

Unlike most of the kids, who raced to their desks and opened their books for last-minute cramming, Keith stolled in with an air of confidence. Becka's stomach started jumping when she realised he wasn't going to his usual seat. He was heading directly towards her. He dropped his books on the desk just behind hers. "Anyone sitting here?"

Dumbly, Becka shook her head.

"Well, someone's sitting here now," he announced, hitting her with the full force of his smile.

Patty, who was listening, put a hand over her mouth and looked at Becka wide-eyed. Becka understood her reaction. Whenever a boy liked a girl, he moved to the seat just behind hers so he could whisper in her ear and pass notes. It was a tradition of long standing at Green Falls Junior High. In fact, Cat had a boy sitting behind her in every one of her classes.

Now Keith was sitting behind Becka. He was announcing to everyone that he was interested in her.

Becka turned slightly and offered a smile. The smile he flashed back was different from his usual one. It suggested that they shared a special secret. Becka couldn't think of one thing to say. Luckily, she didn't have time to say anything. Mademoiselle Casalls walked in.

"Please put away the books, boys and girls," she said pleasantly. "I am certain you are all well prepared for this test, and you will all do splendidly."

A voice whispered in Becka's ear. "What an optimist."

Becka bit her lip so she wouldn't giggle.

"I will now distribute the tests, but please do not begin them until I say it is time. You will have the entire period to complete them."

"Do we get extra points if we finish early?" Keith murmured.

This time Becka had to clamp her hand over her mouth. How was she ever going to concentrate on this test with Keith whispering in her ear? Even if he didn't, just knowing he was there was going to make her nervous.

She wanted to turn and wish him good luck, but she couldn't. The teacher was getting closer. She placed a test facedown on Becka's desk, but she was looking past her.

"I see you have changed your seat, Keith," she said.

"Yes, I mean *oui*. Is that okay?"

Becka didn't understand why Mademoiselle Casalls hesitated. People changed seats all the time. Finally she nodded, handed him a test, and moved on.

"All right, you may commence," she announced.

The room became silent except for the scratching of pens and pencils. With all the mental power she could gather, Becka forced Keith out of her mind.

The questions were about what she'd expected. She was particularly glad to see that they had to conjugate the verb *aller*. Surely Keith would remember that.

She finished before the end of the period and spent the rest of the time going over her answers. Then the bell rang. Students dropped the tests on the teacher's desk as they went out.

Keith left the room before Becka, but he was waiting just outside the door. Behind his back, Patty gave Becka a thumbs-up sign and scurried away.

"How'd you do?" Keith asked.

"Okay, I think," Becka said. "How about you?"

"Okay," Keith said, his eyes twinkling. "I think."

"Did the tutoring . . . was I a help?" Becka asked shyly.

"You bet," Keith replied.

"Then maybe we can study together again sometime."

"Yeah, maybe." Keith gave her a salute. "See ya."

As he walked away, Becka realised they'd been standing just under a poster announcing the forthcoming dance. She wondered if he'd noticed it.

Cat sat on the gym bleachers with the other

members of the pep club and half listened to committee reports. She was thinking about her success as a matchmaker. She had been pleased when Becka reported that Keith had changed his seat in their French class. It was a good sign. She was going to have to work more on Josie and Red. Josie wasn't exactly being cooperative. But with Cat's help, Josie and Becka could both become . . . well, maybe not as popular as Cat, but socially acceptable, at least.

She remembered so clearly how both of them had embarrassed her when they first started at Green Falls Junior High. They were definitely improving. Getting them both a decent love life would make the biggest difference.

As for her own love life . . . well, she had Todd. But she couldn't get that secret admirer out of her mind. Would she ever hear from him again?

She felt Marla's elbow in her ribs. "Get a load of Heather."

The pep club president was prancing down the bleachers. She had on a fabulous outfit, a long pink sweater with a short purple skirt and purple leather boots. She had a new haircut, too. And she was looking very pleased with herself.

"What's she so happy about?" Cat wondered out loud.

Heather stood before the crowd and gave

91

them all a warm, toothy smile. "I just want to remind you all that the pep club is co-sponsoring the dance next week along with the student council. So we have to support the dance, and I want to see every one of you there."

"Too bad she can't provide dates for us to go with," Britt muttered.

"Who is *she* going with?" Cat asked.

"I don't know," Marla said. "But I'll find out."

The meeting was over, and Cat left with her friends. Passing the library, she saw Red coming out. "You guys go on ahead," she told the others. "I'll catch up."

She waved to Red. "Hi. Going home?"

"No, I'm meeting Josie at the gym."

Cat clapped her hands. "Oh, Red, I'm so glad!"

Her enthusiasm startled him. "Why?"

"Red, weren't you listening to me at Luigi's? Josie likes you."

"Of course she likes me," Red said patiently. "We're friends."

Cat sighed. "You know, Red, for a smart guy you can be really dense. Josie *likes* you. Get it? Okay, maybe she doesn't act like it, but I'm her sister. I *know*."

Red suddenly became very interested in his shoes. "Uh, yeah, okay. Look, I better get going."

Well, she'd definitely gotten through that time, Cat decided as she ran to catch up with her friends. She wondered if there was such a thing as a career in matchmaking.

When Cat got home, she dropped her books on the foyer table. Something there caught her eye. She blinked and looked again. It was a plain white envelope with her name and address. She snatched it up and ran to her room.

Tearing open the envelope, she pulled out the white sheet of paper and sat down on her bed.

Dear Cat,

At night I dream of you, and all day long you never leave my thoughts. I see your beautiful face, I hear your sweet voice, I smell your perfume. I even feel you in my arms. But you're only a vision. Will our love ever become a reality?

I don't know how much longer I can continue to worship you from afar. The pain in my heart is becoming unbearable. Somehow, some way, we must meet. I hope you feel the same. For I know you are my one and only, now and forever love.

Cat fell back on her bed. For a moment she lay perfectly still, enjoying the warm, glowing sensation that surrounded her. Then she jumped up and ran to the phone in Annie and Ben's room.

Just as she was about to grab it, the phone rang. "Hello?"

"Cat, it's me," Marla announced. "Listen to this."

"No, you listen first," Cat said. "I got another letter." She read it over the phone.

She was gratified by Marla's shriek. "It sounds like he's desperate! Oh, Cat, this is so incredible!"

"No kidding. Marla, I've just got to get to Dream Burger again. If he's there and he sees me, maybe he'll get up the nerve to speak. What's *your* news?"

"I don't know any details," Marla reported, "but rumour has it that Heather's bringing a high school boy to the dance."

"A high school boy!" Cat gasped. "So that's why she's been looking so happy."

"At least now you know she's not after Todd," Marla said.

After she hung up, Cat stood there for a moment and considered the news. She supposed it was reassuring to know that Heather didn't have any rotten scheme in mind to get Todd back. But the thought of Heather walking into a junior high dance with a high school boy annoyed her.

Especially since she knew there was a high school boy madly in love with *her*.

One thing Becka especially liked about Mademoiselle Casalls was that she always had tests graded the day after they were given. Tuesday was no exception. As the teacher began distributing the tests at the end of class, Becka waited anxiously. She wasn't actually worried for herself. She was thinking about Keith.

The teacher was taking her time, murmuring words of praise or encouragement to each student, so Becka had the opportunity to develop a real fantasy. Keith wouldn't get a D or an F this time. He'd get a C, maybe even a B minus. He'd be so happy and so grateful to Becka for her help that, in a burst of appreciation, he'd ask her to the dance.

"Becka." The teacher's voice broke through her daydream. She was smiling. "Excellent, as usual."

"Thank you," Becka said, accepting her test, which had a big red A on the front.

She didn't dare turn around, but she strained to listen as Mademoiselle Casalls moved to the desk behind her. She hoped to hear something like "Good, Keith" or "Much better." But she heard nothing.

The teacher returned to the front of the room and the bell rang. Becka whirled around in her seat. "How did you do?" she asked eagerly. As soon as the words flew out of her mouth, she regretted them. What if he had blown it again?"

But she needn't have worried. Keith held up the test so she could see the grade.

Becka gasped. "An A?"

Keith grinned as he stuck the papers in his notebook and rose. Becka got up, too, feeling just a little dizzy.

"Wait till I show this to Coach Meadows," Keith said. "Pretty terrific, huh?"

"Terrific," Becka echoed automatically. But her mind was reeling. An A? Keith Doyle got an A in French? No wonder Mademoiselle Casalls was studying him with a sceptical expression as he and Becka moved with the rest of the class towards the door. Just as they reached it, her voice was heard over the hum of conversation. "Keith? Would you remain behind a moment? I'd like a word with you. And Becka, you too, please."

Stiffly, Becka followed Keith back to the teacher's desk. As soon as the last student had left the room, she spoke. "Keith, I was rather amazed by your sudden improvement. And coming so soon after you changed your seat. Can you explain this?"

Keith smiled easily. "Becka's been helping me. She's been giving me tutoring sessions."

Just one session, Becka thought. And not a

very productive one. But when Mademoiselle Casalls asked, "Is this true, Becka?" all she replied was, "*Oui*, mademoiselle."

The teacher nodded, but her eyes seemed to pierce Becka's thoughts, and Becka shivered. Then Mademoiselle Casalls turned her gaze to Keith and her eyes narrowed. "I see. That will be all, for now."

Keith walked ahead of Becka to the door. By the time Becka came out into the hall, he had disappeared. She slowly walked to her next class and tried very hard to push the suspicions out of her mind. Maybe he'd just studied very, very hard. Maybe he'd decided to take his schoolwork seriously. But the rumours Josie had reported to her about Keith kept coming back to her.

Stop it, she scolded herself. *You're jumping to conclusions. You don't know what's going on. You've got absolutely no evidence whatsoever.*

But an *A*? . . .

Josie slammed her locker door shut and looked at the locker across the hall. Where *was* Red, anyway? He always went by his locker after the last class. For once, she didn't have basketball practice, and she wanted to go riding.

Finally, she spotted him coming down the hall. "Red!" she called.

He looked up. For a second his mouth started to form his usual slow, easy grin. But then it turned into something that looked more like a nervous twitch.

"You want to go riding today?" Josie asked him.

"Today?"

"Yeah, today. In about an hour."

He shifted his books from one arm to the other. His face started to redden. "I don't know. Maybe. We could, but . . ." His voice trailed off.

"Look," Josie said impatiently, "either you want to go riding or you don't."

"Um, I've got a lot of homework."

"Oh. Okay." Josie started to turn away.

"Wait," Red said. "If, I mean, if you really want to, I don't know . . ." He was starting to stammer.

"Red! What's the matter with you?"

Now his face was flaming. "Nothing."

Josie was perplexed. "Well, I'm going home. If you want to ride later, call me."

He didn't meet her eyes, but he nodded and went to his locker. He got his coat, closed the door, and walked away.

Josie was still staring after him in bewilderment when Cat came by. "Earth to Josie. Come in, Josie."

"Oh. Hi."

"What's up?"

"It's Red. I wonder if he's feeling all right. He's acting so weird."

"How do you mean, weird?"

Josie tried to explain. "I don't know. All nervous and flustered or something."

Cat laughed gaily. "Josie, that's normal! That's the way guys act when they're in love!"

Josie was about to give her usual response to that suggestion – a groan, a roll of the eyes, and an order to cut it out. But for some reason, Cat's remark didn't trigger that reaction. She looked at her sister uncertainly.

Cat patted her shoulder. "Don't freak out. Just let it happen! You'll see, Josie." Her eyes glazed over. "Being in love . . . it's incredible." She floated away down the hall.

Now Cat was the object of Josie's curious scrutiny. She'd never talked like that about Todd before.

"Are you going straight home?" asked Becka, who had just walked up. When Josie nodded, she said, "Tell Annie and Ben I've got a *Green Gazette* meeting."

"Today? I thought you had meetings on Mondays."

"There must be something special going on. I found a note from Jason on my locker." She didn't sound particularly enthralled with the notion. Her expression was listless.

Jason Wister came tearing up the hall. "Becka, are you coming to the meeting?"

"Yeah. What's the big deal, anyway?"

Jason's face was flushed with excitement. "I've got big news. Dr Potter called me to his office this afternoon. He read the editorial in the *Gazette*. You know, the one about how we need an honour code."

"That's good," Josie said. "It's nice to know the principal actually pays some attention to what students think."

"And he liked it!" Jason continued. "He said he thinks there's more cheating going on than he suspected. And he's going to form a committee to look into writing up a policy."

Josie punched him on the shoulder. "The power of the press! Good going! Becka, isn't that great?"

"Yeah," Becka said. "Great." But her voice was flat.

Jason didn't pick up on it. He grabbed Becka's arm. "Come on, I can't be late for my own meeting." Becka allowed herself to be dragged away.

Now Josie had a third person to wonder about. What was the matter with everyone, anyway? Shaking her head, she headed to the exit. Whatever it was, she hoped it wasn't contagious.

Seven

"No basketball practice for two afternoons," Todd told Cat as they strolled down Main Street that afternoon. "I feel like I'm on vacation. I mean, I'm sorry Coach Meadows has the flu, but it's great having some free time for a change."

"Yeah, great," Cat said, only half listening.

"Some of the kids want to go bowling tomorrow after school," Todd went on. "Want to come?"

"Sure."

"By the way, I told Alex we'd double with him and Sharon on Saturday night."

"What's Saturday night?"

"The dance!"

"Oh yeah, right." How could she have forgotten? Maybe because she had other things on her mind.

"Is that okay with you?" Todd asked.

"Is what okay?"

"Doubling with Alex and Sharon! Hey,

what's the matter with you? You're a regular space cadet."

"It's nothing," Cat said. "Yeah, doubling's fine." But there wasn't much enthusiasm in her voice. When Todd and Alex got together, they acted like clowns.

"You hungry?" Todd asked.

Cat shrugged. Todd took that for a yes. "Let's go to Luigi's."

"Wait," Cat said suddenly. "Not Luigi's. You know, I've got this major craving for a hamburger."

Todd considered this. "We could go to the coffee shop."

"Dream Burger has much better hamburgers," Cat said.

"Dream Burger!" Todd gazed at her in amazement. "What do you want to go there for?"

"Like I said, they've got good hamburgers."

"But we don't hang out at Dream Burger," Todd said.

"We don't have to hang out there," Cat argued. "We'll just have a hamburger and leave."

Todd shook his head. "That's a high school place, Cat. We're not exactly welcome there."

"I don't see any sign on the door that says no junior high students allowed," Cat retorted. "Come on, Todd. It's a free country. We can eat anywhere we want."

Todd glanced at the entrance to Dream Burger

as if he actually expected to see a sign proclaiming NO JUNIOR HIGH STUDENTS. "I don't think that's a great idea."

"Please," Cat wheedled. "I've been there before and nobody hassled me."

"With who?"

"Marla and her sister Chris."

"That's different," Todd said. "Chris is in high school."

Cat pouted. "Honestly, Todd. I never thought you were the kind of person who would be afraid to go into a place just because a lot of high school kids are there."

"I never said I was *afraid*," Todd replied. He looked at the restaurant again. Reluctance was clearly displayed all over his face. But Cat knew he'd give in. He always did.

"Okay," he said finally. "But let's not stay too long."

"That's fine," Cat agreed. Hopefully, she wouldn't need long. All she wanted was a chance to look around and enough time to be seen.

Of course, there wasn't much she could do there with Todd by her side. But if *he* was there and they made eye contact, at least she could put a face on her daydreams.

Dream Burger was noisy and crowded. There were no empty booths, so Cat and Todd took seats at the counter. Todd's expression was uneasy as he drummed his fingers on the countertop. Looking

103

at him, Cat marvelled at the difference a setting could make in a person. At school, Todd was cool and confident. Here, he seemed to shrivel. He looked just as out of place as he had in the French restaurant.

Cat swivelled around on her stool, and her eyes swept the room. Compared to the guys in here, Todd looked almost geeky. And there were lots of guys to compare him to. Tall ones, short ones, light-haired guys, dark-haired guys . . . she had no idea if one was her secret admirer. He might not be here at all, she warned herself. But then again, he might.

She thought she saw one or two guys glance her way. But there was no look of recognition in anyone's eyes.

"Hey, what do you have to do to get some service in here," Todd grumbled.

The guy sitting on his other side turned slightly. "Maybe you got to be a couple of years older."

Todd looked at him sharply. "What did you say?"

The guy sneered. "You heard me, kid."

"Let me hear you say it again."

Cat grabbed his arm. "Todd," she whispered, "don't start anything."

Todd pushed her hand off. The other guy gave a snide laugh. "Hey, that's a hot babe you got there. She deserves better."

With alarm, Cat watched Todd get up. "Want to talk about this outside?"

"Sure. Me and my buddies would enjoy that." With that, two more guys at the counter turned towards Todd with grins that weren't exactly friendly.

"Todd, let's get out of here," Cat said urgently. When he didn't move, she put more emphasis into her words. "Todd! *Please!*"

He grabbed her arm and pulled her towards the door. Behind them, she could hear the guys at the counter laughing.

"They're just a bunch of jerks," Cat said when they got outside.

She'd never seen Todd look so angry. "See? Now are you satisfied?"

Cat was startled by his tone. "It's not my fault you almost got into a fight!"

"I told you I didn't want to go in that place!"

"Why are you making such a big deal about it?" Cat asked.

Todd started walking rapidly. Cat had to run a few steps to catch up with him. Then he stopped and looked at her. "You know, Cat, sometimes I get the feeling you're taking advantage of me."

Cat wasn't sure how to react to that. She took a chance and tried an injured, hurt expression. "Todd. How can you say that?" She reached out and stroked his arm.

For the first time ever, that little gesture didn't

bring a smile. She decided to try another tactic. Gazing up at him seriously, she said, "Todd, I simply don't understand what you're talking about. Exactly what do you mean?"

She knew he wouldn't be able to elaborate. Todd wasn't very good at expressing himself. He made a stab at it, though. "It's like . . . sometimes I think you just use me."

"For what?"

"I don't know." Now he was definitely uncomfortable. "Forget it. I've got to get home."

They walked along, side by side. Every now and then, Cat stole a look at his face. But it told her nothing.

At lunch the next day, Josie listened carefully as the boys discussed the condition of the basketball team. Since Alex, Dave, and Jake had all played the year before, they had something to compare this year's team with.

"I'm not worried," Alex said. "Todd's got the speed, even if he can't shoot."

Jake frowned. "Yeah, but if Todd hurts his knee again, we're going to be in trouble. I still wish we had one more forward who could really move."

"Well, we might get one," Dave said. "I think Coach Meadows is going to put Keith Doyle back on the team."

"You're kidding!" Jake explained. "You mean, he's actually getting decent grades?"

"It's amazing, right?" Dave chuckled. "Leave it to Keith to work out a system."

"What kind of system?" Josie asked.

"You should know," Alex said. "Your sister's part of it."

"Becka?" Josie was confused. "You mean, he's got people tutoring him?"

Dave laughed ruefully. "No, he's got people letting him copy their work."

It took a moment for the implication of his statement to sink in. "Are you saying Becka's letting him cheat off her?"

"How do you think he got an A on that French test?" Alex asked.

Josie remembered Becka telling Cat that Keith had moved to the seat behind her. So this was the result of Becka's stupid crush. For a while, she actually thought Becka was becoming less of a wimp. Obviously, she was wrong.

Well, it wasn't *her* problem. Still, she found herself taking quick glimpses across the room to where Becka was sitting with her friends. Abruptly, she rose. "Excuse me," she muttered, and marched across the cafeteria.

"I have to talk to you," Josie said.

Becka looked a little surprised by her tone. "Have a seat."

"Not here," Josie said. "Privately." When Patty and Lisa raised their eyebrows, she added, "No offence." Turning back to Becka, she said,

"Meet me in the rest room outside the gym." She knew that at lunchtime it was deserted.

Without giving Becka a chance to protest, she whirled around and headed for the door. She didn't turn to make sure Becka was following her. If Becka was back to being that big a wimp, she'd follow Josie's orders without question.

When she reached the rest room, she did turn, but there was no sign of Becka yet. She was probably apologising to Patty and Lisa for Josie's rudeness. Josie went inside and paced the area by the sinks and mirrors.

Why did she care what Becka did? Then the answer hit her. Becka was a Morgan. And Josie hated the thought of any Morgan girl letting some sleazy playboy cheat off her just because she wanted a date. It was too sickening for words.

Finally, the rest room door opened and Becka came in. But she wasn't alone. Cat, her eyes bright with curiosity, followed her.

"What are *you* doing here?" Josie demanded, although she had a hunch. Becka must have figured out what Josie had discovered, and she'd brought along Cat for support. Becka never could fight a battle on her own. And Cat was so boy crazy, she'd probably approve of Becka's stupidity.

"Becka said you were excited about something," Cat replied. "What happened? Did Red ask you to go to the dance?"

"This is a lot more important than any dumb dance," Josie said. She fixed Becka with the look she knew made Becka cringe. "Don't you have any pride at all?"

Becka's face was all innocence and bewilderment. "What are you talking about?"

"Don't give me that," Josie snapped. "You let Keith Doyle copy the answers from your French test. And don't even try to deny it. He's been bragging about it to the guys."

"Is that all?" Cat rolled her eyes. "You're acting like Becka committed a crime or something."

"She practically did!" Josie stated. "Cheating is wrong. Even you know that."

"But Becka didn't cheat," Cat protested.

"Oh yes she did," Josie retorted. "Didn't you read that article in the newspaper? It said that if one person allows another to cheat, the first person is just as much at fault. If we really had an honour code, Becka would be just as guilty as Keith."

Cat brushed her words away. "That's ridiculous. We don't even have an honour code."

"It's still wrong," Josie insisted.

Cat gave her a withering look. "Josie, when will you ever learn that sometimes you have to do things to get a boy's attention?"

Josie's voice rose. "But he's just using her! And she's letting him! She's being a colossal wimp!"

"Both of you, shut up!"

Josie and Cat jumped at the unfamiliar energy in Becka's voice. Josie was particularly unnerved by Becka's reaction. She'd assumed Becka would whimper, cry even, or at least look extremely upset. She certainly hadn't expected an expression of fierce determination.

When Becka spoke again, her tone was steady. "First of all, I didn't *let* Keith cheat. I didn't know he was copying my answers. And second . . ." She paused and took a deep breath. "I am *not* a wimp!"

There was a moment of silence. "Okay," Josie said. "I believe you didn't know he was cheating. But he's going to keep right on doing it. You better tell the teacher."

"Are you nuts?" Cat asked. To Becka, she said, "You must go right on pretending you don't know what he's doing."

Becka looked at Cat. She looked at Josie. Then she went to the mirror and pulled out a hairbrush from her bag.

"Well, what's it going to be?" Josie demanded.

"Listen to *me*," Cat urged. "I'm the one who wants to help you."

Becka pulled the brush through her hair. Then she turned to Cat. "Yeah, I know. But this time I don't need your help." Her eyes shifted to Josie. "Or yours." She tossed the hairbrush back

110

into her bag and went to the door. She opened it and paused for one last comment. "I can take care of myself, believe it or not."

Cat didn't believe it. "Now you've got her all confused," she accused Josie once Becka had gone. "Why don't you just mind your own business?" She stalked out of the rest room before Josie could respond.

I really shouldn't blame Josie, Cat thought as she walked back to the cafeteria. Josie didn't *have* any of her own business to mind. How could Cat expect Josie to understand what a girl would do for love when she'd never been in love?

A plan for Josie began to form in her mind. Deep in thought, she didn't see Todd until he was right in front of her. "Hey, I gotta tell you something," he said.

Cat looked up vaguely. "What?"

Todd's eyes seemed to be focused on a point past her. "Um, it's about this afternoon."

"What about this afternoon?" Cat asked with just a hint of impatience. Now that she'd had this bright idea, she wanted to put it into action. Her eyes roamed the cafeteria.

"I know I said we'd go bowling. But something's come up, and—"

"Oh, that's okay," Cat said quickly. She didn't much like bowling anyway. Then she spotted the person she was looking for. "I'll see you later," she told Todd and hurried away.

"Red! Wait a minute. I need to talk to you."

He paused. "I have to get to class."

"I'll walk with you," Cat said. She matched her footsteps with his long stride. "It's about the dance. You know, Saturday night. I think you should ask Josie to go with you. She really wants to go, and she wants to go with *you*. I know you think you guys are just buddies, but she's feeling something else about you. Now, if she knew I was telling you this, she'd kill me." She realised she was chattering and hadn't allowed Red to get a word in. But Red hadn't even tried. In fact, he looked speechless.

"So call her, okay?" Cat asked. "Tonight." Without waiting for a reply, she ran off.

Becka clutched her books tightly as she waited by Keith's locker after the last bell. She needed something to hold on to. Automatically, her eyes lit on the poster hanging on the wall. She wished she didn't want to go to the dance so much. In her mind, she saw herself walking in with Keith, arm in arm. She could see the admiring looks of her classmates. She heard the music. She had the feeling Keith was a good dancer. It was something about the way he moved. There was a swagger to his walk. She saw it now as he came towards her.

"Hi," he said, punctuating his greeting with that incredible smile.

Becka steeled herself. *Why* did he have to look so good? This wasn't going to be easy. "Hi. I wanted to ask you something."

He twirled the combination on his lock. "Ask me no questions, I'll tell you no lies." He winked. "Just kidding. What's up?"

"It's about the French test."

"What about it?"

Becka forced the words out. "Did you . . . did you copy my answers?"

She was watching his hands. They didn't falter as he finished dialling his combination and opened the locker door. When he spoke, his tone was casual.

"I talked to Coach Meadows. He said if I can keep making grades like that, he's letting me back on the team." He pulled out a sweater. "Test grades aren't going to be enough though. There's homework, too. That's fifty percent of the grade, right?"

"Right," Becka replied softly.

"Maybe I could take a look at yours."

Becka tried to swallow, but the lump in her throat made it too painful. "You want to start copying my homework." It was a statement, not a question.

"I'll change a few answers so Casalls won't catch on," Keith assured her. "Actually, I should have done that on the test. Old Frenchy was suspicious."

At least he wasn't a liar, Becka thought dully. Suddenly, she couldn't bear to look at him. Her eyes went back to the poster.

When she didn't say anything, Keith turned towards her. His eyes followed hers. "Got a date for the dance?"

"No."

"Want one?"

Becka forced herself to face him. "You want to take me to the dance?"

"Sure. I mean, after all you've done for me . . ."

"You don't need to do me any favours," Becka said.

"I don't mind."

"But I do." Becka could feel her face getting hot. At least she knew she wasn't going to cry. She was too mad to cry. "Besides," she continued, "you don't owe me anything. See, you're not going to be copying my homework. And if you don't change your seat tomorrow, I'll be changing mine."

Despite her anger, she almost enjoyed the stunned look on Keith's face. She didn't allow herself to enjoy it for long. But she knew it was still there as she turned her back on him and walked away.

Eight

For once, Cat could understand why people liked doing good deeds for other people. She was feeling almost saintly as she walked home from school. What a good sister she was! She knew her suggestion to Red had made an impact. He'd ask Josie to the dance, they'd realise they were really in love, and Josie would start behaving like a normal girl. As for Becka, Cat felt sure she'd take her advice about Keith and not Josie's. After all, Becka had always looked up to Cat. Now Becka could have a date for the dance, too.

She recalled a Sunday school teacher back at Willoughby Hall who had told the orphans that a person who did nice things for other people was always rewarded. If that was true, Cat was due for something wonderful very soon.

"Hi," she called out as she entered Morgan's Country Foods. Annie looked up from the counter where she was ringing up purchases.

"Hi, honey. Have a good day?"

"Very good," Cat replied.

Annie gave the customer his change and beckoned for Cat to come closer. "I think your day's about to become even better. Something arrived for you at home."

"What?"

"Go look. It's on the table in the foyer."

Cat ran out of the store and across the street. Entering the house, her eyes darted to the little table. Then she gasped.

Sitting there was a huge bouquet of flowers. They weren't just regular flowers from someone's garden, either. They were all arranged with bows and wrapped in cellophane. A little envelope stapled to the paper displayed the name of a florist. Scrawled across the envelope was the name Catherine Morgan.

For a moment, Cat just stood there, frozen in a state of ecstasy. No one had ever sent her flowers before. When she recovered from her shock, she carefully pulled the envelope off the cellophane. Her hands were trembling as she removed the card.

The message was brief and to the point. "We must meet. Tonight, ten o'clock, Escapade. Your one and only, now and forever love."

She read it twice to make sure she wasn't seeing things. Clutching the card to her heart, she closed her eyes and let out a sigh of enormous

116

satisfaction. So the Sunday school teacher was right.

She opened her eyes when she heard the front door open. "Wow," Becka exclaimed, taking in the bouquet. "Whose are those?"

"Mine! And guess who they're from?"

Becka's eyes widened. "Your secret admirer?"

Cat nodded happily. "And guess what he wrote on the card?" Before she could go on, the door flew open again and Josie entered. "Nice flowers," she said.

"They're for Cat," Becka told her.

Josie gaped. "Todd sent you flowers?"

"No," Cat shoved the card in her pocket. "They're from someone else."

"I didn't think Todd was that goofy," Josie commented. "Who sent them? They must have cost a fortune."

Cat avoided the question. "Well, boys do crazy things."

"Yeah," Becka sighed. "Really dumb things, too."

"Are you talking about Keith?" Josie asked. Becka nodded.

Cat frowned. "You mean he still hasn't asked you to the dance?"

Becka studied the floor. "Oh, he asked me."

"Becka!" Cat turned to Josie in triumph. "See? I told you!"

But Becka's next words came as a shock. "I

said no. It was just a bribe. He only asked me so I'd let him copy my homework and cheat off my tests."

Now it was Josie's turn to be triumphant. "And you wouldn't let him. That's super, Becka, I never knew you were that gutsy."

"You call it gutsy," Cat murmured. "I call it stupid."

"No boy's worth getting into trouble for," Becka said. "Or doing something you know is wrong."

Cat could only shake her head sadly. She hadn't expected Becka to be such a goody-goody. Thank goodness she hadn't shown her the card from the flowers. Gathering them in her arms, she swept past the others and went up to her room.

There, she had a chance to look at the card again and think. Escapade. That was the club she'd heard about, the one that was letting in underage kids. It was on Green Street, she remembered. And he wanted her to be there at ten o'clock.

This was going to take some planning. She considered the possibilities. Then she got up and walked out of the room. She could hear Josie and Becka downstairs, talking. She hurried into Annie and Ben's room, shut the door, and went to the phone.

"Marla, it's Cat. Wait till you hear this. *He*

wants to meet me tonight at Escapade."

The screech on the other end was extremely satisfying. But Cat didn't even give it time to die down before she continued. "I need your help." Speaking rapidly, she told Marla what she wanted her to do. Then she heard footsteps on the stairs. "I have to go," she said in a rush. "Thanks!"

Opening the door, she practically collided with Annie. Annie seemed startled at finding her in their bedroom with the door closed. "I – I had to talk to Marla about something private."

Annie's eyes twinkled. "Telling her about the flowers?"

"Exactly," Cat said, glad she didn't have to make up a major lie. She started down the stairs.

"Who were the flowers from?" Annie called after her.

Cat laughed lightly. "Just some silly boy at school. He's got a crush on me."

"You mean Todd's got competition?"

"Looks like it!"

They were all just sitting down to dinner when the phone rang. Cat leaped up. "I'll get it!" She tore into the kitchen. "Hello?"

"Uh, hi, it's Red. Can I speak to Josie?"

"Hang on." She went back to the dining room. "Josie, it's for you, Red."

"Tell him I'll call him back after dinner."

"You tell him," Cat said.

Sighing, Josie rose and went into the kitchen.

"Cat got flowers today," Annie told Ben as she passed him a bowl of beef stew.

"Flowers!" Ben exclaimed. "From whom?"

"Just a boy," Cat said.

Ben shook his head in amazement. "Thirteen-year-old boys must be a lot more romantic than they were in my day," he mused.

Cat tried to picture Todd – or any other boy at school – sending her flowers. Not very likely.

"Boys must have a lot more money, too," Annie added. "It's a huge bouquet."

Both Annie and Ben were looking at Cat with curious interest. Cat plunged her spoon into the stew. "This is delicious."

Josie returned, and she looked disturbed. This drew Annie and Ben's attention away from Cat. "Is something the matter with Red?" Annie asked.

"Yeah." Josie sat down. "He just asked me to the dance."

Cat clapped her hands. "See? I was right again! Red *is* in love with you!"

Ben almost choked on his stew. "What?"

Annie was startled too. "Josie! I had no idea. I thought you and Red were just good friends."

"That's what I thought, too," Josie said glumly.

"It's strange," Becka murmured. "You think

120

a guy is one way and he turns out to be another."

"I think this is fabulous," Cat stated firmly. "Are you going to get a new dress? You should have a manicure, too, and—"

"Hold on," Josie interrupted. "I haven't even told him whether or not I'll go. I said I'd have to think about it."

"But you *have* to go!" Cat exclaimed. "You can't hurt his feelings. Here he's finally gotten up the courage to ask you out. If you turn him down, it could absolutely destroy him!"

"Now, Cat," Ben said, "I wouldn't go that far. I've been turned down by a girl or two in my time, and I survived."

"Red might be more sensitive," Cat argued.

"Josie certainly doesn't have to go on a date with Red if she doesn't want to go out with him." Annie noted.

"I like being with Red," Josie said. "But why do we have to go on a *date*? And I hate dances."

"You've never even been to one," Cat pointed out.

"Yeah, but wearing a dress, dancing . . . yuck."

The phone rang again. Ben started to rise, but Cat got up first. "Hello?"

"Hi, it's Marla. Here's your call."

Cat waited a few seconds. Then, loudly, she said "I'll have to ask and see if it's okay. I'll call you back."

121

In the dining room, she announced, "That was Marla. She wants me to come over tonight to work on this project we have for pep club."

"Tonight?" Ben frowned. "What about your homework?"

"I did most of it in study hall," Cat fibbed. "And I can finish what's left before I go."

"But it's a weeknight," Annie said. "Can't you and Marla work on this project after school?"

"Marla baby-sits after school every day," Cat explained. To support her case, she added another lie. "And we, um, can't work this weekend because . . . because we have to have it done by Friday." Strange, how she was stumbling over her words. Lies usually came so easily to her.

She could feel Becka and Josie looking at her sceptically. It was very hard to meet Annie's eyes, or Ben's. "It's really important. And I'll be in trouble with the pep club if we don't get this done." She turned on every ounce of charm she possessed. *"Please?"*

"How is Cat getting home from Marla's?" Annie asked Ben.

"She said Marla's sister would drive her home. But I told her to call and let us know when she was leaving. What time is it?"

Annie looked at her watch. "Almost ten."

Ben's brow furrowed. "She'd better call soon."

"You know how Cat loses track of the time," Becka said.

"What are you defending her for?" Josie grumbled.

"Are you angry at Cat?" Annie asked.

Josie sighed. "No. It's just that she keeps bugging me to go to this dance with Red. I wish she would quit trying to make me and Becka act like her."

Becka smiled. "That's just the way Cat is. Besides, you don't have to listen to her."

"But I don't want to hurt Red's feelings," Josie went on. "I guess it wouldn't kill me to go to one dance." She got up. "I'm going to call him now."

She was just reaching for the phone when it rang. "Hello?"

The voice at the other end was muffled, and Josie could barely make out the words, "Mr Morgan, please."

"Just a minute. Ben, it's for you," she called out.

Ben joined her in the kitchen and took the phone. "Hello?" There was a pause. *"What?"*

Josie watched his expression in alarm. Something was wrong.

"Who is this?" Ben demanded. He stared at the receiver, then slowly replaced it.

Annie came in. "Who was that?"

"I don't know. It was a female voice. She asked me if I knew where my daughter was. Then she said Cat is at Escapade."

Annie went pale. "The nightclub?"

"Maybe it was a prank," Josie suggested.

"What's Marla's number?" Ben asked. Annie picked up the Green Falls telephone directory and flipped through it. As she recited the number, Ben dialled it. "Hello, Mrs Eastman? This is Ben Morgan. Is Cat there?" His face hardened. "I see. Thank you." Hanging up, he turned to Annie. "Cat hasn't been there all evening."

Annie's hand flew to her mouth. Ben strode out of the kitchen, went to the hall closet, and pulled out a jacket. "Exactly where is this Escapade?"

It was chilly outside. Cat hugged her sweater closer. Glancing down at her jeans, she wished she could have worn something a little more spectacular for their first meeting. But Annie and Ben would have become suspicious if she'd dressed up just to go to Marla's.

Nervously, she looked up at the neon sign proclaiming this to be Escapade. There were no windows, so she couldn't see inside. She'd been standing out there for five minutes, and she'd seen several adults go inside. This was definitely not a kids' place. But the older girls had said anyone could get in. And somewhere in that place waited her one and only, now and forever love.

The thought gave her strength. Trying to look like she went into this kind of place every night, she opened the door. A man standing just inside muttered, "Five dollars."

Cat fumbled in her purse and pulled out a bill. The man barely glanced at her as he took it. Cat moved into the main room.

It took a few minutes for her eyes to become accustomed to the darkness. Between the dim lighting and the deafening music, she felt a little dizzy. Once her eyes adjusted, she made out a lot of figures on the dance floor. So many people . . . how was she going to find him? She'd just have to let him find her.

Along one wall was a counter with stools. Cat edged around the dancers and made her way there.

"What'll it be?" a man behind the counter asked.

"Um, a Diet Coke, please," She lifted herself onto one of the stools. The man brought her Coke, and Cat started sipping it. She wasn't thirsty, but it gave her something to do.

She felt so uncomfortable. She wasn't sure if it was this place or what she'd had to do to get there. Funny, telling little white lies had never bothered her before. She used to tell them all the time back at Willoughby Hall, to get out of chores and stuff like that. And she'd told some when she first came to the Morgans', mainly to avoid working at the store. At school, she never had a problem inventing stories.

Why did she feel so creepy about it this time? It was a dumb question. In her heart, she knew. It had something to do with lying to Annie and Ben. Lying to people who trusted her, who loved her.

But it was love that had brought her here, too. She'd had no choice.

Where was he, anyway? It was too dark to read her watch, but it had to be after ten by now. Surely he could see her sitting there. She certainly felt conspicuous enough. She swivelled on her stool to survey the room.

"Cat."

The voice came from behind her. It was unmistakably male. It was also unmistakably familiar. Slowly, she turned. Ben stood there, his arms folded across his chest, his face stern.

Cat had a pretty good suspicion all the charm in the world wouldn't get her out of this one.

Nine

On Saturday evening, Cat sat cross-legged on her bed and for the hundredth time in three days, bemoaned her fate. "Grounded. For two weeks. *Two weeks!*"

Sitting beside her, Becka patted her on the back. "Try to look on the bright side. It could have been for a month."

"And I didn't even meet him," Cat wailed.

"If he really loves you, he'll find a way to meet you," Becka said.

Cat's eyes drifted to the bouquet, which was still sitting on the dresser. The flowers were starting to turn brown and wilt. She hadn't had any more letters.

"What did Todd say when you told him you couldn't go to the dance?" Becka asked.

Cat shrugged. "He didn't say much. He didn't even act all that upset."

Becka nodded. "Boys don't show their feelings like girls do."

"How do you know so much about boys all of a sudden?" Cat asked.

"I'm learning," Becka replied. "Where's Josie?"

"In the bath. Isn't it weird? Of the three of us, she's the only one going to the dance."

Becka grinned. "And she's the only one who doesn't *want* to go."

Cat couldn't help grinning back. Then they both started to giggle.

"What's so funny?" Annie stood in the doorway.

"Josie," Becka said. "Going to a dance."

Annie smiled slightly. "I have to admit, she hasn't been particularly excited about this. Maybe we can all pitch in and get her spirits up." She came in the room. Standing by the girls, she stroked Cat's hair. Cat looked up. There was so much warmth in Annie's eyes. It truly amazed her. Despite what she'd done, Annie and Ben still loved her.

Josie, wrapped in a robe, stomped in. "Well, I'm clean."

"That's a start," Cat said. She got up. "Now, what are we going to do about your hair?"

Josie stepped back. "I'm not letting you stick those hot things on my head again."

"But it's so straight!"

"I like it straight," Josie insisted. "And no make-up either."

128

"You're hopeless," Cat grumbled.

"What are you going to wear?" Becka asked.

Josie flopped down on her bed. "I haven't even thought about that."

"*I* have," Annie said, and hurried out.

"Cheer up," Becka said to Josie. "It might be fun."

Josie wrinkled her nose. "I doubt it. I still can't figure out why Red wants to go."

Annie reappeared, carrying a bag from Danielle's Boutique, one of the nicest stores in town. She held it out to Josie.

"Oh, wow," Cat breathed as Josie pulled a dress from the bag. It was a deep midnight blue, simple but elegant, with long sleeves and a dropped waist. Josie held it in front of her and turned to the mirror.

"The colour's perfect for you," Becka said.

"It brings out your eyes," Annie added.

They all watched while an expressionless Josie examined her reflection. Finally, her face broke into a smile. "I guess if I have to wear a dress, it might as well be a pretty one." She turned and hugged Annie. "Thanks."

Cat watched in envy. She should be the one with the new dress. And it was her own fault she wasn't.

It didn't take Josie long to get ready. Cat was able to talk her into just a little make-up.

"How about some jewellery?" Annie suggested.

Josie wiggled the finger that held her little ruby ring, identical to the ones Becka and Cat wore. Annie and Ben had given them to the girls, to celebrate their becoming a family. "Isn't this enough?"

But Annie insisted on lending her some tiny pearl earrings, and she contributed a spray of her best perfume.

"Darling, you look beautiful," Annie said.

Privately, Cat thought that was an exaggeration, but she had to admit Josie didn't look half-bad. They all went downstairs.

"Who is this gorgeous creature?" Ben cried out as they entered the living room.

"I'm not sure," Josie said. "I certainly don't feel like me. Especially in these shoes." The heels weren't very high, but she was teetering in them. "How am I supposed to dance in these? I can't even dance in flat shoes."

"Well, you're going to have to," Cat said. "That's what you do at dances." She looked at the clock on the mantel. "Where is Red anyway? The dance started at eight, and it's already quarter after."

"Maybe he's got cold feet," Josie said. "Mine are freezing."

But just then the doorbell rang. On unsteady feet, Josie went to the door. Red stood there. He produced a rather sickly smile for her. And he was unusually awkward as he greeted the others and shook hands with Annie and Ben.

"Are you sure you two don't want a ride over to school?" Ben asked.

"No thanks," Josie said. "We'll walk."

"Hope she makes it," Becka whispered to Cat.

Red turned to Josie. "Ready?"

"Yeah." Her face was as grim as his. Together they walked out.

Cat shook her head. "You'd think they were going to a funeral, not a dance."

"Well, maybe they'll start enjoying themselves once they're there," Annie said, but her tone didn't carry much hope.

The phone rang. For once, Cat didn't jump up to get it. Who'd be calling her when everyone was at the dance? She was startled when Annie called to her from the kitchen.

"Maybe it's *him*," Becka hissed in Cat's ear. Cat ran to the kitchen and picked up the phone. "Hello?"

"Hi, it's me."

"Oh. Hi, Marla. You sound funny."

"I'm calling from the pay phone outside the gym. I can't talk any louder or someone will hear me."

"How's the dance?" Cat asked.

"It's okay. But Heather just walked in. And you're not going to believe who she's with."

"Some high school boy, right?"

131

"No, that was just a rumour. Cat, maybe you better sit down."

Suddenly, Cat knew what Marla was about to tell her. "Just say it, Marla. She's with Todd, right?"

"Yeah."

Cat stamped her foot. "That creep!" she raged. "Just because I'm grounded, he goes running back to that witch! Oh, I'm never going to speak to him again! Never!"

"I just thought you'd rather hear it from me," Marla whispered into the phone. "It'll be all over school by Monday."

And I'll be the girl who got dumped, Cat thought as she hung up the phone. Her eyes were burning. *Oh, Todd,* she thought. *How could you do this to me?* And did he have to take Heather, his ex-girlfriend and her number-one worst enemy?

It was all so embarrassing and humiliating and totally awful. She grabbed a napkin and wiped her eyes. There was no way she was going to cry over Todd. She'd much rather strangle him. And then a thought occurred to her that *really* made her want to cry. Now she wouldn't even get nominated for homecoming queen!

"You look very nice," Red said in a strained voice.

"So do you," Josie replied. Then they both

lapsed into silence. Josie thought about all the time she spent with Red. They usually never stopped talking. Now, as she hobbled along by his side, she couldn't think of a thing to say.

"They're having a live band at this dance," Red said.

"That's nice."

There was another awkward silence. "Have you ever been to a dance before?" Red asked.

"No."

"Then, how come . . . why do you want so much to go to this one?"

Josie stared at him. "Who said I wanted to go to the dance?"

"Cat. She said you'd be really hurt if I didn't ask you."

Josie stopped walking. "Cat told me you'd be really hurt if I told you I didn't want to go."

They stared at each other for a second. Then Red averted his eyes. Josie looked away, too. "Red . . . did Cat tell you I was, uh . . ." She tried to think of a way to say this without sounding too sickening. "That I wanted to be . . . more than your friend?"

Even in the darkness, she could see him blush.

"Well, yeah. Sort of."

Josie groaned. "She's been trying to convince me that you're the one who's, um, getting romantic."

133

They were both finding it impossible to look each other in the eye. Finally, Red asked the question. "Do you?"

"Do I what?"

He practically choked on the words. "Want to be . . . more than friends?"

The answer came easier to Josie. "We already are. You're just about my *best* friend. But I'm not interested in anything like . . . you know."

The relief on his face was clear. "Same here. Do you really want to go to this dance?"

"Not particularly. Do you?"

Red shook his head.

"Well, we have to do something," Josie said.

Red brightened. "How about bowling?"

"Bowling? Dressed like this?"

"Why not? There are no rules about clothes, just shoes. And we can get those there."

Josie grinned. "And I'll be able to walk." She linked her arm in his. "Let's go."

They did get a few odd glances in the bowling alley, particularly after Josie changed into bowling shoes. They didn't exactly go with the dress she was wearing. But she didn't care. She concentrated on trying out several balls before selecting the right one.

Red looked a lot more relaxed, too. "Hey, what do you think Cat would say if she knew we ended up here?"

"She'd say we were both very sick," Josie replied.

Red touched his forehead. "I feel pretty good myself. How about you?"

Josie stood in front of the lane and aimed her ball. "I feel fabulous." She rolled the ball. "A strike! I got a strike!" She threw her arms around Red. Then, very quickly, she withdrew them.

But Red was grinning. And he didn't even blush.

Ben came into the living room.

"Who were you talking to on the phone?" Annie asked.

"The mayor. It seems there's been one positive result of Cat's little adventure the other night. It provided evidence that Escapade *has* been letting underage kids in. Now the mayor's got proof he needs to order the place closed."

"Gee," Cat said. "So I've really done something good for the town."

"In a manner of speaking," Ben agreed. "But don't get the idea that it's going to reduce your sentence."

Cat's face fell. Ben put a gentle hand on her shoulder. "Two weeks isn't that long."

"It's not just that," Cat said. "It's Todd. He took Heather to the dance at school."

"Oh, Cat," Annie murmured. There was real compassion in her voice.

Ben looked sorry, too. "Well, he's a real jerk, then. They talk about women being flighty. Sometimes I think men are worse."

"No kidding," Becka muttered.

"Oh, dear," Annie said. "Have you had a bad experience, too?"

"Yeah." Becka told them about Keith.

When she finished her story, Annie groaned. "Men." She tossed a pillow at Ben.

Ben responded with an injured look. "Hey, don't blame the whole sex for a couple of rotten apples. Believe me, girls, there are a few good guys out there."

"He's right," Annie said. "I found one, didn't I?" She leaned over and planted a kiss on her husband's cheek.

"I think," Ben said slowly, "that our daughters need a little cheering up. Any ideas as to how we might accomplish that?"

"I only know one sure cure for depression," Annie said. "Chocolate. Unfortunately, there's none in the house."

"Then I say we go in search of some," Ben said. "Come on, girls, we're going to Brownies."

There weren't many people in the restaurant. It was too early for the after-movie crowd. And all the kids their age were at the dance. They settled in a booth and gave their orders to the waitress.

There was a question in Cat's head that had

been nagging her. She hadn't wanted to bring it up before. But now seemed the right time. "Ben, how did you know I'd gone to Escapade the other night?"

"I got a phone call."

"Who from?"

"I don't know. It was a female voice, though."

"Cat," Annie said, "you never told us *why* you went there."

Cat started to fabricate a story. But for some reason, she stopped and decided to tell the truth. "A guy asked me to meet him there."

"What guy?" Ben asked.

"I don't know." All of a sudden, she felt a little silly. "I have this . . . secret admirer. He's been writing to me."

"And he sent her those flowers," Becka piped up. "Isn't it romantic?"

"Where did you meet this secret admirer?" Annie asked.

"I haven't actually met him. He saw me at Dream Burger. He wrote that he couldn't get me out of his mind."

"And he called her – what did he call you?" Becka asked.

Cat reddened. "His one and only, now and forever love."

"Good grief," Annie said. She didn't look impressed.

Ben was actually frowning. "Cat, that could

have been very dangerous. You don't know anything about this person. He could have been a criminal."

"Oh, no," Cat said. "Everyone at Dream Burger is in high school."

"Even so," Ben began, but Becka suddenly clutched Cat's arm.

"Cat, look."

Cat's stomach turned over. Walking into Brownies were Todd and Heather. They sat down at a table near the entrance.

Annie and Ben saw them, too. Both grimaced.

"That's the girl he picked over you?" Ben asked. "He's dumber than I thought. And I question his eyesight."

Cat smiled sadly. "Thanks." It dawned on her that she didn't have any make-up on, not even lipstick. And just in case they saw her . . . "Excuse me a minute."

In the rest room, she made some repairs to her face. She was brushing her hair when the door swung open. Heather sauntered in.

"Why, Cat," she said sweetly. "What a surprise. Who are you here with?"

Cat kept her head high. "My parents."

Heather raised her eyebrows. "Your parents. On a Saturday night?" Her lips twitched, as if she was trying to keep from laughing.

"Why aren't you at the dance?" Cat asked.

"It was boring," Heather said airily. "Too

many seventh-graders crowding the dance floor. Todd hates crowds, you know." She pulled out a comb and ran it lightly over hair that was already perfect.

Cat stared at her own reflection. *My eyes are so much greener than hers,* she thought fiercely.

"Of course," Heather continued, "if we'd known you were here, we wouldn't have come. It must be so painful for you to see Todd now." She put the comb back in her purse and went to the door. Opening it, she paused and looked back. "But don't be too sad, Cat. I'm sure any day now, you'll find your one and only, now and forever love."

For an instant, Cat froze. Then she whirled around. But Heather was gone. Only her parting words lingered in the air. *Her one and only, now and forever love.* What her secret admirer had called her. How could Heather have known.

Then, like a lightening bolt, it hit her. Suddenly, everything made sense. She knew how the secret admirer had learned her name. She knew why he'd never tell her his. She knew why he didn't show up at Escapade.

There *was* no secret admirer. It was a set up, a prank, Heather's finest scheme so far. She had seen Cat coming out of Dream Burger. She had sent the letters and the flowers. She had made the phone call to Ben.

And Cat had fallen for it all. She turned back

to the mirror and faced herself. The strangest assortment of feelings were churning inside her. First, she wanted to cry over the loss of the boy who never even was. Then she wanted to laugh at herself for being such a fool.

But it wasn't long before a stronger emotion took over. Anger. And a burning desire for revenge.

She'd get back at Heather for this. She could always figure out a way to get Todd back. Of course, she wasn't so sure she wanted him back. Maybe she'd have to come up with some other way to make Heather suffer. Something really horrendous. . . .

She didn't know what, or how, or when. But she'd come up with something. Nobody pulled a stunt like this on Cat Morgan and got away scot-free. Heather was going to *pay*.

Thoughts of revenge improved her mood. But she still felt like such a fool. She spoke to her reflection. "Cat, for a smart girl, you can be really stupid."

The rest room door opened and Becka came in. "Hey, are you okay? You've been in here forever."

Cat turned around, and Becka stepped back in alarm. "You look you're ready to kill someone!"

"I am," Cat said grimly. "But don't worry. It's not you. Come on." She started towards the door. "Now I'm in *serious* need of chocolate."

140

Here's a sneak peek at what's ahead in the exciting fifth book of THREE OF A KIND:
Cat Morgan, Working Girl

Cat walked at a steady pace, her face set in a grim expression. Glancing at her watch, she quickened her step. She knew what Miss Andrews' reaction would be if she was late. This was only her second real working day at the Green Falls Inn. She wished it was her last.

Her thoughts went back to Friday. It had been a disaster. She couldn't do anything right, at least not according to Miss Andrews, the manager. Cat left streaks on the windows, she didn't sweep properly, and she broke one of the stupid china figurines on the lobby mantel while she was dusting. For two hours, Miss Andrews had hovered over her, scolding and snapping and complaining. Well, what did she expect? Cat Morgan was *not* cut out to be a maid.

Somehow, she'd managed to keep up a brave front at home over the weekend. She couldn't very well let Ben and Annie know how miserable she was, not when she was working for their friends. Even thinking about her new dress from Danielle's Boutique didn't bring much comfort, considering what she was going through to get it.

In her eyes, the Green Falls Inn no longer looked pretty and quaint. It was beginning to resemble a torture chamber. With extreme reluctance, she opened the door and went in.

"Morgan!"

Cat flinched. "Yes, Miss Andrews?"

"What are you waiting for? Get into your uniform immediately."

Cat went into the little bathroom behind the reception desk and took off her skirt and sweater. Then, with a grimace, she slipped into her uniform and tied the apron around her waist. She tried to avoid the mirror, but years of habit forced her eyes automatically in that direction.

For once, she didn't smile and preen at the image she saw. Her reflection revolted her. Grey had to be her very worst colour. It made her skin look yellow. The uniform was baggy and shapeless. And that wretched apron! It was like a sign, telling the whole world she was a maid.

Scowling, she pulled her hair back in an elastic band, the way Miss Andrews insisted she wear it. One lock refused to be gathered and fell down the side of her face.

I look like Cinderella, Cat thought. *Before* the visit from her fairy godmother. She could only be grateful that all the guests here were from out of town, and she wasn't likely to ever see any of them again.

Out in the lobby, Miss Andrews' piercing eyes hit Cat. "Follow me." She led Cat to a storage closet, where she took out a can of furniture polish and a nasty-looking rag. "Do the banister."

Cat took the rag gingerly between two fingers and went to the stairs.

Miss Andrews snatched the rag out of her hands. "Like this!" She rubbed the railing vigorously. "Haven't you ever polished furniture before?" She snorted. "Are you afraid of ruining your nails?"

Cat pressed her lips together tightly so the response she was forming in her head wouldn't come out of her mouth. A rush of conflicting emotions battled inside her. On the one hand, she wanted to inform this witch that she had lived in an orphanage for thirteen years and had done her share of drudgery. Not to mention the fact that she had regular chores at home.

"Okay, get to work."

Cat rubbed until the manager left the area. Then she examined her hands. Already, the polish was leaving brown streaks. Gook was collecting under

her fingernails. The polish on a nail was chipped.
Waves of self-pity engulfed her.

Two women came down the stairs and stepped
past her as if she were invisible. Well, who *would*
notice a maid? Oh, the shame of it all. . . .

Step by step, she mounted the stairs, dragging
the rag across the banister. Thank goodness, her
friends couldn't see her now. Her lunchmates
knew she was working here, but she'd managed
to avoid telling them exactly what she did. Her
reputation would be in shreds.

Finally, Cat reached the top. Then she
stepped back down, glancing at the banister as
she went. It didn't look any different to her.

Miss Andrews was nowhere in sight. Thankfully, Cat collapsed on the bottom stair. Through
the railing, she felt a cold breeze as the door to
the Inn opened.

Sally Layton, the owner said, "Good afternoon. May I help you?"

A woman's voice replied, "Yes, we're meeting
the Hudsons for tea. Have they arrived?"

"I'll call their room," Sally said. "Could I have
your name, please?"

"Mrs Beaumont."

Cat froze, then slowly turned her head to
get a look. A tall woman with streaked blond
hair, wearing a mink coat, stood there. She
wasn't alone. Cat swallowed and almost choked.
Standing beside Mrs Beaumont was Heather.

Cat Morgan,
Working Girl

For Amy Cimino

One

Josie Morgan lay sprawled on the living room floor with the *Green Falls Daily News* spread out in front of her. She pushed her unruly red hair out of her eyes and examined the front page. Scanning the headlines, she grimaced. There was a war going on in a country she'd never heard of, crime rates were up right here in Vermont, and a five car pile-up on a road just outside Green Falls had resulted in a lot of injuries.

"Why isn't there any good news?" she muttered.

"Ick!" Cat Morgan exclaimed from her place on the couch. She was also reading the paper. "This is disgusting!"

"No kidding," Josie agreed. "Wars, bank robberies, car accidents . . ."

"That's not what I mean," Cat said. "Look at my hands!"

Josie looked. Cat's fingers had black smudges on them. Josie had the same smudges on her own hands.

"I knew there was a good reason not to read

5

the newspaper," Cat grumbled, gazing at her dirty hands in dismay.

Swaying in the rocking chair, Becka Morgan glanced up from *her* newspaper. "It's not permanent, Cat. It comes off with soap and water."

"Maybe I don't particularly feel like washing my hands every time I turn a page," Cat replied. As she spoke, she automatically smoothed back a lock of hair that had escaped from her barrette. Then she let out a little shriek. "Oh, no! Now it's in my hair, too!"

"That's okay," Josie said cheerfully. "Your hair's as black as the ink. It won't even show."

"But I'll know it's there," Cat moaned. "And I just washed it this morning." With her hands stretched stiffly out in front of her, she rose from the couch and hurried to the little bathroom off the hallway.

"This is interesting," Becka said, turning back to the newspaper. "The public library is having a special exhibit of books by authors from Vermont."

Josie made no response. Only Becka would find something like that interesting. Bored and depressed with all the grim headlines, Josie pushed page after page aside. Then she brightened. "Hey, here's something good!"

"What?" Becka asked.

"The Giants have traded Rob Fenster to the Patriots!"

"Huh?"

"Football," Josie explained.

"Oh."

Josie turned another page. Then she started laughing.

"What's so funny?" Cat asked, returning with clean hands.

"This ad on page twenty-six," Josie replied. "Listen to this: 'An amazing scientific breakthrough! Now you can get rid of unsightly freckles and birthmarks. Use this remarkable *Invisicream* daily and watch those spots disappear!'"

Cat picked up her copy with two fingers and gingerly turned the page. "Why don't you get some of that stuff?"

"What for?" Josie asked.

"To get rid of your freckles, dummy."

"Maybe I like my freckles," Josie retorted.

Becka slipped off the rocking chair and went to the mirror that hung over the fireplace. She touched a tiny brown mark on her chin. "I wonder if that *Invisicream* would make this birthmark disappear."

Josie rolled her eyes. "Becka, *Invisicream* doesn't work. Nothing gets rid of freckles and birthmarks."

"Then why would it say that?"

"Because they're trying to get you to buy the stuff. It's all made up."

"How can you be sure?" Becka was still studying her birthmark. "It's in a newspaper. A newspaper wouldn't print something that's not true."

Josie eyed her impatiently. Becka could be so naïve sometimes. "It's an *ad*, Becka. Somebody paid to have this put in the newspaper."

Becka went back to the rocking chair. "I still don't think it would be in there if it wasn't true. Newspapers don't lie. I should know. I work for a newspaper."

Cat directed scornful eyes at her. "The *Green Gazette*'s not a real newspaper."

"Sure it is," Becka said. "Just because it's only for Green Falls Junior High doesn't mean it's not a real newspaper. We even take ads."

"Personally, I like the ads best," Cat remarked. "Like this one, on page six."

Josie turned to page six.

"Are you talking about this ad for Danielle's Boutique?" It was a photo of three girls wearing fancy dresses.

"Check out the dress in the middle," Cat said. "Isn't it gorgeous?"

Josie shrugged. A dress was a dress to her — something she was occasionally forced to wear instead of jeans.

A wistful sigh escaped Cat's lips. "I think it's positively elegant. It would be so perfect for the Turnaround."

8

"The *what?*" Josie asked.

"The Turnaround. It's a dance the pep club's going to have next month. Girls are supposed to ask boys for dates."

"Oh." Josie lost interest. Dances appealed to her about as much as dresses. Just last month, she and her friend Red MacPherson had almost gotten conned into going to one. Luckily, they had escaped in the nick of time.

"I love this dress," Cat said dreamily. "Black velvet, white lace collar, dropped waist . . ."

Josie tuned Cat out. Becka didn't seem to be listening either. She was engrossed in a newspaper article.

Well, that isn't surprising, Josie thought. Becka would read anything. An earthquake could hit and she wouldn't notice. When she wasn't reading, she was daydreaming about what she'd read. Josie could never understand that. She'd much rather do things than read about them.

If Becka was puzzling to her, Cat was mystifying. All she cared about was how she looked, what she wore, who she dated. Who would ever guess the three of them were related? Looking at them wouldn't give anyone a clue.

Becka had fair, frizzy hair and a penchant for crazy, gypsyish clothes. Cat had glossy black hair and emerald green eyes. She was always perfectly groomed and dressed in the latest fashion. As for herself . . . *how would*

9

I describe myself? Josie wondered. Tall, lanky, short red hair, and perpetually skinned knees from playing basketball. Luckily, they were almost always hidden by the faded blue jeans she wore.

About the only thing they had in common was their age – thirteen – and their last name. Of course, there was no reason why they should look alike, act alike, *be* alike, even though they were all Morgans. Only five months ago, they had been unrelated orphans. Then Annie and Ben Morgan had come along and adopted all three of them. Practically overnight, they went from being orphanage roommates to sisters.

Josie heard the back door of the house slam. A moment later, Annie Morgan appeared in the room. The fresh, multi-coloured smudges on her smock announced that she'd been out in her studio, painting. "Hi, girls," she called. Her eyebrows went up as she saw what they were doing. "Since when have you guys become newspaper readers?"

Cat answered for them. "Since the principal started requiring it. We're supposed to read the paper every day. Can you believe it? How could he do this to us?"

"Well, it's not exactly torture to read a newspaper," Annie replied.

"It is for me," Cat murmured.

Becka explained, "Dr Potter decided we should all be more aware of current events. He thinks we waste time in homeroom, so from now on we'll spend the period talking about the news."

"It's so ridiculous," Cat said. "*I* don't waste time in homeroom."

"What do you do there?" Josie asked. "Add another layer of eye shadow?"

Cat made a face at her, but she didn't argue. *Probably because it's true,* Josie thought.

Annie perched on the arm of the couch, and Cat looked up at her hopefully. "Maybe you could write our teachers a note to get us out of it. Like, you could say the news is too violent or something."

Annie laughed. "No way, honey. I think Dr Potter's idea is excellent. We should all be aware of what's going on in the world."

"But everything that's going on is so depressing," Josie complained.

"That's not true," Becka said. "There's an article on page ten about how the standard of living has improved in eastern Europe. It's fascinating."

"Maybe if you live in eastern Europe," Cat countered. "We live in Green Falls, Vermont."

"Now, Cat," Annie gently reprimanded her. "We're all people, and we need to care about what happens to people all over the world.

11

Come on, I'll bet there's something in this newspaper you'd enjoy reading about."

Cat considered that. "Actually, I did find something interesting." She held up the ad for Danielle's Boutique. "Isn't this dress pretty?"

"Very pretty," Annie agreed.

"It would be nice for a special, dress-up occasion, wouldn't it?" Cat said casually. Then she snapped her fingers. "I almost forgot! The pep club's having a dance next month!"

Josie and Becka exchanged looks. Cat was never good at being subtle. Annie looked at her in amusement. But she shook her head. "It's also pretty expensive, Cat."

Cat dropped her innocent act. "Seventy-five dollars isn't so much for a really nice dress," she objected. "And it's going to be a very special dance, Annie. Everyone's going to get really dressed up."

Annie's face became serious. "Cat, I'd love to be able to get you that dress. But—"

Before she could get any further, the front door opened and Ben Morgan came in. For a moment, he just stood there, very still.

"Ben, what's the matter?" Annie asked in alarm.

A slow smile spread across his face. "Nothing. I'm just taking a minute to absorb this happy scene. Home sweet home, and all my

12

lovely ladies together. It's a very nice change after a day in Morgan's Country Foods."

Josie grinned. "Didn't any lovely ladies come into the store this afternoon?"

"No ladies at all, lovely or otherwise," Ben told her. "No men either, for that matter."

"Ben!" Annie exclaimed. "Are you saying we had no customers at all?"

Ben pulled off his jacket. "Okay, I'm exaggerating. Maybe we had two or three." He was still smiling, but Josie detected little lines of concern around his eyes.

Annie got up and went to the window. "Maybe it's the weather. It's been awfully cold today, and it looks like snow. Some people don't like to go out much in the winter."

"They still have to eat," Ben said. "What I don't understand is the maple syrup. Sales have been really low. Don't people eat pancakes and French toast any more?"

"Of course they do," Annie replied. "But I guess they're buying their maple syrup somewhere else."

"All sales are down," Ben said. He joined her at the window. "We need to do bills today."

"Do we have to?" Annie sighed.

"Mmm-hmm. The mortgage is due. And the home-improvement loan payment. I think we should go over the budget, too. The heating bills have been staggering."

Hearing this conversation made Josie uneasy. She got the feeling her parents wanted to talk privately. "I'm going upstairs," she announced, gathering up her newspaper.

Becka had picked up on the atmosphere, too. "I'll come with you."

Only Cat seemed totally unaware of what was going on. She stayed where she was, still looking at the dress ad. "Cat," Josie said, "we're going upstairs."

"Mmm."

Becka leaned over the couch. "Come with us and I'll tell you what's in the newspaper. Then you won't have to read it." That got a response. Cat left the couch and followed them upstairs.

They all had their own rooms now. When they'd first been adopted, there had been only one bedroom available for them in the old, slightly ramshackle farmhouse. Becka had gotten the next renovated room. Just two weeks ago, Ben had finished painting the third. Cat had made a big show of graciously offering the new bedroom to Josie. It hadn't been all that generous, considering that the original bedroom was twice the size of the new one.

The three girls gathered in Cat's room. Becka climbed onto the bed and curled up, wrapping her arms around her knees. Her eyes were dark with worry. "Do you think Annie and Ben are having money problems?"

"It sure sounds like it," Josie said. "Maybe it's just a temporary thing."

"What are you talking about?" Cat asked.

"Annie and Ben," Becka said. "Didn't you hear what they were saying just now?"

"They were talking about maple syrup."

Josie groaned. "Where do you think our money comes from? Believe it or not, Cat, it doesn't grow on trees."

Cat sighed. "I guess there's no point in bugging them about this dress, then."

Josie felt like she was about to explode. "Honestly, Cat, you're so greedy!"

That accusation didn't bother Cat. She'd heard it before. She twisted the little ruby ring on her finger. "I wonder how much this is worth."

"Cat!" Becka gasped. "You wouldn't sell your ring for a dress, would you?"

Josie was a little shocked, too. Even though she wasn't into jewellery, the identical ruby rings they all wore were special. Annie and Ben had given the rings to them as a symbol of their birth as a family.

"No, I guess not," Cat admitted.

Josie tossed the newspaper on the bed.

"Hey, don't get that nasty black ink on my bedspread," Cat warned.

Josie wasn't listening. Something on the back page of the paper had caught her eye and she

15

snatched it back up. She read the ad in the For Sale column and she whistled.

"What is it?" Becka asked.

"Listen to this: 'For sale. One gelding quarter horse, ten years old, sixteen hands.' "

"Sixteen hands!" Cat exclaimed. "He must be deformed!"

Josie shot her a scathing look. "No, dummy, that's how horses are measured. Wow, would I love a horse like that."

"We've already got a horse," Becka pointed out.

"Maybelline?" Josie shook her head. "She's a sweet old nag, and I love her, but you guys don't ride her and I do. She can barely move."

"How much does that horse cost?" Becka asked.

Josie smiled. "Only four hundred dollars. That's really cheap."

"Four hundred dollars!" Cat yelled. "And you're calling *me* greedy?"

Becka was taken aback, too. "You can't ask Annie and Ben for four hundred dollars, Josie. Not when they're worried about money."

"Don't be silly. I'm not planning to ask them for any money," Josie assured her sisters. Still, she couldn't help wondering what colour the horse was.

"Okay, Becka, tell me what's in the newspaper," Cat demanded.

As Becka launched into a lecture on eastern Europe, Josie looked at the ad again. For as long as she could remember, she'd wanted a horse of her own. A lively, spirited horse who could jump over fences, take her galloping across the fields . . . but where in the world would she ever find four hundred dollars?

Maybe there was a cheaper horse for sale. She scanned the listings. There weren't that many, and before long she realised she was looking at the wanted ads. One of them caught her eye.

WANTED: Companion for elderly woman, ten hours weekly, five dollars an hour. Student preferred. For more information, call Mrs Daley.

A tingle shot through her. Ten hours a week at five dollars an hour. That meant fifty dollars a week. She did some rapid calculations. In eight weeks she could have four hundred dollars.

Stop it, Josie scolded herself. Whoever this elderly woman was, she probably wanted someone older, more experienced, not a thirteen-year-old eighth-grader. Even if the woman did offer her the job, Annie and Ben might not give her permission to take it. Besides, she had school, homework, basketball practice, work at the store, chores at home – when would she have time for a part-time job?

Still, it wouldn't hurt to ask Annie and Ben. And she could call this Mrs Daley for more information.

"I'm going to help Annie with dinner," she announced. Carefully, she tore out the ads for the horse and the job and stuck them in her jeans.

Two

At Cat's lunch table, the main topic of conversation was the same as it had been the day before, and the day before that.

"I don't know who to ask to the Turnaround." Sharon Cohen said.

"Me neither," Karen Hall echoed.

"I think I'm going to ask Alex Hayes," Britt Foley announced.

"Why?" Marla Eastman asked.

"Three reasons," Britt replied. "He's not going with anyone, he's taller than I am, and I'm pretty sure he'll say yes."

Trisha Heller clutched her throat. "What if you asked a guy and he said no?"

"I'd die," Sharon and Karen said simultaneously.

Cat shuddered along with the rest of them, although personally, she couldn't imagine anything like that ever happening to her.

"I might ask Jeff Wilson," Marla mused. "Who are you going to ask, Cat?"

"I haven't decided yet." Cat surveyed the noisy, crowded cafeteria. There were plenty of guys around, but none of them grabbed her eye.

"Well, I've got some news that might help you decide," Britt said. "I heard something very interesting last period." Britt glanced at another table. The others turned, too, and Cat knew immediately who Britt meant. Heather Beaumont sat there, surrounded by her usual group of adoring fans.

"Don't keep us in suspense," Marla ordered. "Tell!"

Britt leaned across the table, and the other girls automatically moved in closer. "I was talking to Pam Wooster. You know, she's on the tennis team with Eve Dedham. Wait till you hear what Eve told her."

She paused again and smiled mysteriously. Cat could tell that Britt was enjoying this and wanted to drag it out as long as possible. "Come on," she said impatiently. "Get to the point."

"Okay. Eve told Pam that Heather and Todd had a serious fight at Luigi's yesterday. And Pam said that Eve thinks she's going to break up with him."

Cat studied her fingernails. "What does that have to do with who I take to the Turnaround?"

The others gave her reproving looks. "Get real, Cat," Marla said. "He was your boy-friend."

It was a totally unnecessary reminder. "*Was,*"

Cat said. "Past tense. I wouldn't take Todd Murphy back on a silver platter."

She meant it, too. In the ongoing war between Cat and Heather Beaumont, Todd had been a major weapon. But even before Heather had managed to lure him away in the last battle, Cat had been getting bored with him.

She took another look at the pretty blonde holding court just three tables away. She had to admit, Todd's main appeal had been the fact that he was Heather's boyfriend when Cat first came to Green Falls. But if Heather had no use for him any more, why should she?

The others still looked sceptical. "I've got more important things on my mind right now," Cat told them. "Like, what I'm going to wear to the Turnaround. I saw a fabulous dress in the newspaper yesterday, but it's really expensive." She sighed. "I wish I was old enough to get a part-time job."

"I know what you mean," Marla agreed. "My sister just got an after-school job. She's going to be making tons of money, not to mention the discount."

"What discount?" Britt asked.

"She's working at Danielle's Boutique, and she gets a twenty per cent discount on anything she buys there."

"Danielle's Boutique!" Cat exclaimed. "Marla, that's where my dress is! Quick, somebody,

21

what's twenty per cent off seventy-five dollars?"

Trisha, the maths wizard, whipped out a pencil and did a quick calculation on her napkin. "Sixty dollars," she announced.

Cat groaned. "It's still way too much."

"It wouldn't matter anyway," Marla said. "Chris isn't supposed to buy stuff with the discount for anyone but herself. She won't even get me anything."

"Danielle's gives credit," Karen said. "You get three weeks to pay it off and you only have to put ten per cent down. That's – what?"

"Seven dollars and fifty cents," Trisha stated.

"I can come up with *that*," Cat said, "but where am I going to get . . . how much, Trisha?"

"Sixty-seven dollars and fifty cents."

"Right. How can I come up with sixty-seven dollars and fifty cents in three weeks? How do kids our age make money?"

"There's baby-sitting," Marla suggested.

Cat wrinkled her nose. "Little kids. Ugh."

"Dog walking?" Karen offered.

That appealed to Cat about as much as baby-sitting.

"My brother shovels snow," Sharon mentioned.

Britt giggled. "Cat couldn't do that. She'd ruin her nails."

"Very funny," Cat retorted. She leaned back in her chair. "I wonder who Heather's going to take to the Turnaround if she breaks up with Todd?"

Marla grinned. "She's probably waiting to find out who you want to ask, and then she'll ask him first."

"That sounds like something she'd do," Cat murmured. "Hey, that's not such a bad idea. Maybe *I'll* find out who she's planning to ask."

"Shh," Trisha whispered. "Here she comes."

Heather, accompanied by two friends, passed their table, but she didn't even glance at them. So she didn't see the piece of paper that flew out of her notebook and landed on the floor right by Cat.

Cat scooped it up. It was a newspaper clipping. She frowned as she studied it. "Why would Heather be interested in oil prices?"

"Check out the other side," Trisha said.

Cat turned it over. Then she practically choked. "This is it! My dress!" She showed the ad for Danielle's Boutique to the others. "It's the one in the middle."

"It's gorgeous," Marla exclaimed. She peered closer. "There's a little check mark over it."

"I'll bet Heather's planning to buy it," Britt said.

Cat wanted to cry. "She can't! It's mine!"

"Not unless you buy it before she does," Marla said. "You and Heather are probably around the same size. And Chris told me

23

Danielle's only orders one or two dresses in each size."

"Oh, well," Britt said, "you wouldn't want to show up in the same dress she's wearing anyway."

Cat gritted her teeth. "I want that dress. I'm going to Danielle's this afternoon and putting it aside."

"But how are you going to get the rest of the money in three weeks?" Marla asked.

"I don't know," Cat said. "I'll find a way." She would, too. If she wanted something badly enough, she could always figure out a way to get it. And knowing Heather was interested in this dress made her want it even more.

When the last bell rang, Becka hurried out of class. She had a *Green Gazette* meeting, and there was something she had to do first.

She ducked into a rest room, went directly to a mirror, and examined the birthmark on her chin. She couldn't see any change in it yet. Maybe it was too soon. She'd only just bought the *Invisicream*.

Funny, that birthmark had never bothered her before. But just a week ago, when she was working at the store, a small child had asked, "What's that spot on your chin?" Ever since then, it had looked bigger and darker to her.

She got the silver tube out of her purse and

squeezed a little cream out. She dabbed it on her chin and rubbed it in. She dropped the tube back in her purse just in time. The rest room door swung open and Josie burst in.

"Hi," she said hurriedly to Becka.

Becka's mouth fell open as Josie pulled off her jeans. She whipped a skirt out of her knapsack and put it on. Becka couldn't remember the last time she'd seen Josie in a skirt.

"What are you doing?"

"I've got an interview," Josie said. "There's an old lady who wants a part-time companion. Ben and Annie said I could apply. If I get hired, I'll get five dollars an hour. I could have enough for that horse in eight weeks!"

She washed her hands and ran back to the door. "Wish me luck," she yelled as she tore out.

Becka didn't. She stood there and shook her head in annoyance. Her sisters were so selfish. All Cat could think about was getting money for a dress. Josie wanted money for a horse. No one seemed to care that the Morgan *family* was having money problems. Except her. And she couldn't think of anything to do to help them.

By the time she got to the *Green Gazette* meeting, it had already started. Jason Wister, the editor of the newspaper, was handing out story assignments.

"Tom, can you catch a ride on the bus with

the football team Friday to cover the game?"

"Yeah. Can I take photos, too?"

"Sure," Jason said. "Take as many as you want. But they won't go in the newspaper. We don't have any money in the budget for photos."

A chorus of groans filled the room. "A newspaper without any pictures looks so crummy," someone said.

"I know," Jason replied. "But we can't afford them unless we have more money to spend. And the only way we can get more money is if we sell more ad space. If you guys would work harder at soliciting ads, we could have pictures."

"How are we supposed to solicit ads?" One of the students asked.

"Just go around to businesses and stores and ask them. Tell them how an ad can improve their business, increase their sales, that sort of thing."

"It really works," one girl piped up. "My mother bakes fancy cakes for special occasions, like weddings and birthdays. She took an ad in the *Gazette* last year, and kids must have shown it to their parents, because she got a lot more orders."

Becka sat up straight. That was what Annie and Ben needed – advertising! Why hadn't she thought of that before? If it worked for birthday cakes, it would work for a food store.

Her mind was reeling. Some people in town probably didn't even know the store was there. One little advertisement would get people to start thinking about Morgan's Country Foods. They'd come out of curiosity, if nothing else, and end up buying. Sales would skyrocket!

She leaned back in her seat with a pleased smile. She, Becka Morgan, was going to help make the Morgan family fortune.

Standing on the doorstep of a pretty, well-kept cottage, Josie took a moment to smooth down her hair and pull up her knee socks. She took a deep breath and pressed the doorbell.

The woman who answered the door couldn't have been Mrs Daley. She was an attractive, fair-haired woman in jeans and a flannel shirt.

"Hi, I'm Josie Morgan. I called about the job."

"Oh yes, come on in, Josie." Josie entered the house and looked around curiously. It was an old-fashioned-looking room, with large, dark, carved furniture. There was a big oriental rug on the floor.

"I'm Sue Campbell, Mrs Daley's companion."

Josie's face fell. "Oh no, you mean, she's already hired someone?"

The woman smiled. "No, I'm the full-time

companion. We're looking for someone to come in for a couple of hours, a few days a week, to stay with Mrs Daley while I do the grocery shopping, run errands, that sort of thing."

"Oh, I see." Josie decided Mrs Daley must be pretty decrepit, if she needed someone with her every minute. "Is Mrs Daley . . . very old, Miss Campbell?"

"Call me Sue. As for Mrs Daley, old . . . ? Well, in some ways, yes. In other ways, not at all."

Josie found out what she meant soon enough.

"Is that the child who's come about the job?" A tiny woman stood under the arch leading to the next room.

Josie bristled at being called a child. But she supposed that, compared to this woman, she was a child.

Her hair was grey, and she walked with a cane. Moving very slowly, leaning heavily on the cane, she approached Josie. "Let me take a look at you."

While she did, Josie took the opportunity to look *her* over. Her grey hair was almost as wild and unruly as Josie's. She wore baggy trousers and an old sweater with holes that had been darned. She looked sort of shabby, and Josie wondered how she could afford a full-time companion.

"I'll bet you're an athlete," Mrs Daley stated.

Startled, Josie nodded. "Yes, I play basket-ball for Green Falls Junior High. How could you tell?"

"Scabby knees," Mrs Daley said. "I always had scabby knees when I was your age. What's your favourite basketball team?"

"Uh, the Celtics."

"Mine, too!"

Josie gaped at her. Mrs Daley's eyes were as bright and lively as a child's. "What are you wearing that skirt for?" the elderly woman demanded. "Your legs must be freezing."

"I . . . I thought you might want someone who dresses nicely."

"Nonsense," Mrs Daley barked. "A good, heavy pair of jeans is what I want to see you in. You have jeans, I presume?"

Josie nodded. "That's usually all I ever wear."

"Good." She peered at Josie's face closely. "Aha! You don't wear make-up."

"Well, no, I—"

"Excellent! I'm tired of seeing these young girls messing themselves up with all that junk. Now, would this job interfere with your schoolwork?"

"I don't think so."

"How about your sports?"

"I guess it depends on when you'd need me," Josie replied.

"We're pretty flexible around here. We aim to please. Isn't that right, Sue?"

"Yes, ma'am," Sue replied with a twinkle in her eye.

"Don't *ma'am* me," Mrs Daley snapped. "You're going to frighten this child. She'll think I'm some sort of tyrant, and she won't want to come work here. Do you want to work here? What's your name, anyway?"

"Josie. Josie Morgan, ma'am." The *ma'am* slipped out before she could stop it. Mrs Daley grimaced, but then she grinned.

"Well, I suppose that's all right. Respect's a good thing for a young person to have. Don't see much of it these days." She paused. "Josie. I like that. It's not one of these fancy, newfangled names. It's got a good, solid sound. Well, Josie Morgan, you want this job?"

Josie's head was spinning. "I . . . I guess that depends. What would you want me to do?"

"You'd be a companion. That means you keep me company. You a good reader?"

"Okay, I guess."

"Good. My eyes don't work the way they used to. Can you fix a cup of tea?"

Dumbly, Josie nodded.

"Wash windows?"

Josie looked at her in dismay. Mrs Daley's lips twitched, then she burst out laughing.

"That was a joke, my dear." She turned to

30

Sue. "I think she'll do. What do you think?"

Sue smiled warmly. "I think she'll do just fine."

Josie could tell from the way Sue looked at Mrs Daley that there was real affection between them. She wasn't surprised. Once she recovered from her surprise at the oddness of this old lady, she had an idea she'd feel the same.

They worked out a schedule of two hours after school three days a week, and four hours on Saturday. Josie left with the promise that she'd be back the following day.

She wanted to race home and tell everyone, but there was something else she wanted to do first. She stopped at the nearest pay phone and reached in her pocket for the ad.

She stuck in her coin and dialled the number. "Hello, my name is Josie Morgan. I'm calling about the horse you have for sale. Could I come over and see him?"

She got directions from the person on the other end of the line and hung up. Her heart was thumping as she started walking. What if he wasn't the horse of her dreams? What if he was lazy and slow, or wild and unmanageable?

No, it wasn't possible. Somehow, she just knew it. Everything else was working out perfectly. This horse was going to be perfect, too.

Three

"She's nothing like what I expected," Josie told Annie several days later as they cut up vegetables for a salad. "She's so . . . different."

"How?" Annie asked.

"Well, I thought old people were all cranky and mean and out of it. Mrs Daley's totally real. She's into basketball, and she likes action movies, and she's funny. She's more like a friend than a boss."

"She sounds like an interesting person," Annie said. "I'd like to meet her sometime. Does she have any family here in Green Falls?"

"I don't think so," Josie replied. "At least, no one ever comes to visit while I'm there. And if she had family, she wouldn't need a paid companion." She tossed a mound of cucumbers into the salad bowl. "Working for her doesn't seem like work. I have such a good time, I feel funny taking money from her."

Annie paused in the middle of cutting up a tomato. "Are you sure it's not interfering with your schoolwork?"

Josie began measuring out oil for the salad

dressing. "No. In fact, I think it helps. I made a schedule, and I'm sticking to it."

"What about basketball practice?"

Josie grinned. "That's no problem. Some parents have been complaining to Coach Meadows about all the time we spend in practice. So he cut it back to just Tuesday and Thursday afternoons. I'm working at Mrs Daley's Monday, Wednesday, Friday, and Saturday afternoon. So it's perfect!" She took a piece of lettuce and dipped it into her dressing. "Try this. Does it need anything?"

Annie popped the lettuce into her mouth. "It's delicious. I don't know how you do it. Whenever I make dressing, it's either too oily or too vinegary. Has Mrs Daley discovered your culinary expertise?"

"My what?"

"Your talent in the kitchen."

"Not yet," Josie told her. "She doesn't eat much. She says her taste buds don't work the way they used to. I want to come up with something that appeals to her." She considered it. "Maybe a cheese soufflé."

Annie gazed at her lovingly. "You're some girl, Josie Morgan. I'm proud of you."

Josie blushed. "Thanks."

"Now, what are you going to do with all that money you're making?"

This was the perfect time to tell her about the

horse. She was just about to when Ben walked in. "Something smells unbelievably fantastic in here. Could it be . . . is it possible that we're having what I think we're having?"

"It's Josie's lasagna with her special secret sauce," Annie informed him. Ben clutched the sink and pretended he was about to faint with delight.

Annie gave Ben a look of mock frustration. "Would you believe that she won't even tell *me* what's in it?"

"Mrs Parker made me promise," Josie apologised. She remembered the day that the Willoughby Hall cook taught her the recipe, then swore her to secrecy.

Ben ruffled Josie's hair. "Well, as long as you're here to cook it, we don't need to know. But maybe when you go away to college—"

"I'll ask Mrs Parker," Josie promised.

Ben took a deep whiff of the aroma coming from the stove. "Sally and George are in for a treat. By the way, what time are they coming?"

"Around seven," Annie said.

"Good. I'll have time for a shower, a change, and maybe even a little nap."

"Rough day?" Josie asked.

"Boring day," Ben replied. "You know, sometimes sitting and doing nothing in an empty store is more exhausting than waiting on a hundred customers."

The sparkle in Annie's eyes seemed to dim. "Business hasn't picked up?"

Becka came into the kitchen just in time to catch that. "Don't worry," she said. "When our ad comes out in the *Green Gazette*, we'll have more business than we can handle. Have you written it yet, Ben?"

Ben closed his eyes and hit himself on the side of the head. "I forgot. I'm sorry, Becka."

Becka put her hands on her hips and eyed him sternly. "I want you to do it right away. Ben, you used to be in advertising back in New York. You must know how powerful a well-developed advertisement can be."

Ben looked at her in amusement. "How do you know so much about advertising all of a sudden?"

"I found some of your old advertising magazines up in the attic and I've been reading them. It's fascinating! Why do people buy one brand of toothpaste instead of another that's exactly the same? Because of the advertising! It makes the customer *think* one brand is better."

"I know, I know," Ben said. "I remember it well. Boy, am I glad to be out of that business. But I'll write your ad right away," he added hastily. "As soon as I've had a shower."

"I'll go set the table," Becka said and went back out into the dining room.

"Business will get better," Annie assured Ben.

"I hope so. For all our sakes." He took one last long sniff and left.

"Josie? What's wrong?"

"Huh? Oh, nothing." She felt Annie's eyes on her. She busied herself chopping a garlic clove and turned away so Annie couldn't see her face. It was burning, and she suddenly felt crummy.

Here she was, about to tell Annie she was saving her money to buy a horse, when they were so worried about their business. If she was a truly good daughter, she'd offer all her earnings to them.

"Josie, I'll finish up here," Annie said. "You can go wash up, and—" she stopped.

"And what?" Josie dumped the chopped garlic into the pan of melted butter.

"Well, I was going to say you could change your clothes if you'd like." She glanced at Josie's sweatshirt, which held traces of the lasagna ingredients. "But you don't have to if you don't want to."

Annie is so nice, Josie thought. Some mothers would order their daughters to dress up when company came for dinner. Annie gave her the choice. It made her feel even worse.

"Don't let the garlic burn," she said and went out.

It seemed as if a dark, gloomy cloud had just settled on her head. Was she a rotten daughter,

36

or what? Morgan's Country Foods could be in real trouble, and all she'd been able to think about lately was that horse.

She shivered as she recalled her first look at him. He was simply beautiful, chestnut brown with a shiny coat. She remembered the way he shook his head and whinnied when she stroked him. He was the horse she'd dreamed about. Even his name was perfect – Sunshine. As she climbed the stairs, she could see herself riding him on a sunny day, his mane flapping in the warm breeze . . . but Sunshine was a horse. Annie and Ben were her parents.

Cat was coming out of the bathroom, her head wrapped in a towel. "How was your old-lady-sitting today?"

"Don't call her that," Josie snapped. "She's a senior citizen, not an old lady."

She expected Cat to respond with a sharp retort. Instead, she just shrugged and mumbled, "Okay, okay. Sorry." Her face was despondent.

Was she worried about the store, too? Josie wondered. Curious, she followed Cat into her room. "What's your problem?"

Cat flopped down on her bed and raised a mournful face. "Remember that ad I showed you? The beautiful dress at Danielle's Boutique?"

"Yeah, why?"

"I put it aside on credit. I figured I'd find a job fast and have enough money to pay it off in three weeks. But it's been *days,* and I still haven't found anything."

"Have you tried?"

"Sure I have! I went to every store in town and asked them if they wanted a model. But nobody's interested."

"I don't think there's a big demand for models in Green Falls," Josie commented. "What happens if you don't pay for the dress in time?"

"They keep my down payment. And I don't get the dress." Cat cocked her head to one side and looked at Josie thoughtfully. "You must be making a lot of money, working for that old – uh, that senior citizen."

Josie's eyes narrowed. "What about it?"

"You could give – I mean, *lend* me the money to pay for my dress."

"How would you pay me back?"

"Out of my allowance. I could give you a little each week."

Josie uttered a short laugh. "That would take forever! Besides, if business at Morgan's Country Foods doesn't improve, we may not even be getting allowances." She paused. "I've been thinking . . . maybe I should give Annie and Ben the money I'm making. To help out."

Cat shook her head. "They'd never accept it."

She's right, Josie thought. Annie and Ben wouldn't take money from their daughters.

"But *I* would," Cat said. "So you might as well lend some to me."

"I can't," Josie said. "I'm saving it."

"For what?"

"That horse I saw advertised in the newspaper."

Cat stared at her for a second. Then she fell back on her bed. "A horse? You're going to spend all that money on a dumb horse?"

Josie hadn't expected her to understand. "Look, it'll take me eight weeks to save the money for the horse. After that, I can lend you some."

"It'll be too late!" Cat wailed.

"Then . . . I'm sorry." Josie left and went to her own room. Peering into her closet, she sighed. Then she pulled out a dress. It wouldn't kill her.

Cat hit the button on the blow dryer and aimed it at her hair. A horse. Her sister was making tons of money, and she was going to blow it all on a stupid horse. What a waste. And the most beautiful dress in the world was just waiting for Cat at Danielle's Boutique.

It wasn't fair. If she could just get a job, she'd have her dress.

To cheer herself up, she envisioned Heather

going into Danielle's Boutique, her purse crammed with money and credit cards, and asking to see that particular dress in size five. The saleslady would tell her the only size five had been reserved. Maybe she'd tell Heather *who* had reserved it.

A satisfied smile crossed Cat's face as she pictured Heather's furious expression. Or maybe it would be even better if the saleslady didn't tell Heather, and Heather wouldn't find out until Cat walked into the Turnaround.

Her smile faded. It wasn't going to happen. Not unless she figured out a way to come up with sixty-seven dollars and fifty cents.

She didn't bother to put on any make-up. It was only a couple of friends of Annie and Ben's coming over. She slipped into some corduroy pants and a shirt and went downstairs.

"Do you need any help?" she asked as she came into the dining room.

Annie placed a pair of candlesticks in the centre of the table. "I think we're all set, Cat." She disappeared back into the kitchen.

Becka smiled at Cat. "Funny how you always manage to show up just when everything's done."

Cat looked at the table. "Becka, knives go on the *right* side of the plate, forks on the left."

"Then you can switch them around," Becka replied.

Cat slumped down into a chair, put her elbows on the table, and rested her chin in her hands. "Who are these people coming for dinner?"

"Sally and George Layton. Ben and Annie knew them back in New York. They bought the old Green Falls Inn, and Ben says they've fixed it up really nice."

Cat looked up. "They're re-opening the old inn?" With Becka's nod, an idea sprang into her head. "I'll be right back." She ran out, ignoring Becka's cry of, "Hey, what about the knives and forks?"

So the Laytons are opening the old inn, Cat thought. They'd need people to work there. There must be something she could do, like . . . like what? Then it hit her. She could be the receptionist! She saw herself wearing a nice dress, greeting guests, registering the wealthy people who came to ski in Vermont. It was the perfect job for her!

Up in her room, she began to apply make-up. Not a lot, just enough to look a little older, more sophisticated. She twisted her hair into a chic knot. Then she pulled off her clothes and threw on a simple shirtwaist dress.

Just as she slipped her feet into neat flats, the doorbell rang. Josie raced past Cat's door. Cat wasn't going to run. She wanted to make an entrance.

She waited until she heard a chorus of voices

41

in the living room. Then she proceeded, slowly and gracefully, down the stairs.

"And here comes our third daughter, Catherine, better known as Cat," Ben said.

"How do you do?" Cat asked. She extended a hand, first to the woman, then to the man, and smiled. "It's a pleasure to meet you. Welcome to Green Falls!"

Behind Annie's back, she could see Josie rolling her eyes. Becka had a hand over her mouth, like she was trying to stifle giggles. Cat didn't care. She could tell from the couple's faces that she was definitely making an impression.

"I can't believe you've got three daughters," George Layton said later as they all moved into the dining room.

"You're very lucky," Sally said.

"We know," Annie joined in as she carried a steaming pan of lasagna out of the kitchen. "They bring us a lot of joy."

"And an occasional nervous breakdown," Ben added with a smile.

Cat stiffened. She hoped he wasn't about to start telling stories – like about the time she'd sneaked out of the house to go to a nightclub.

But she should have known Ben wouldn't betray family secrets. "Annie's right," he said. "Having a family has been the best thing that's ever happened to us."

"And how's your store doing?" George asked.

Annie and Ben exchanged looks. "It has its ups and downs," Ben said.

"It's going to be more up from now on," Becka reminded him. "Do you have the ad ready for me? The deadline's tomorrow."

Ben groaned. "I knew there was something I was supposed to do."

Becka sighed. "How about if I write it for you?"

"Be my guest," Ben said. He turned to the Laytons. "Becka's the writer in the family. She works on her school newspaper. And you should see the essays she does for her English class."

"Josie's our athlete," Annie told them. "She was the first girl to get into her school's basketball team."

"Wonderful!" Sally exclaimed. "By the way, this lasagna's delicious. When did you learn to cook like this? I didn't think you two even knew where the kitchen was in your apartment back in New York."

Annie laughed. "I've been learning, but I can't take credit for this. Josie made it."

"You've certainly got some talented daughters," George remarked.

Before anyone could ask Cat what *her* speciality was, she broke in. "I understand you're re-opening the Green Falls Inn."

Sally nodded. "The day after tomorrow."

"Becka's right about advertising," George

said. "We took one small ad in a Boston newspaper, and we've already got reservations coming in."

"What did you say in your ad?" Becka asked him.

"Oh, we just described the inn, how charming and quiet it is, and how close to the ski slopes." He winked at Ben. "I didn't exaggerate too much."

"George and I worked at the same advertising agency in New York," Ben explained to the others. "There were times when we were forced to exaggerate to come up with a halfway decent ad." He shook his head ruefully.

Cat spoke casually. "I suppose you're hiring people to work there."

"That's what I've been doing all day," Sally said. "Interviewing people."

"Do you have everyone you need?" Cat turned to Annie and Ben. "After hearing Josie talk about her job, I think I'd like one, too."

She couldn't blame Annie and Ben for being startled. Cat had never been known for her willingness to work.

But the Laytons were looking at her with interest. "We could always use another pair of hands," George said. "If it's all right with your parents."

Annie and Ben looked at each other. "Well,

I suppose it's okay," Annie said. "If it's not too many hours."

"Why don't you come by the inn tomorrow after school and we'll talk about it," Sally suggested.

Cat was dying to ask how much money they'd pay her. But that would have to wait. She wouldn't want them to think she was *greedy*.

Becka scrutinised her face in the bathroom mirror. The birthmark was still there. Was it a little lighter, maybe? No, she couldn't honestly say she saw any difference in it at all. Josie was right. The ad had lied.

Becka went back to her bedroom and shut the door. Then she sat down at her desk, turned on the desk lamp, and began chewing on a pencil.

Morgan's Country Foods. What could she say about Morgan's Country Foods that would make people want to buy stuff there? She thought about the ads she'd seen in newspapers and magazines, the commercials she'd watched on television. They all made wonderful promises and guarantees. That's what got people to buy the products. They exaggerated, according to Ben and George. If *Invisicream* was any example, they lied, too.

She thought for a while. Her creative juices started to flow, and she began to write.

Four

The next day, Cat left her class and hurried to her locker. She didn't want to be late for her meeting with the Laytons at the inn.

"Uh, hi, Cat." Todd, her ex-boyfriend, was standing by his locker. Out of the corner of her eye, Cat could see the lopsided grin that used to make her heart flutter. She glanced at him briefly, just to let him know she'd heard him. Then she breezed past him without speaking.

She caught a flash of his crestfallen face. *Serves him right,* she thought. Still, memories flooded her mind. Football games, movies, Luigi's for pizza. For a second, she almost felt wistful. Then she recalled that it was *always* football games, movies, Luigi's for pizza. Boring. Even so, she would have liked to have been the one who dumped him, not the other way around. And to be dumped for Heather Beaumont. The thought still rankled.

Cat reached her locker and started turning the combination. A group of boys passed, reminding her that she still had to figure out who to ask to the Turnaround. Now that she knew she was actually going to get that dress, she could get excited about the dance. If only she could think of a guy worth wearing it for. . . .

She opened the locker. Just as she was putting on her coat, she saw Britt and Marla running down the hall.

"I'm so glad we caught you," Marla said breathlessly.

"We were afraid you'd already left," Britt gasped.

"What's up?" Cat asked, eyeing them curiously.

Britt's face was flushed with excitement. "Wait till you hear what we found out!"

"Britt was in the bathroom," Marla began, "and—"

"Oh, let me tell it," Britt pleaded.

"Somebody tell me!" Cat demanded. "And quick! I have to get to the inn."

Britt took a deep breath. "I'd just come out of study hall, last period. I went into the rest room. You know, the one by the media centre, near the water fountain . . ."

"Yes, yes, I know," Cat said impatiently.

"Anyway, I went into one of the stalls. And guess who came in?"

"Britt, just tell her," Marla ordered.

"Heather and Blair Chase. Honestly, that Blair is such a dork. She tags after Heather like—"

"Britt!" Cat and Marla shrieked in unison.

"Okay, okay. I heard Blair ask Heather if she was going to take Todd to the Turnaround. And Heather said no, she broke up with him."

"Is that all?" Cat slammed her locker shut. "I told you, there's no way I'm asking Todd. Besides, I wouldn't want Heather's rejects."

"Wait, she hasn't gotten to the good part," Marla said. "Britt *tell* her."

"So Blair asked Heather who she *was* going to ask. And Heather said – are you ready for this?"

Frustrated, Marla finished for her. "She wants to ask Sid Belcher."

Cat's mouth fell open. "Sid Belcher! Britt, are you sure she said Sid Belcher?" When Britt nodded, Cat shook her head in disbelief. "No way."

"There's nothing wrong with my hearing. She said it loud and clear." Britt's forehead puckered. "Funny, Heather's usually so secretive about who she likes. And they must have known I was in there. They were right behind me in the hall. Kind of strange, don't you think?"

"What's really strange is Heather Beaumont asking Sid Belcher to the Turnaround," Cat said. "Why would she ever be interested in a greaser?"

Marla considered that. "Well, he's sort of

interesting looking. If you like the type."

Cat made a face. She simply could not picture Heather with a boy who wore a skull and cross-bones earring and sweatshirts with the sleeves cut off to display his tattoo. Privately, Cat suspected it wasn't a real tattoo. But it didn't matter. It still looked gross.

"Very weird," Cat murmured. "Look, I've got to go."

Marla and Britt walked along with her. "So what are you going to do?" Marla asked.

"About what?"

"Remember the other day when you said you'd like to find out who Heather was going to ask to the dance so you could ask him first?"

Cat was aghast. "Marla, you're not saying I should ask Sid Belcher!"

"You have to admit, it would be a great way to get even with her," Britt said.

"Are you nuts? Forget it!"

"You could ask him now and then break the date right before the dance," Marla suggested.

Cat wrinkled her nose. "That's an awfully mean thing to do. Even to a greaser."

"Yeah, I guess you're right," Marla said.

Cat sighed. "Too bad she isn't planning to ask someone more, more . . ."

"Human?" Marla asked.

"Right. See ya later." Cat left the building and began walking rapidly. She'd told Sally

49

Layton she'd be at the inn at three-thirty, and it was past that now. She wasn't really worried, though. After all, the Laytons were friends of her parents. She'd get the job whether or not she was on time.

As she walked, she considered the news she'd just heard. Heather with Sid Belcher . . . never in a million years would she have put those two together. Heather was so into being cool. Sid was the kind of person who smoked cigarettes in the boys' room and got suspended. Totally uncool.

It was too bad. It would have been fun to snag the boy Heather liked – but no way was she going after Sid. At least Cat would have the dress Heather wanted. That was something.

The Laytons had done a terrific job with the inn, Cat thought as she approached it. The last time she'd seen the building, its outside was peeling, windows were broken, and it looked generally rundown.

Now it gleamed and shined and looked positively elegant. If she had to work, this was a nice place to do it, Cat decided happily. She turned the brass knob on the front door and walked inside.

The lobby area was lovely, full of antique furniture, including a grandfather clock. Two flowered sofas faced each other, with a pretty rug between them. The reception desk was polished wood, with an old-fashioned telephone on it. Cat could see herself standing behind it, greeting guests, answering the phone.

What she didn't see was any sign of the Laytons. Of course, the inn wasn't scheduled to open until tomorrow, but Sally or George had to be around somewhere. "Hello?" Cat called. When there was no response, she slipped off her coat, sat down on one of the sofas, and picked up a magazine from the coffee table.

"What are you doing?"

Cat turned her head in the direction of the harsh voice. A woman with a face like a prune stood there.

Cat smiled brightly. "Is Sally Layton around?"

"Who wants to see her?"

"I'm Cat Morgan."

The woman nodded shortly, as if she recognized the name. But it didn't change her sour expression. "They told me you'd be coming at three-thirty. It's now four o'clock. I will not tolerate tardiness."

Cat stared at her in bewilderment. What was it to her if Cat was a little late? "I'm supposed to see Sally Layton about a job here."

The woman sniffed. "You're seeing me."

"Um, excuse me, but who are you?"

"I'm Miss Andrews, the housekeeper." She surveyed Cat and shook her head. "You don't look like you're going to be much of a maid."

Cat couldn't have heard correctly. "Did you say – a maid?"

"What size dress do you wear?"

Dazed, Cat managed to mumble, "Size five. Why do you want to know?"

"For your uniform, of course."

"Uniform?" Cat asked faintly.

"Your hours are three-thirty to five-thirty, Monday, Wednesday and Friday. You will report to me. As I said, you must be on time."

Cat swallowed. "What – what exactly will I be doing?"

Miss Andrews gave a look that clearly indicated her opinion of Cat. "What do you think a maid does? You'll sweep, dust, mop . . ."

The horrid words continued to come, but Cat wasn't hearing them anymore. She was in a state of shock.

"Your move," Mrs Daley barked.

Josie contemplated the chequerboard. She saw a place she could move to where Mrs Daley could jump her. Should she do it? No, Mrs Daley wasn't some little kid she had to go easy on. She'd want to win only if she could do it on her own. Josie moved her chequer somewhere else.

Mrs Daley's face was expressionless. Then the corners of her lips twitched. She picked up a chequer, jumped Josie's three remaining ones, and won the game.

"I didn't see that!" Josie wailed as Mrs Daley threw back her head and laughed.

"You're going to have to open your eyes if you want to beat me, child!"

"How did you learn to play chequers so well?" Josie asked.

"Many years ago, when I was skiing in the Swiss Alps, I broke my leg," Mrs Daley said. "Laid me up for a month. So I mastered every game I could get my hands on." She shook a finger at Josie. "For your own sake, never invite me into a game of poker."

"You've been everywhere, haven't you?"

"Just about, my dear. Never got to go to college, though. In my day, some parents didn't believe in education for a girl. But travel is a great education in itself."

"Of all the places you've travelled to, what was your favourite?" Josie asked.

Mrs Daley shook her head. "I don't believe in having favourites. There's something good to be said for every place I've been. Just like there's something good about every person I've known."

"I love hearing you describe your travels," Josie told her. "You make countries sound so much more interesting than my geography teacher at school."

53

"There are photos from some of my trips over there on that table," Mrs Daley said.

Josie had noticed the huge collection of framed photos on the corner table, but she hadn't examined them. She didn't want Mrs Daley to think she was nosy. But now that she had permission to look, she went over to the table.

"Wow, where's this old building? It looks like it's hundreds of years old."

Mrs Daley squinted. "Bring it closer, Josie." When Josie did, she scrutinised the photo. "Try more than a thousand years. That's the Forum, in Rome."

Josie put the photo back. There were so many interesting looking ones, she didn't know which to ask Mrs Daley about next. Snow-capped mountains, beautiful lakes, forests, castles, Heather Beaumont – Josie stopped. What was a photo of Heather Beaumont doing here?

"What are you looking at now?" Mrs Daley demanded, peering at her.

Josie brought the photo over to her. "Isn't this Heather Beaumont?"

"You know her?" Mrs Daley asked.

"Sure. She's in my class at school."

Mrs Daley nodded. "That's right. She would be in the eighth grade now."

"Why do you have a picture of her?"

"She's my granddaughter."

"Heather Beaumont is your *granddaughter?*"

"Something wrong with your hearing? That's what I said. Why do you look so surprised?"

"I don't know. I guess because you never mentioned having a granddaughter."

Mrs Daley grunted. "Maybe that's because sometimes I forget I have one."

Josie looked at her sceptically. There was nothing wrong with this woman's mind.

Mrs Daley grinned. "I don't mean that literally. She just doesn't come around to visit much. Only when her mother, my daughter, makes her."

How could a neat person like Mrs Daley be related to someone as creepy and snobby and mean as Heather Beaumont? "That's terrible," Josie stated. "If I had a grandmother, I'd visit her all the time."

"You don't have any grandparents?"

Josie shook her head, and Mrs Daley eyed her keenly. "Child, I don't know much about you. I'm always telling you stories about myself, but I haven't heard any stories from you. Tell me about yourself."

Josie busied herself putting photos back the way they were. "There's not much to tell."

"Nonsense," Mrs Daley stated. "Everyone's got a story. I want to hear yours." She rapped her cane on the floor. "Come here."

It was a direct order. Reluctantly, Josie left

55

the table and sat down in a chair across from the woman. "My life's not very interesting," she said.

"I'll decide what's interesting and what's not. I'm the boss here. I pay your salary, right? Well, okay, my son-in-law does. In any case, I'm in charge and I want to know about you. Start talking."

Josie had to smile. There was something about Mrs Daley that reminded her so much of Mrs Parker, the cook back at Willoughby Hall who had been Josie's closest friend. Like Mrs Parker, Mrs Daley was gruff on the outside but warm and kind on the inside. They were both real, no-nonsense, down-to-earth people.

Josie had the feeling she could trust Mrs Daley the way she had trusted Mrs Parker. So she started to talk.

"I was born in Texas." That was easy. Now came the hard part. "My parents were killed in a car accident when I was five." She tried to speak matter-of-factly, but she choked a little. Clenching her fists, she waited for the automatic look of pity she'd seen so many times to appear on Mrs Daley's face. But it didn't come.

Josie relaxed. She should have known. Mrs Parker never gave her those awfully pitying looks either.

"Go on," the elderly woman said.

"I was sent to live with a cousin in Vermont.

But she – she had her own kids and she didn't really want me. I went to some foster homes, but they didn't work out. So I was put in an orphanage. Willoughby Hall."

"How long were you there?"

"Till last July. I was adopted, by Annie and Ben Morgan. We live on Church Road. Our store, Morgan's Country Foods, is right across the street."

"I believe I met them when they first moved to Green Falls," Mrs Daley said. "So the Morgans adopted a thirteen-year-old girl? They're brave people."

Josie grinned. "They adopted *three* thirteen-year-old girls." She told Mrs Daley about Cat and Becka. Before long, she found herself telling Mrs Daley all about their experiences back at Willoughby Hall, and their life for the past five months with the Morgans.

Mrs Daley was a great listener, nodding, laughing, exclaiming at all the right times. "If your parents have a store, how come you're working here?"

"I needed to make some money. You see, I want to buy a horse."

"Aha! I knew it!"

"You knew what?"

"I just knew you'd be a horse lover." Her eyes became soft. "When I was your age, you couldn't drag me off my horse. A person would have thought there was glue on the seat of my riding britches."

Josie nodded fervently. "That's how I'm going to be. What was your horse's name?"

"Moonlight."

"Hey, that's sort of a coincidence! The horse I want to buy is called Sunshine."

"How much does this Sunshine cost?"

"Four hundred dollars. I figure I'll have enough saved up in eight weeks."

"I see." Mrs Daley was quiet for a minute. "You plan to quit coming here then?"

"Oh no!" Josie exclaimed. "I'm going to have to go on making money to keep him. I haven't told my parents about Sunshine yet, but I'm going to be responsible for him. I have to feed him, and I want to buy a good saddle, and some riding boots. Besides . . . I *like* coming here."

Mrs Daley beamed at her. "And I like having you here. Now, is the owner of Sunshine going to hold on to him until you have the money?"

"Not exactly. He said if he gets another buyer before then, he'll have to sell him. But no one's come to see the horse besides me. I'm just hoping no one will before I get all the money saved up."

"Sounds to me like you're taking a risk. Look, I've got a little money put aside. How

58

about if I lend you the four hundred dollars now?"

Josie breathed in sharply. What a great friend Mrs Daley was! To be able to buy Sunshine right now, today maybe, and not have to worry that someone else would buy him first . . . it was so tempting.

But she shook her head. It wasn't right. Annie and Ben wouldn't approve of her borrowing the money. And she wouldn't feel good about it herself.

"Thanks a lot, but I think I'd better wait until I earn it."

She saw approval in Mrs Daley's eyes. "I can't say I blame you. Something always seems more yours when you pay for it with your own hard-earned money."

Josie grinned. "Except that it hasn't been very hard earning *this* money."

Mrs Daley's eyebrows shot up. "Oh, no? Hmm . . ." She looked around the room. "Seems to me those windows are getting a little dirty."

They both started laughing.

Five

The *Green Gazette* arrived from the printer every Monday just as school was letting out. Becka, like most students, usually waited until Tuesday morning to pick up her copy and read it in homeroom. But this particular Monday, she waited impatiently just outside the school entrance for its arrival.

Finally, the car bearing the words GREEN FALLS PRINT SHOP pulled up in front of the school. A man jumped out, carrying a stack of newspapers tied with twine in each hand. Becka followed him into the school.

The man had barely finished cutting the twine before Becka grabbed the first copy. She disregarded the articles and news, and went directly to the back of the newspaper where the ads were. Her eyes scanned the page. Sports Stuff, The Town Shoppe . . . there it was!

She read the words she'd written with pride. In all modesty, she had to say it was a very creative ad. If this didn't help business, nothing would.

She felt very good about herself. Cat was

working for a dress, Josie was working for a horse. Only Becka was working to help her family. Ben and Annie would be so happy.

As she re-read the ad, savouring each and every word, two girls she didn't know picked up copies of the newspaper. She didn't pay any attention until she heard one of them say to the other, "Hey, did you see this ad?"

"Wow," the other one replied. "That's amazing."

Becka couldn't resist. "Which ad are you talking about?"

"Morgan's Country Foods," the first girl told her. "Look what it says about their maple syrup!"

Becka made a big show of widening her eyes and raising her eyebrows. "My goodness! That's remarkable!"

As the girls walked away, she overheard the other one saying, "I'm going to show this to my mother." Becka wanted to jump for joy. It was going to work! She saw Cat coming towards the exit and ran to her.

"Cat! Look at my ad!" She thrust the paper in Cat's face. Cat pushed it away.

"Not now, Becka." With her head down, she stalked out the door.

Becka gazed after her in mild curiosity. What was the matter with *her?*

Cat walked at a steadfast pace, her face set

in a grim expression. Glancing at her watch, she quickened her step. She knew what Miss Andrews' reaction would be if she was late. This was only Cat's second real working day at the Green Falls Inn. She wished it was her last.

Her thoughts went back to Friday. It had been a disaster. She couldn't do anything right, at least, not according to Miss Andrews. Cat left streaks on the windows, she didn't sweep properly, and she broke one of the stupid china figurines on the lobby mantle while she was dusting. For two hours, Miss Andrews had hovered over her, scolding and snapping and complaining. Well, what did she expect? Cat Morgan was *not* cut out to be a maid.

Somehow, she'd managed to keep up a brave front at home over the weekend. She couldn't very well let Ben and Annie know how miserable she was, not when she was working for their friends. Even thinking about her new dress didn't bring much comfort, considering what she was going through to get it.

In Cat's eyes, the Green Falls Inn no longer looked pretty and quaint. It was beginning to resemble a torture chamber. With extreme reluctance, she opened the door and went in.

From the lobby, Cat could see into the dining room. Guests were sitting at tables, having afternoon tea. Conversation and laughter drifted out into the lobby. Cat felt even more sorry for herself.

"Morgan!"

Cat flinched. "Yes, Miss Andrews?"

"What are you waiting for? Get into your uniform immediately."

Cat went into the little bathroom behind the reception desk and took off her skirt and sweater. Then, with a grimace, she slipped into her uniform and tied the apron around her waist. She tried to avoid the mirror, but habit forced her eyes automatically in that direction.

For once, she didn't smile and preen at the image she saw. Her reflection revolted her. Grey had to be her very worst colour. It made her skin look yellow. The uniform was baggy and shapeless. And that wretched apron! It was a sign, telling the whole world she was a maid.

Scowling, she pulled her hair back in an elastic band, the way Miss Andrews insisted she wear it. One lock refused to be gathered and fell down the side of her face.

I look like Cinderella, Cat thought. *Before* the visit from her fairy godmother. She could only be grateful that all the guests were from out of town, and she wasn't likely ever to see any of them again.

Emerging from the room, she passed Sally Layton behind the reception desk. The woman gave her a slightly anxious smile. "Hello, Cat. How is everything working out?"

Cat forced a return smile. "Just fine."

"Good, good. Miss Andrews, I'll be in the dining room if anyone wants me."

Miss Andrews' piercing eyes hit Cat. "Follow me." She led Cat to a storage closet, where she took out a can of furniture polish and a nasty-looking rag. "Do the banister."

Cat took the rag gingerly between two fingers and went to the stairs. The ornate carved railing along its side looked perfectly fine to her. But Miss Andrews was standing there, so Cat poured a little polish on the rag and stroked the wood.

"Not like that!" Miss Andrews barked. "Put some elbow grease into it!"

Elbow grease. What a disgusting expression. Cat polished a little faster.

Miss Andrews snatched the rag out of her hands. "Like this!" She rubbed the railing vigorously. "Haven't you ever polished furniture before?" She snorted. "Are you afraid of ruining your nails?"

Cat pressed her lips together tightly. *Don't say it, Cat*, she warned herself.

"Just what I need," the housekeeper muttered. "Some little pampered princess working here."

A rush of conflicting emotions battled inside

Cat. On the one hand, she wanted to inform this witch that she had lived in an orphanage for thirteen years and had done her share of drudgery. Not to mention the fact that she had regular chores at home. On the other hand, she rather liked having the image of a pampered princess.

"Are you listening to me?" Miss Andrews asked.

Are you saying anything worth listening to? Cat wanted to ask. She quickly drummed up a mental picture of her dress and replied, "Yes, ma'am."

"Then get to work."

Cat rubbed until the housekeeper left the area. Then she examined her hands. They were covered with brown streaks. Gook was collecting under her fingernails. The polish on one nail was chipped.

Waves of self-pity engulfed her. She felt like she was back at Willoughby Hall, a poor, neglected orphan, slaving away. Okay, she hadn't been neglected at Willoughby Hall, and no one ever treated her like a slave. The Green Falls Inn was definitely worse than an orphanage.

Two women came down the stairs and stepped past her as if she was invisible. Well, who *would* notice a maid? Oh, the shame of it all. . . .

Step by step, Cat mounted the stairs, dragging the rag up the banister. Thank goodness her friends couldn't see her now. Her lunchmates knew she was working here, but she'd managed to avoid telling them exactly what she was doing. Her reputation would be in shreds.

Finally, she reached the top. Then she stepped back down, looking at the banister as she went. It didn't look any different to her.

Miss Andrews was nowhere in sight. Thankfully, Cat collapsed on the bottom stair. Through the railing, she watched as the door to the inn opened. A man and a woman, both carrying suitcases, entered.

"This is charming," the woman exclaimed.

"A real New England inn," the man said.

Cat glanced at them with disinterest. Then she saw a boy, also carrying suitcases, come in after them.

He looked about her age, not very tall, but absolutely *adorable*. His hair was so blond it was practically white. And he had a tan — something unheard-of at this time of the year in Vermont.

Sally Layton bustled out of the dining room. "You must be the Hudsons."

The man put down his suitcase and shook hands with her. "Howard and Joan. And this is our son, Bailey."

Bailey, Cat mused. *What a neat name.*

"Welcome to the Green Falls Inn. If you'll come sign in over here, I'll show you to your rooms."

As Sally led them to the desk, Cat moved back slightly, but it was too late. Sally saw her sitting there, and she frowned slightly. "Uh, Cat, maybe you could help with the luggage."

Cat rose and went over to them.

"Take this one up to room four," Sally said, pointing to one.

Cat was aware of the boy's eyes on her. She was in agony, thinking of how she must look. She grabbed the suitcase and started back up the stairs. She was almost halfway up when she heard footsteps behind her.

"Here, let me take that."

The fair-haired boy took the suitcase from her hand. "If you'll just show me where my room is . . ."

With her head down, Cat hurried up the rest of the stairs. Once on the landing, she pointed towards the room. But he didn't move.

"My name's Bailey Hudson."

For a moment, Cat was taken aback. It was the first time a guest of the inn had spoken directly to her. Bailey had a nice smile, not crooked like Todd's but full and wide and showing even white teeth. Under normal circumstances, Cat would know exactly how to behave when meeting a really cute guy for the first time. But how could she flirt when she was dressed like a maid?

"And your name's Cat. I heard the lady downstairs call you that. I've never known anyone with that name."

Cat found her power of speech. "It's really Catherine. Catherine Morgan. Cat's a nickname."

"Oh. It's neat." He glanced towards the window at the end of the hall. "You know, this is the first time I've ever seen real snow. I'm from California."

"Wow. I've never been there. I've never been out of Vermont."

"California's pretty cool. It's sunny most of the time, and it's a great place for surfing. But it must be nice living in a place that has four seasons."

Cat listened in awe. Most of the boys she knew could barely string two sentences together.

"Morgan!"

Miss Andrews seemed to have materialised out of nowhere. "Cat! Don't bother the guests," she hissed. "You have work to do. Come downstairs."

"Excuse me," Cat mumbled, her face hot and burning with embarrassment. She turned away from Bailey and followed the housekeeper back downstairs, passing the Hudsons and Sally Layton on their way up. Back in the lobby, Miss

Andrews handed her another rag and pointed.

"Dust," she commanded.

Once again, Cat felt like Cinderella, only now she'd just met the prince. Too bad he was just visiting. But maybe that was for the best. He couldn't like her, knowing she was a maid.

Why weren't there cute, interesting guys like that at school? In frustration, Cat slapped the rag at the table. It hit the rim of a bowl of candy and the bowl tipped over, spilling candy all over the floor.

Miss Andrews magically appeared again. "What happened?"

"The bowl tipped over."

"All by itself?" The woman folded her arms. "What are you waiting for *this* time? Pick it up!"

Cat got down on her hands and knees and began picking up the candies. She had to crawl under the table to reach them all. Suddenly, a gust of cold air told her the front door had opened. She heard Sally Layton saying, "Good afternoon. May I help you?" A woman's voice replied, "Yes, we're meeting the Hudsons for tea. Have they arrived?"

"I'll call their room," Sally said. "Could I have your name, please?"

"Mrs Beaumont."

As in *Heather's mother?* Cat wondered. Cat turned her head to get a look. A tall woman with streaked blonde hair, wearing a mink coat, stood there. She wasn't alone. Cat swallowed and almost choked. Standing beside Mrs Beaumont was Heather.

Still on her hands and knees, Cat edged backward, praying that Heather wouldn't look down. This couldn't, *couldn't* be happening to her. Sally Layton put down the telephone and returned to the Beaumonts.

"The Hudsons are coming right down. Won't you have a seat?" To Cat's horror, Sally led them to the twin sofas. Sitting there, Heather would have to see her.

For once, Cat had a little luck. Just as Heather and her mother started following Sally, a voice trilled from the stairs. "Gloria! How lovely to see you again!"

From her hiding place, Cat could see Mrs Hudson and Bailey join the Beaumonts, and she heard Mrs Hudson introduce Bailey to Heather. Cat gritted her teeth as she watched Heather toss her head so her blonde curls bounced on her shoulders.

Thankfully, they all moved into the dining room, and Cat relaxed slightly. She didn't get to stay that way for long.

"What are you still doing there?" Miss Andrews said.

Sally Layton turned, and for the first time saw Cat under the table.

"Uh, just getting the last pieces," Cat said.

"How long does it take you to pick up candy?"

Cat had no answer for that. She quickly picked up the remaining ones. Emerging from her cave, she stood up and noticed with resignation that the front of her uniform was smudged with dust. She hoped the housekeeper wouldn't see it. Cat was supposed to have swept under there on Friday, but she had figured no one would notice if she didn't.

Miss Andrews was deep in conversation with Sally Layton. Their backs were to Cat, but Sally turned slightly and cast a worried look in her direction. She quickly averted her eyes when she realised Cat was watching. Cat had a pretty good idea who they were talking about.

She emptied the candies in a wastebasket and made a few ineffectual swipes at the front of her uniform. She looked at the grandfather clock in the corner and stifled a groan. Forty-five minutes left. With one nervous eye on the entrance to the dining room, Cat approached Miss Andrews. "What would you like me to do now?"

Miss Andrews and Sally exchanged looks. Miss Andrews sighed. "Go upstairs and . . . and look in the rooms. Check to see if there are fresh flowers in the vases."

"You can put in more water if they need it," Sally said.

"But *try* not to spill it," the housekeeper added. She handed Cat the master key.

What a relief. At least this would put her out of the general vicinity of the dining room, and Heather Beaumont.

When Cat reached the top of the stairs, she leaned against the wall and closed her eyes. Heather Beaumont. Of all the people she didn't want to run into. If she hadn't been under that table, Heather would have seen her. It was too unbelievably gruesome to think about.

Now, if she could just dawdle up here till Heather left . . . Cat started moving very, very slowly. She went to the first door, unlocked it, and went in. She checked the two vases and pulled out a few limp flowers.

Then she went to the next room and did the same. In the third room, she added some water to the vases. No one was staying in there, so she spent a few moments poking around, looking at the pictures on the wall, admiring the fancy soaps in the bathroom, and feeling the thick, plush towels.

She was unlocking the door to the next room when she heard voices on the stairway.

"How big is the junior high? How many students?" Cat recognised Bailey's voice.

"I don't know. I never counted." That was followed by an all-too-familiar tinkling laugh.

Frantically, Cat turned the key, scurried into

the room, and closed the door. She was about to allow herself a sigh of relief when she heard a key in the lock!

Cat ducked into the bathroom and pulled the door closed. A second later she heard Bailey's voice. "Gee, I thought I'd locked it. This is my room."

Wildly, Cat wondered if they could hear her heart pounding through the bathroom door. It certainly sounded loud enough to her.

"It's nice," Heather replied. "I mean, for a little place like this. Of course, it's nothing like the hotel we stay in when we go to New York. That place is like a palace. Our rooms there are twice this size."

"This rooms suits me okay," came Bailey's easy reply.

"How long will you be staying here?"

"Just till our house is finished being painted. Friday or Saturday. That's when the movers are supposed to arrive from California."

"When will you start coming to school?"

"Next Monday, after we get settled in."

It took a few moments for the significance of his words to penetrate Cat's panic. When they did, she wanted to sink to the floor. This boy, this adorable Bailey Hudson, wasn't visiting Green Falls. He was *moving* to Green Falls. Next week, he'd be at Green Falls Junior High. She'd see him, in the halls, in the cafeteria, maybe in a class or two. He'd say, "Didn't I see you working as a maid at the Green Falls Inn?" Other kids would hear him.

But she had someone else to worry about first. "What are the bathrooms like here?" Heather asked.

"Like ordinary bathrooms," Bailey replied.

"Could I see it? I'd like to brush my hair."

Cat was momentarily paralysed. But her finely tuned instincts took over. She whipped off her apron and stuffed it under the sink. Just as the doorknob started to turn, she grabbed it and pushed.

Heather almost toppled over. Cat wasn't sure if it was from being pushed by the door or from the shock of seeing Cat come out of Bailey's bathroom.

Heather recovered quickly. "What are *you* doing here?"

Think, Cat ordered herself. *Think!* She laughed lightly to give herself time. "Why, Heather, what a surprise. The owners here are friends of my parents. They invited me over to see the new inn."

Heather wasn't completely satisfied. "What are you doing in *this* room?"

"Well, if it's any of your business, I thought it was empty." She turned to Bailey. "I'm very sorry." With her eyes, she tried to communicate a message: *Please don't tell! Don't let her know*

I'm a maid! It was so hopeless. How could she expect him to figure out what she was thinking? He didn't even know her!

Bailey was watching them both with interest, his eyes darting back and forth between them. Then that big smile appeared. "Like I said, I guess I forgot to lock the door."

Luckily, Heather was still so startled by Cat's appearance that she didn't seem to notice the awful grey dress. But given more time, Cat knew she would.

"Excuse me," Cat said. She brushed past Heather and sauntered out, closing the door behind her. Her hands were shaking as she fumbled with the key and went into the room next door. How many close calls could a person have in one day?

She pressed her head against the door. A few seconds later, a faint voice drifted up from somewhere downstairs. "Heather!" Then she heard Bailey's door open.

"Coming, Mother. It was nice meeting you, Bailey. Maybe we can get together after school later this week."

Cat couldn't hear Bailey's reply. But she could imagine it. She'd seen Heather's effect on boys at school when she turned on the charm.

What a crummy break, Cat thought. Cute boys were not a dime a dozen at Green Falls Junior High. Bailey would definitely be welcome. And

Heather had already sunk her claws into him. Oh, why couldn't Cat have met him for the first time at school, where she could have had a fighting chance?

Cat listened for Heather's footsteps on the stairs. Then she quietly opened her door and stepped out into the hall. She waited for the goodbyes. Finally, for what seemed like the first time that day, she exhaled.

Miss Andrews would be looking for her any minute now. She might as well go downstairs. She closed the door behind her, locked it, and headed down the hall.

"Cat?"

Bailey was standing outside his door, holding out an apron. Cat thought she detected a twinkle in his eyes.

"Is this yours?"

"Thank you." Cat took the apron and fled down the stairs.

Six

On Wednesday, Josie sat at lunch with her usual companions, all members of the basketball team. They were discussing the schedule of games, which would start in January. As interested as she was, Josie couldn't seem to pay attention. Her thoughts, and her eyes, kept drifting to a table on the other side of the cafeteria. There was something she wanted to do, but she didn't know if she had the guts to do it.

Observing Heather Beaumont, Josie once again experienced the feeling of disbelief she'd felt when Mrs Daley had first told her about Heather. How could a kind, funny, down-to-earth woman like Mrs Daley have such a horrible granddaughter? Horrible wasn't too strong a word for Heather. Josie could think of worse adjectives. Why, if Heather had gotten her way, Josie wouldn't even be on the basketball team.

And yet, Mrs Daley seemed to care about the girl. Just the other day, Josie had had to get something for the elderly woman from her bedroom. In there, she'd seen several framed photos of Heather at different ages.

Maybe that wasn't so surprising. Mrs Daley had to care about Heather. After all, she *was* her grandmother. But Heather didn't even bother to visit her. Josie thought that was disgusting. Even if Mrs Daley didn't show it, Josie knew she must be hurt by Heather's neglect. She hated the thought of that wonderful woman feeling bad. As much as she didn't want to do this, she felt like she owed it to Mrs Daley.

Before Josie could lose her nerve, she got up and strode purposefully across the room. When she reached Heather's table, she stopped and coughed loudly.

Heather and her two girlfriends turned towards Josie. Eve Dedham started to smile, but that little friendly gesture was stopped by Heather's sharp glance.

"What do *you* want?" Heather asked.

Josie steeled herself. "I want to talk to you about your grandmother."

She might as well have said she wanted to talk about the solar system. Heather's expression changed from contempt to utter bewilderment. "My grandmother?"

"Mrs Daley. I've been working for her, and—"

Heather interrupted. "*You've* been working for *my* grandmother?" She was beginning to sound like a parrot.

78

"Yes, just part-time." As she spoke, Josie tried to see something of Mrs Daley in Heather's face, but found nothing.

Heather had recovered her composure. "That's very interesting, Josie. Maybe you'll earn enough money to get some decent clothes."

Josie ignored the insult. "What I wanted to tell you is that I think your grandmother is lonely. It would be nice if you dropped by to see her once in a while."

Heather's pale green eyes became dangerously dark. "I don't see how that's any of your business."

"I like your grandmother," Josie replied simply. "She's my friend."

Blair, Heather's tag-along friend, sneered. "You must be pretty desperate for friends if you're hanging out with an old lady."

Josie bit her tongue to hold back a retort. She didn't want to start an argument. Besides, it wasn't her place to speak up for Mrs Daley when her own granddaughter was there.

But Heather didn't make any attempt to defend her grandmother. Her small, cold eyes were still fixed on Josie. They gave Josie the creeps.

"Hey, Heather," Blair said, "there's Sid Belcher." She started giggling like a hyena. Heather's eyes darted from Josie to Blair to the greaser who was ambling by. Then she put a hand over her heart.

"Ooh, every time I see him I get goose bumps. He is *so* incredible."

"Sid Belcher?" Josie blurted out. She took a furtive look at the boy with the slicked-back hair and torn sweatshirt. He was *awful*.

Heather turned back to Josie. "Was there anything else you wanted?"

"No." Josie walked away, shaking her head. What a waste of time that had been. She saw Cat beckoning her and went to her table.

"What were you talking to Heather about?"

"I told her she ought to visit her grandmother."

Cat's reaction was similar to Heather's. "Her grandmother?"

"Mrs Daley. The woman I work for."

Cat's eyes widened. "Your Mrs Daley is Heather's grandmother?"

Josie could see Cat's brain clicking away. "Don't get any bright ideas. I'm not using Mrs Daley so you can get back at Heather for something." She sighed. "Heather never visits Mrs Daley. When I told her she should, all she wanted to do was giggle about some guy."

"What guy?" Marla asked.

Josie made a face. "Sid Belcher."

"See?" Marla and Britt said to Cat in unison.

"Unbelievable," Cat breathed. Her eyes

searched the cafeteria and rested on Sid Belcher, leaning against a wall with a couple of his greaser buddies. "What does she see in him?"

Before anyone could hazard a guess, Becka joined them. "Hi. Are you guys working after school?"

When both Cat and Josie nodded, Becka said, "Too bad."

"Why?" Josie asked.

"I was hoping you could help out at the store. We might get a big crowd."

"Are you kidding?" Cat asked scornfully. "There hasn't been a big crowd in there for ages."

"I know. But by now, people might have seen my ad in the *Green Gazette*. Have you heard people talking about it?"

The girls all shook their heads. "I haven't even read the *Gazette* yet," Cat said.

"Me neither." Josie looked at Becka curiously. "It's been out for two days now. Were there any more customers in the store yesterday?"

"No," Becka admitted. "Well, I guess I'll go to my locker."

"I have to go, too," Josie said. "See you later, Cat."

Cat nodded, but her eyes were still on Sid Belcher. Was there anything at all about him that was even slightly attractive? There *had* to be, if Heather was really interested in him. Cat thought maybe she should strike up a conversation with him sometime and find out what his secret appeal was. The idea didn't exactly thrill her. Another face crossed her mind. Bailey Hudson. But that was pure wishful thinking. . . .

"Is the inn really nice?" Marla asked. "Maybe we could come by and see it."

"Yeah," Britt said. "How about today?"

Cat gave them both a weak smile. "Gee, I wish you could, but, um . . . the Laytons don't like people who aren't guests coming by."

It was a pretty lame excuse. From the doubtful looks on her friends' faces, she didn't think they bought it. But thank goodness, they didn't press the subject.

When Josie arrived at Mrs Daley's that afternoon, the older woman was giving Sue Campbell a list. "Check to see if they have those little chocolate cream puffs at the bakery. Maybe you could pick up a small cake, too."

"What's going on?" Josie asked.

Mrs Daley's bright eyes were sparkling even more than usual. "My granddaughter called a few minutes ago. She's coming by for a visit!"

Josie's mouth dropped open. "Heather? She's

coming here today?" Josie was stunned. She'd only made a little suggestion to Heather, which didn't seem to have been appreciated. But she must have gotten through to her! Josie gave herself a mental pat on the back.

"And it's about time," Sue stated. "How long has it been since she last came to see you?"

"Now, now," Mrs Daley remonstrated. "Heather means well. But she's a teenager. She's got more important things on her mind than visiting an old lady."

What could be more important than visiting your own grandmother? Josie wondered. But she didn't say anything. Mrs Daley obviously didn't want to hear anything negative about Heather.

Sue left the house with the shopping list, and Mrs Daley began hobbling about, rearranging some magazines on the coffee table and plumping pillows on the sofa.

"Here, let me do that," Josie offered. "You sit down."

"You're a good girl, Josie." Mrs Daley eased herself onto the sofa. "I must admit, I'm a little tired. Ever since Heather called, I've been so excited. Sue was right. It's been a long time since I've seen her. The past few times I went to their house for dinner, she wasn't even home. I *am* looking forward to this visit."

Josie smiled. She hoped she'd be able to hold on to her smile once Heather arrived. She wasn't much of an actress. "Maybe when Heather gets here, I should leave the two of you alone," she suggested.

"Nonsense! I'm planning a real tea party, and I want you to join us."

"But you two will have so much to catch up on," Josie argued.

"That makes no difference," Mrs Daley replied. "As I recall, the last time I saw Heather we had some difficulty carrying on a conversation. I suppose there's a generation gap. It will be a lot more pleasant for her if there's someone else her own age here."

Not when that someone else is me, Josie thought. She hoped her face hadn't revealed her reaction, but Mrs Daley was peering at her keenly. For someone whose eyesight wasn't too great, she certainly had no problem reading expressions.

"Don't you like my granddaughter?" she asked bluntly.

Josie hesitated. She thought about all the nasty stunts Heather had pulled on Cat. Of course, in all fairness, Cat had managed a few schemes of her own, too. But she remembered how Heather had tried to arrange for Becka to get hit in the face with a pie in front of the whole school. And how she'd made Todd lie to Coach Meadows, telling him that none of the boys wanted Josie on the basketball team. How could she say anything about Heather without letting on that, in her opinion, the girl was practically evil?

It was best to say nothing at all. "I guess I just don't know her very well."

"Well, here's a chance for you to get to know her," Mrs Daley stated.

Josie's insides were queasy, but she managed a bright smile. "That's right. Now, what can I do to help you get ready?"

"Is there anything you can do with my hair?" the woman asked hopefully, patting her unruly grey mop.

"I'm no hairdresser," Josie replied, "but I'll give it a shot."

By the time she'd tamed Mrs Daley's hair with a brush and a few bobby pins, Sue was back from the bakery. Josie helped arrange the pastries and the cake on plates and set water to boil for tea. Then Sue took off on more errands, and Josie settled down with Mrs Daley to wait for Heather. She was about to suggest a card game when the doorbell rang.

"I'll get it," Josie said. She stretched her lips into a grin and went to the door.

"Hi, Heather." She forced some warmth into her words.

Heather's smile was even more artificial than

her own. "Hello, Josie. So nice to see you. Grandmother, dear! It's been ages!"

Whose fault is that? Josie asked silently as Heather brushed her lips against her grandmother's cheek. "I'll get the tea," Josie announced, leaving Heather and Mrs Daley together on the sofa.

She took her time in the kitchen. Despite what Mrs Daley had said, Josie felt sure they'd need some time alone, to talk about private family stuff. But when she returned with the teapot, the living room was silent.

"Tell me about your classes," Mrs Daley said to Heather. "Do you have good teachers? Are you enjoying school?"

"I told you, grandmother, everything's fine." Heather seemed more interested in watching Josie pour tea. "How long have you been working here?"

"This is my second week. If you can call it working. It's more like fun for me." She handed a cup of tea to Heather.

Heather took a sip, eyeing Josie thoughtfully over the rim of her cup. "How did you find out about this job?"

"I read about it in the *Green Falls Daily News*. It's weird. I was complaining about having to read newspapers for school. But if it wasn't for that assignment, I probably never would have found out about this job."

"Is that where you saw the ad for the horse, too?" Mrs Daley asked.

"What horse?" Heather asked.

There was something about the way her expression became suddenly alert that made Josie uneasy.

"Oh, just a horse I'm saving up to buy. His name is Sunshine. He's a ten-year-old quarter horse."

"That's nice," Heather said.

The room fell silent. "Do you like horses, dear?" Mrs Daley asked Heather.

"Not particularly." Heather turned back to Josie. "Aren't horses very expensive?"

Josie nodded. "It's going to take me a while to save all the money I need."

"I do wish you'd let me lend you the rest of the money," Mrs Daley said.

Heather rose. "I have to go now."

Mrs Daley's face fell. "So soon? Heather, you just got here!"

"I've got shopping to do, Grandmother. There's a big dance coming up at school. I had the most perfect dress all picked out. But when I went to Danielle's Boutique to buy it, someone else had put it aside! Isn't that awful?"

Josie wondered why Heather was directing that remark at *her*. "Awful," she murmured.

Mrs Daley pointed to the untouched plates. "But you haven't eaten anything!"

"I'll be back again soon," Heather said. She threw a quick kiss in her grandmother's direction. "Bye, Josie."

Mrs Daley struggled to get to her feet, but Heather was out the door before she could stand up. Josie watched as the woman sank back heavily into her seat and gazed wistfully at the closed door. She had a strong urge to wrap her arms around Mrs Daley, but her natural reserve held her back.

Then Mrs Daley turned back to Josie and smiled a little sadly. "How would you like to adopt a grandmother?"

That was all it took for Josie to drop her reserve.

Becka sat behind the counter at Morgan's Country Foods with her elbows on the countertop and her chin resting in her hands. A man stood over by the fruit bins, picking out apples. A woman strolled down an aisle, pausing to examine the selection of jams. That was it – two customers. Becka had expected customers to be beating down the door by now.

"Why so glum?" Ben asked.

"I don't understand," Becka said. "I thought my ad was going to help business."

"Don't worry about it," Ben said. "You did what you could."

Annie stroked Becka's hair. "Every business goes through slumps, honey. We'll come out of this one sooner or later."

"But it was such a good ad," Becka insisted. "I can't figure out why it didn't work."

"Maybe people didn't see it," Annie suggested. "Actually, I don't think we ever saw it. Did we, Ben?"

"No, but I'm sure it was a persuasive masterpiece."

"I thought so, too, but I guess I was wrong." Becka fumbled in her knapsack for a copy of the *Green Gazette*. She opened it to the ad page and handed the paper to Annie. Ben read it aloud over his wife's shoulder.

"A message from Morgan's Country Foods. Do you want to lose weight? Are you losing your hair? Is your face breaking out? Then try our all-natural miracle foods and watch your problems disappear."

Listening to the words, Becka closed her eyes and once again marvelled at how convincing the ad sounded. Surely there were fat people and bald people and people with bad complexions in Green Falls. Why weren't they here?

Suddenly, she realized that Ben and Annie were oddly silent. She opened her eyes. Her parents' expressions were startling. Instead of the beaming, proud faces she expected to see, both of them looked completely aghast.

"Becka!" Annie gasped. "How could you write something like this?"

Becka fumbled with her words. "Because . . . because I figured people would buy anything that could help them lose weight or grow hair."

Ben gazed at her in horror. "But nothing we sell in this store does that!"

Did they think she was stupid or something? "I know that," Becka replied. She looked at them in confusion. What were they getting so upset about?

"Then why did you write this?" Ben asked. His voice was getting louder.

"To get people to buy the stuff we *do* sell. To make it all sound special."

"But Becka, what you've written here – this isn't true!" Annie exclaimed.

"It doesn't have to be completely true," Becka said. "It's an ad." She noted with alarm that Ben's face was getting red. "Ads lie all the time. I bought some stuff that was supposed to get rid of my birthmark and it didn't work."

Now Ben's face was taking on a purple hue. "That doesn't mean you have the right to lie. Becka, this is false advertising! Do you know what kind of reputation we could get if we make false claims about our goods?"

Becka shrunk back.

"Ben, calm down," Annie said. "She didn't know any better. Honey, we realise you just wanted to help. But something like this can do more harm than good. Like that stuff you bought for your birthmark. Since it doesn't do what it said it would do, you wouldn't buy it again, would you? Or recommend it to your friends?"

"I guess not," Becka admitted.

"And it's not just bad business," Annie continued. "It's morally wrong to lie like this."

Slowly, Becka nodded. What Annie said made sense. But there was still something Becka didn't understand. "How do all those ads get away with lying? I saw an ad for shampoo once that said it would make my hair look shinier. I tried it, and it didn't make my hair shinier at all."

Ben's face was beginning to return to its normal colour. "Some ads do lie. Or at least, exaggerate and stretch the truth. But that doesn't make it right. That's one of the reasons I got out of the advertising business. I'd write ads and then I'd feel ashamed, because I knew I wasn't being totally honest about a product."

Becka hung her head. "I'm sorry."

Ben tousled her hair. "At least you've learned something from this."

"Can we just forget I ever wrote this?" Becka asked.

Ben shook his head. "No, honey, I'm afraid you'll have to make up for it. You have to write a retraction."

"A what?"

"A retraction. Another ad saying that the statements made in this ad were not true, and that there's nothing sold at Morgan's Country Foods that will help a person lose weight or grow hair or . . . what was the other one?"

Becka felt silly even saying it. "Clear up a bad complexion."

"You have to apologise for printing misleading claims. And the ad should be printed in the next copy of your newspaper."

Becka thought of how Jason and the rest of the staff would react to that. "Everyone's going to think I'm pretty goofy."

"Maybe," Ben said. "But it's better for people to think you're goofy than to think you have no ethics. Right?"

Becka sighed. "Okay." She slid off her stool. "I'll go write it now."

"And put the Closed sign on the door, please," Annie called to her. Becka did and walked out. As she headed across the road, a car pulled up and a man she'd never seen before got out. He started towards the store.

"We're closed," Becka called to him.

"Oh, too bad," he said. He looked disappointed.

"Was there something special you wanted?" Becka asked. She was thinking she could run back in and get it for him, if it was really important.

"I came about this," he said, holding up a newspaper. It was the *Green Gazette*, and as Becka drew closer, she saw that it was opened to the page with her ad.

At least one person had been attracted by it. But that didn't lift her spirits. "I guess I'd better tell you, none of that is true."

The man's eyebrows went up. "You mean, there's nothing sold here that aids weight loss or hair growth?"

"No. Nothing at all." Becka wondered why he was so interested. He looked pretty thin to her. But maybe his hair was thinning on top, where she couldn't see it.

"How do you know this?"

"Because I'm Becka Morgan. My parents own this store. And I wrote the ad."

"I see." The man studied her. "Did your parents approve of this ad?"

Becka shook her head fervently. "They're making me write a retraction."

"I see," he said again. "Why did you make these claims in the first place?"

Becka hesitated. It wasn't really any of his business. But there was something about his friendly eyes, his interest, that made her feel

93

like talking. "Because business hasn't been so good lately. We haven't been getting a lot of customers. And I thought it would be okay to lie a little – okay, a lot – if it would get people to come in. But my parents said it was wrong. That's why I have to write a retraction."

The man smiled. "Well, good luck with it, Becka." He started back towards the car.

"Come again," Becka called after him. "Everything we sell is really good. And all natural. And not too expensive."

The man smiled and waved. Strangely enough, she felt better, maybe because the man hadn't laughed at her. Confessing out loud hadn't been so hard. Now she had to put it on paper, and hope her classmates wouldn't laugh either.

Seven

Cat wore an unusually cheerful smile when she entered the dining room at breakfast the next morning. "What are you so happy about?" Becka asked.

"It's Thursday," Cat replied.

Annie handed her a glass of orange juice. "What's special about Thursdays?"

"No work."

Ben put the newspaper down and raised his eyebrows. "Isn't the job going well?"

"Oh, no, it's fine," Cat said quickly. "It's just that, well, sometimes it's nice not to work. Becka, would you pass the toast, please?"

Becka shoved the plate of toast in Cat's general direction. As Cat buttered a slice, she added, "I really like counting my money."

"How much have you saved?" Josie asked.

"Twenty dollars. How about you?" She didn't care for the smug expression that crossed Josie's face.

"Seventy dollars."

"Seventy!"

95

Ben winced. "Cat, sweetie, don't scream so early in the morning."

In a slightly less loud shriek, Cat asked, "How did you save seventy dollars already?"

Josie bit into her toast, chewed, and swallowed before answering. "I work more hours than you, I started my job before you, and I guess I make more money."

Cat frowned as she considered this. "How long do you have to work before asking for a raise?"

"Longer than a week is usually advised," Annie replied dryly. "Cat, I wouldn't hit Sally and George up for a raise just now. They've only had the inn open for a week, and they're probably struggling."

"Getting a business on its feet takes time," Ben added. "As we all know."

"Maybe they should advertise," Josie said with a mischievous glance in Becka's direction.

"Yeah," Cat chimed in. "Stay at the Green Falls Inn and – and grow six inches."

"Girls, don't tease," Annie remonstrated.

"Very funny," Becka muttered.

Cat returned to the original subject. "If I had seventy dollars, I could get my dress off credit right now."

"Credit," Josie repeated. She snapped her fingers. "That's why Heather gave me the evil eye yesterday. She said she'd wanted to buy a dress at Danielle's Boutique, but someone had already taken it. And she gave me the meanest look. Cat, did Heather want the same dress as you?"

Cat nodded. "I guess she found out that I was the one who put it on one side. I'll bet she's mad!"

Annie looked at her curiously. "Why does that make you so happy?"

Cat scrambled in her mind for a reasonable explanation. Somehow, for months she'd managed to keep her ongoing war with Heather Beaumont a secret from her parents. Instinct told her they wouldn't exactly approve. "Well, Heather's not the nicest girl in the world. And it's fun knowing I've got something she wants."

Ben shook his head reprovingly. "That's not a very good attitude, Cat. What are you going to do next, steal her boyfriend?"

Cat practically choked on her juice. "Uh, could you guys hurry up? I want to get to school early. I have to do something before homeroom."

"I'm ready if you are," Annie said.

On the way to school, a light snow began to fall. "Look at those greasers," Becka said as they got out of the car. "Sitting on the steps in the snow."

She and Josie hurried towards the entrance.

Cat lagged behind. As soon as her sisters disappeared into the building, Cat casually edged towards one of the guys on the steps.

"Think we're going to get a real snowfall?" she asked.

Sid Belcher sneered at her. "What do I look like, a weatherman?"

Cat pretended he'd just said something funny. She tossed her head, laughed brightly, and gave him a sidelong look. It was a move she'd used a zillion times, and it never failed to have an impact.

Until now. "What's so funny?" Sid growled.

"What do you think?" Cat asked in a teasing voice.

"How should I know? You're the one who's laughing."

Cat tried to recall if they'd ever actually met before. "I'm Cat Morgan."

"Your name's Cat?" His lips parted, revealing yellowish teeth. "You got claws?" He started laughing at his own unamusing joke. It was an ugly laugh that matched his face.

Cat gave up and went on into the school. She'd always thought she'd do anything to upset Heather Beaumont. But there were limits.

Josie was beat. Basketball practice had gone on much longer than usual. Coach Meadows was trying to make up for cutting back on the practice sessions. Now it was almost six o'clock, which meant she wouldn't be able to go see Sunshine and be home in time for dinner. The snow had stopped, but there was plenty of wet slush to walk through. She'd left her wool scarf back in the locker room, but she didn't have the energy to go back and get it. She was cold, hungry, and totally exhausted.

She cheered up by reminding herself that it wouldn't be too much longer before Sunshine would be there at home, waiting for her. And her mood improved considerably when she walked into the house.

Ben was at the fireplace, stoking a blazing fire which cast a warm glow over the living room. Becka was curled in the rocking chair, a book in her lap. In the dining room, Cat was setting the table for dinner. Good smells floated out from the kitchen, where Josie could hear Annie singing.

"Boy, is it good to be home," Josie sighed, slipping out of her coat.

"Honey, you should have called me," Ben said. "I would have picked you up."

"Oh, that's okay. Something smells great," Josie said.

Annie came out from the kitchen. "Chilli and cornbread. Josie, take those wet shoes off right this minute. I don't want you catching cold."

Josie happily obliged. She used to think she'd

hate having people fuss over her. But every now and then it was very pleasant.

The phone rang in the kitchen. "I'll get it," Annie said.

"I turned in my retraction to the *Green Gazette*," Becka announced.

"Did the editor give you any grief about it?" Josie asked.

"Not really. In fact, Jason told me this was the first time the *Gazette* ever printed a retraction. He said it made him feel like it was a real newspaper." She made a little face. "I still feel pretty stupid about it."

"Look at it this way," Josie said cheerfully. "It's more publicity for the store."

Annie called from the dining room. "Josie, Ben, would you come back here for a minute?"

"Sure," Josie said. "Did you burn the cornbread?" Annie had yet to completely master the mysteries of cooking. But one look at Annie's face told her that whatever it was, it had nothing to do with food. Cat's curious eyes followed Josie as she went through the dining room to the kitchen.

"What's the matter?" Ben asked once the three of them were together.

Annie's face was troubled. "That was a Mr Beaumont on the phone."

"Heather's father?" Josie asked, puzzled. "Why would he be calling here?"

Annie spoke in a soft voice. "He's also Mrs Daley's son-in-law."

A sudden fear gripped Josie. "Oh no! Has something happened to Mrs Daley?"

"No, dear, she's fine," Annie said hastily. "But . . ." She seemed to be having a hard time saying something. Josie waited anxiously.

Annie bit her lip. "Mr Beaumont doesn't want you to work for Mrs Daley any more."

Josie heard the words, but they didn't sink in right away.

"Why not?" Ben asked.

"He wouldn't say. All he told me, and I quote, was that 'Josie's services are no longer required.'"

Now that Josie had absorbed the message, she immediately reached for the telephone.

"I'm going to call Mrs Daley and find out what this is all about."

Annie put a gentle restraining hand on Josie's arm. "He also said you weren't to call her or see her."

Josie gasped. "But that's crazy! Mrs Daley likes me! She wouldn't want me fired!"

"Darling, I know you feel awful about this," Annie said. "But Mr Beaumont is a member of her family, and we have to respect his wishes."

"But this doesn't make sense!" Josie cried. She simply couldn't believe she wasn't going to see Mrs Daley again. Then something else hit her, and she clapped a hand to her mouth. "Sunshine . . ." she breathed.

"What?" Ben asked.

Josie clenched her fists. There was no point in keeping it a secret anymore. "Sunshine. He's a horse that's for sale. I've been saving my money to buy him. That's why I got the job in the first place."

"Why didn't you tell us about this?" Annie asked.

"Well, you were worried about the store, and I didn't want you to think I was asking for something you couldn't afford. I was going to wait till I had all the money saved and then ask if I could buy him." She felt something wet on her cheek. Furiously, she brushed the tear away.

Annie and Ben exchanged agonised looks. "How much does the horse cost?" Ben asked.

"Four hundred dollars. I've saved seventy."

Ben thought for a moment. "Maybe if I talked to the owner, he'd accept a down payment on the horse."

"You mean, put him on credit?" Josie asked hopefully. "Like Cat's dress?"

Ben nodded. "Where's the phone book?"

Josie told him the owner's name, and Ben looked him up in the directory. Then he dialled.

"Hello, this is Ben Morgan. I'm the father of Josie, the girl who's interested in buying your horse, Sunshine. I wanted to ask if – what?" There was a pause. "I see. Thank you." He hung up.

"What did he say?" Annie asked.

Ben looked like *he* wanted to cry. "Josie . . ."

Somehow, Josie already knew what he was going to say. "He sold Sunshine."

Ben nodded. Silently, with their eyes filled with love and sympathy, he and Annie gazed at Josie. But this was a moment when Josie didn't want any fussing.

"I . . . I think I'll go to my room for a while."

As she passed through the dining room, she was aware of Cat and Becka watching her. "What's wrong?" Cat asked.

Josie was suprised to hear her own voice coming out clear and steady. "I've lost my job. And Sunshine's been sold." Only at the end did her voice crack. She ran up the stairs so she could cry in private.

Standing in the centre of a bedroom at the inn, Cat wondered if losing a job was really such a tragedy. Okay, maybe for Josie it was. She remembered how upset Josie had been the night before, how she couldn't even eat dinner. She had looked the same this morning and had barely touched her breakfast.

Well, it was different for Josie. She'd actually liked working. But as Cat struggled to get a fitted sheet corner off a bed, she thought she wouldn't mind losing this job. And as soon as she had enough money for her dress, she would.

Thinking of the dress made her think of the Turnaround dance, which made her think about a date. She recalled her encounter the day before with Sid Belcher and shuddered. For the millionth time, she wondered why Heather wanted to go out with him. Maybe she was into bad guys. Cat knew there were girls who screamed over those guys in heavy metal bands, with their tough attitudes and tattoos and stringy hair. Not Cat. Even the tantalizing temptation of spiting Heather wasn't enough to drive her in that direction.

No, she wasn't about to go after the date Heather wanted. But at least she'd have the dress.

The sheet corner wouldn't come up so Cat gave it a hard tug. Then she groaned as the sheet ripped.

Naturally, Miss Andrews would choose that minute to check on her work. The housekeeper gazed at the torn sheet in despair. "You are undoubtedly the worst excuse for a maid I've ever seen," she announced. "Morgan, you are positively incompetent. Utterly worthless."

By now, Cat was so accustomed to Miss

Andrews' criticisms and rebukes that they went in one ear and out the other. She didn't even bother to apologise, which seemed to make Miss Andrews even angrier.

"The only reason you're kept on here is because your parents are friends of the Laytons."

"I know that," Cat said airily. "It doesn't bother me in the least." Cat sensed she was being rude, but she was beyond caring.

Miss Andrews pressed her lips together so hard they turned white. Cat tried to find her manners.

"What would you like me to do now, Miss Andrews?" she asked politely.

"We can't afford for you to ruin any more sheets," the housekeeper replied through her clenched lips. "Go downstairs and dust."

Cat scurried out of the room. As she went down the hall, a door opened. "Hi, Cat."

Bailey was grinning. Remembering how he'd witnessed her escapade on Monday, Cat flushed and ducked her head. "Hello," she murmured and kept on walking towards the stairs. He followed her.

"Do you go to the same school as Heather?" Cat nodded.

"I'll be starting there next week."

"That's nice." Cat eyed him warily. He hadn't exposed her secret to Heather. Would he remain as silent at school?

"I hear it's an okay place," he remarked. "I mean, considering that it's a school."

He was trying to be funny. Automatically, without even thinking, Cat went into her act: head toss, bright laugh, sidelong look. Then she felt stupid. How much impact could that have when she was dressed as a maid?

But, to her amazement, she recognised the expression on Bailey's face. She'd seen that same expression on Todd's face, and on the faces of other boys she'd flirted with (not counting Sid Belcher). She caught her breath. Was there a chance, a remote possibility, that he liked her? Even wearing an *apron?* Or was he just leading her on?

There was no time to find out, because his mother stepped out of her room. "Come on, Bailey, we have to get over to the Beaumonts'."

Cat allowed them to pass ahead of her and start down the stairs. But she was pleased when Bailey turned his head and smiled back at her.

For the next hour, Cat listlessly passed her rag over the various pieces of furniture in the dining room, barely moving any bits of dust around. Bailey's cute face was firmly implanted in her brain, and despite her efforts, she couldn't push him out.

He'd be the centre of female attention next week at Green Falls Junior High. There was no doubt about it. Girls would flock to him. There would be Cat, sauntering down the hall in her green sweater, hair loose and flowing, perfectly groomed. Maybe Bailey would forget that he'd first seen her as a maid. . . .

"Aren't you finished in here yet?" Miss Andrews' sharp voice ended her reverie. She ran a finger along a sideboard, then looked at the finger in disgust.

"I'm going into the lobby now," Cat replied quickly, and hurried out.

She returned to her fantasies as she lightly stroked the mantle over the fireplace with her rag. A thought struck her. No, it was too outrageous to contemplate. But then, this was just a daydream, so she might as well indulge herself.

What if . . . what if she asked Bailey to the Turnaround? Suddenly, she could see herself, walking into the decorated gym, arm in arm with him. Everyone's eyes would be on them. What a couple they'd make! Cat in her black velvet, Bailey in a black suit – no, a light-coloured one, to set off his gorgeous tan. She had a clear vision of Heather, with that grungy Sid Belcher, eyeing them in envy as they floated onto the dance floor. Oh, it would be awesome. . . .

The image exploded with a crash. Cat jumped back. Fragments of a big vase that had stood on the mantle just seconds before lay all over the floor.

Miss Andrews came running out of the dining room. Sally Layton flew out from the office behind the reception desk. They both stood there, speechless.

Cat gulped. "Uh, I'm sorry. I guess I wasn't looking where I dusted."

"My vase from China," Sally moaned. She went over to where it had fallen and knelt down.

"Can it be fixed?" Cat asked.

Sally shook her head. "It's beyond repair."

Cat felt awful. "I'm *really* sorry. I'll . . . I'll pay for it." She hated asking the next question, but she had to. "Was it very expensive?"

"I'm afraid so," Sally said, picking up the pieces.

Miss Andrews spoke stiffly. "Mrs Layton, this girl is a walking disaster. She can't dust, she can't sweep, she can't even take sheets off a bed. I've told you this before. I realise that she's the daughter of your friends, but it's my duty to tell you that she has no business working as a maid."

Sally rose from the floor. "I'm sure Cat didn't intend to break the vase," she murmured tentatively, but the housekeeper didn't let her continue. She folded her arms across her chest and faced Sally with a look of determination.

"Either that girl goes or I go."

The look of horror that crossed Sally's face

told Cat she didn't want to lose her house-keeper.

"Oh, Miss Andrews . . ." Sally began, but her voice trailed off as the housekeeper remained steadfast. Sally sighed heavily and turned to Cat.

"Cat, dear, I'm sorry, but it looks like things aren't working out."

Cat froze as she absorbed the implication of the words. "But I've got a dress on credit! I'll be more careful, I promise!"

Her plea seemed to have an effect on Sally, and the woman once again turned to Miss Andrews. The housekeeper shook her head firmly.

"I'm sorry, Cat," Sally repeated. She really did look regretful.

There was nothing left to say. Feeling like her world was crumbling, Cat made her way to the little powder room. In a daze, she removed her uniform and put on her skirt and blouse. She gathered up her schoolbooks and purse and went out.

"I'm truly sorry, Cat," Sally Layton called to her again as Cat dragged herself back through the lobby towards the door. But all the apologies in the world weren't going to pay for that dress.

Cat hadn't bothered to button up her coat, but she didn't even feel the cold as she stepped outside. She was positively numb with shock.

Then she saw a car pulling up. Bailey and his mother got out. Mrs Hudson hurried to the inn, but Bailey stopped when he saw Cat.

"Leaving already?" he asked.

Cat nodded, but she didn't explain. It was bad enough for him to know she had been a maid. How could she admit she'd been a failure as one?

She turned away from him and started walking.

"Wait!" Bailey called.

She paused and let him catch up to her. "I was just talking to Heather," he said. "She was telling me about this dance, this Turnaround thing."

The impact of his words hit her like a rock. No, more like a gallon of water poured on her head when she was already drowning.

"Are you going?" he asked.

Cat couldn't be sure if the word actually left her mouth, or if her lips had just formed it. "No." She whirled around and flew off.

So Heather was taking Bailey Hudson to the Turnaround dance. Everything became very clear. Heather never intended to ask Sid Belcher. It was a setup. She'd planted hints, knowing Britt was in the bathroom when she was talking about him, and again with Josie. Her mean, nasty little mind had assumed that Cat would ask any boy she thought Heather wanted to ask.

And now she'd get the black velvet dress, too. Cat was too upset to do any arithmetic calculations, but she knew that whatever amount of money was needed to pay off the dress, she'd never have it in time.

Heather would be going to the Turnaround with the cutest boy and the prettiest dress. As for Cat, all she knew was that in the entire universe at this moment, there couldn't be anyone more miserable than she was.

Eight

It was like a grey cloud had fallen on the Morgan household, Cat decided the next morning. There wasn't a cheerful face at the breakfast table. Outside, the world sparkled from the sun's rays on the new-fallen snow, and inside the delicious smell of cinnamon rose from the steaming bowls of oatmeal, but neither of those things had any effect on the general atmosphere.

Josie, with her elbows on the table, stirred her oatmeal without lifting a spoonful to her mouth. She was still pale and puffy eyed. Cat wondered if she herself looked as bad. She was certainly entitled to, every bit as much as Josie was.

Becka was eating, but her forehead was puckered, which meant she was worrying. Every few minutes, she let out a soft sigh. Cat couldn't see her expression, but she knew she was totally incapable of making even the slightest attempt at a smile or conversation.

"We're certainly a jolly bunch today," Ben commented. It was his third remark of that type. No one responded. Ben shook his head in resignation and returned to his breakfast.

Annie took a stab at it. In an overly bright voice, she asked, "Do you girls have any special plans for today?"

Three heads moved from side to side.

"Ben and I are doing inventory at the store today," she went on. "We thought we'd take advantage of the quiet. If you don't have anything else to do, you can come and help out if you'd like. We'll turn it into a party!"

This suggestion received three unenthusiastic nods.

Annie sighed heavily. "Girls, I know everything seems bleak right now, but things will get better, I promise. Josie, there will be other horses for sale. Cat, you'll find another dress, one that's more within your means. And Becka . . . Becka, I'm not sure I even know *why* you're depressed.

"My retraction's coming out in the *Green Gazette* on Monday," Becka told her. "I'm afraid everyone at school is going to make fun of me."

It was hard for Cat to drum up any sympathy. Becka's concern was nothing compared to *her* problems.

"If people tease you, just laugh along with them," Annie advised.

Becka managed a wan smile, but it was clear what she thought of that idea.

113

"Ben," Annie said. "Help!"

"What?" Ben asked.

"Look at your daughters! Have you ever seen three more miserable faces?"

Ben made another futile attempt at humour. "They're teenagers. They're supposed to be depressed, right?"

Annie raised her hands in an I-give-up gesture. The phone rang and she leaped off the chair as if she were escaping. Becka let out another of her soft sighs, and Cat turned to her in irritation.

"Quit moaning," she demanded.

Becka became indignant. "Look who's talking. You've been whining non-stop since yesterday."

"I've got a right to," Cat retorted. "I've got *real* problems."

"Some problems," Josie growled. "You can't buy a dumb dress. That's really serious."

"Just as serious as a stupid horse," Cat shot back. "And all Becka's carrying on about is a silly newspaper that no one even reads."

"Oh, yeah? My problems are just as real as yours!" Becka argued.

"All of you, stop it," Ben ordered. "You've got problems. Your mother and I have problems. We're all going to be sympathetic to each other and stop feeling sorry for ourselves. Case closed."

114

That stilled the argument for the time being, but the girls were still shooting hostile looks at one another. Annie returned from the kitchen.

"That was Sally Layton, from the inn. Cat, she'd like you to come by today so that she can give you your pay from yesterday."

"Goody, goody," Cat murmured. "Eight dollars." She got a glimpse of Annie's rebuking face and rose hastily. "I'll go get ready."

Josie got up, too. "I'll do the dishes."

"I'll help you," Becka offered.

"Thanks," Josie said, "but I'd rather be alone." Cat rolled her eyes. Josie sounded *so* tragic.

"You can come to the store with Ben and me, Becka," Annie said.

Cat went up to her room and sat down at the dressing table mirror. Studying her reflection, she decided she didn't look as bad as Josie, but pretty bad, nonetheless. She couldn't go to the inn looking like a pathetic, downtrodden nobody. There was a chance she could run into Bailey. She might as well show him who he *could* have been escorting to the Turnaround.

When Cat finished a careful application of make-up, she put on her newest jeans, a green sweater that made her eyes look like emeralds, and boots. Then she gave herself a satisfied once-over in the mirror. She looked cool, confident, and totally together – the opposite of how she felt.

Beyond her reflection, she saw Josie standing at her door. "Are you going to the store?"

"Yeah, I guess so," Cat said, inserting small gold hoops into her pierced ears. "When I get back from the inn."

"Tell Ben and Annie I'll be there in a little while. I've got something to do first."

Cat noticed that Josie had her parka on. "Where are you going?"

"To see Mrs Daley."

Shocked, Cat tore her eyes from the mirror. "Josie! You can't do that! Mr Beaumont told Annie you're not supposed to see her!"

"I don't care," Josie said. "Look, there's nothing I can do about Sunshine. But I've got to find out why Mrs Daley doesn't want me around anymore."

"You're going to get into trouble," Cat warned. But Josie had her jaw set in that obstinate way that told Cat nothing would change her mind. She stuffed her hands in her pockets and took off.

Cat couldn't help admiring her determination and guts. Of course, she thought that Josie should use them for more important purposes, but still, Cat respected her bravery.

Cat opened her jewellery box and took out the twenty dollars she'd saved from her job. Maybe if she still felt really down after leaving the inn, she'd go buy herself something. That was always a surefire cure for the blues. She went downstairs, got her coat, and left.

Now that she wasn't working there anymore, the inn had stopped looking like a prison. With the clean white snow nestled on its roof and window ledges, it was charming again.

Inside, she glanced around furtively for Miss Andrews and breathed a sigh of relief that the housekeeper was nowhere in sight. Sally Layton was behind the reception desk.

"Hello, Cat, I'm glad you came by. I hope there are no hard feelings."

Cat didn't want to give her the satisfaction of a real response, but the woman sounded so sincere that she relented and forced a small smile.

Sally handed her an envelope. "There's your salary for yesterday. And a little something extra as, well, a show of appreciation."

Cat accepted it with a gracious nod. "Thank you."

"Excuse me, dear. I have to see about something in the dining room." As soon as Sally disappeared, Cat tore open the envelope. As she expected, there were eight dollar bills. And a long, pale blue slip of paper. She pulled the paper out, then drew in her breath sharply.

It was a gift certificate to Danielle's Boutique in the amount of thirty-five dollars! Suddenly, her head was spinning. Was this for real?

Cat snatched a pencil from the desk and a copy of the inn's brochure. On the back of the brochure she scrawled $67.50. That was what she owed on the dress. Then she put down the total amount she'd made working: $28. She added that to $35. It came to $63. She subtracted that from $67.50. Four dollars and fifty cents. Exactly what she had left from this week's allowance.

In amazement, she did the sums over again. It came out the same. There was no doubt in Cat's mind that she was witnessing a miracle. Her heart was beating with excitement. The dress was hers!

Just as she was stuffing the envelope into her purse, she heard a voice say, "Hello, Cat."

Cat looked up. "Hello, Bailey," she said coolly. He was looking slightly less than sure of himself.

"How come you ran off like that yesterday?" he asked.

"I was in a hurry," she said. "Now, let's see . . . oh yes, you were telling me about your date with Heather." Cat assumed a bored expression.

"What date with Heather?"

"For the Turnaround dance."

Bailey scratched his head. "I don't have a date with Heather for the Turnaround dance."

For once in her life, Cat was at a loss for

words. "But, what about . . . I mean, you said—"

"I just said she told me about the dance." He gave her an abashed grin. "Okay, just between us, she *did* ask me. But I didn't say yes."

Cat stared at him blankly. "Why not?"

Bailey suddenly became very interested in his shoes. "Well, because . . . I was hoping *you'd* ask me."

"Becka, would you see if that woman needs any help?" Annie asked hurriedly. She was trying to ring up a sale on the cash register for one customer and point out where the wholewheat flour was to another. Over by the bins of fresh fruit, Ben had a line of people waiting for him to weigh their bags.

Becka sailed off towards the woman who was wandering down an aisle. "Can I help you?"

"I was trying to find your maple syrup."

"I'm afraid we're sold out," Becka replied. But we'll be getting more on Monday. Have you tried our jams?"

The woman brightened. "No, but I'd like to."

Becka led her to the rapidly diminishing selection of jams. Leaving the woman to contemplate the flavours, she hurried away to help another couple who had just walked in.

It had been like that since the store opened.

Of course, they usually did get a few more customers on Saturdays than any other day. But never like this. There hadn't been a moment all morning when there were fewer than a dozen people in Morgan's Country Foods.

They could forget about doing an inventory. There was hardly anything left on the shelves to count and not a minute available to count what *was* there. Becka hadn't stopped moving since they opened the doors, and her ears were ringing from the constant jingles of the cash register and the bell over the door.

Ben and Annie looked just as bewildered as she did. But none of them had had a free moment to talk about it.

Back at the counter, a woman had one bag in her arms and was trying to lift another. "Can I carry one of those to your car for you?" Becka asked.

"No, thank you, dear," the woman said as she got a firm grip on her bags. Then she beamed at her. "Are you the little girl in the story?"

Becka was so startled by the question that she wasn't even insulted at being called a little girl. "What story?"

Annie, too, was looking at the woman in bewilderment. "Becka was in a story?"

"In the newspaper!" the woman said. "You mean, you haven't seen it?"

Becka had a feeling the woman wasn't talking about the *Green Gazette*. Sure enough, the woman set down her bags, fumbled in her purse, and pulled out a clipping. "It's from this morning's edition of the *Daily News*. Here, read it. In fact, why don't you keep it? It's not often that a person gets her name in the paper!" She hoisted up her bags and left.

Annie and Becka put their heads together and read the clipping. It was a regular feature from the newspaper, a column called "This and That," which reported funny little goings-on in Green Falls. At the top was a photo of the man who wrote it. He looked familiar. Becka drew in her breath. "That's the man I talked to on Wednesday when I was leaving the store! I told him we were closed."

"He came back on Thursday," Annie murmured as she read the column.

The first paragraph was about a Girl Scout who had sold more cookies than anyone in the state. The second paragraph was about a family's successful search for a lost dog.

The third paragraph made Becka and Annie gasp in unison.

In an attempt to bolster business at her family's store, Morgan's Country Foods, Becka Morgan, a student at Green Falls Junior High, placed an ad in her school newspaper in which she proclaimed the magical curative powers of the products available in the store. Curious as to these remarkable claims, this reporter visited the store in question, and while he was unable to locate any item which might stem the loss of his hair, he found the sweetest maple syrup, the juiciest jams, the tastiest breads, and the freshest produce available in these parts. Definitely worth a visit! By the way, Becka's parents were not pleased with their daughter's well-intentioned but misleading claims, and Becka has been ordered to write a retraction. It's nice to know our merchants are committed to truth in advertising!

As Becka and Annie looked at each other in astonishment, a man plunked some purchases on the counter. He saw what they were reading and nodded. "You know, I didn't even know this place was here until I read that this morning!"

Another customer fell in line behind him. "Yes, wasn't that cute? And I must say, everything here does look delicious. You'll be seeing a lot of me!"

"That's nice," Annie said, her eyes glassy. "Ben!"

When he joined them, she handed him the

clipping. Still looking dazed, Annie started ringing up the purchases.

"Good grief!" Ben blurted out. "What – how—?"

"Excuse me," Becka said sweetly. "But we've got customers to help." And she sailed off on cloud nine.

Nine

Josie strode along rapidly until she reached the cottage. Then she hesitated. What if Mrs Daley refused to see her? Could she bear having someone she'd thought was a friend slam a door in her face?

She had to risk it. It would be better to know than to always wonder what she had done wrong. She marched up the pathway to the door and rapped firmly.

Sue Campbell opened the door. "Josie!" It was evident she was surprised to see her. Josie waited for Sue's quick smile but it didn't come.

"I'm here to see Mrs Daley."

From the back of the house, a voice rung out. "Who is it, Sue?"

"It's Josie Morgan," Sue called back.

"Well, let her in!"

Sue stepped aside, allowing Josie room to pass. But as she did, she whispered, "Don't upset her, Josie."

Josie was bewildered. "Upset Mrs Daley? Why would I do that?"

Mrs Daley didn't seem at all upset to see her.

She wore a big smile as she hobbled towards Josie. "What a nice surprise! I wondered if I'd ever see you again. Sit down, dear."

Now Josie was really confused. Mrs Daley wasn't faking her pleasure. Then why had Josie been forbidden to visit?

She waited for Mrs Daley to ease herself onto the sofa and then sat alongside her. "It's good to see you, too. How have you been?"

Mrs Daley gazed at her steadily. "I must say, I was rather disappointed in you, young lady. And a little hurt when my son-in-law told me you had resigned."

Josie sat up straight. "Resigned?"

"My daughter's been taking your place," Mrs Daley continued. "Actually, it's been good for both of us. I feel Gloria and I have drifted apart, and this time together is bringing us closer."

Sue peered out the window. "Here comes your daughter now. Oh Mr Beaumont's with her, too. I'll be off now."

Mrs Daley hoisted herself up and went to the door. A wave of panic swept through Josie. "Mr Beaumont?" She couldn't imagine what his reaction would be at finding her there. She looked around the room frantically. Maybe she should hide in the kitchen.

No. She had to face him. It was the only way to find out what was going on, why he had told Mrs Daley she'd quit her job. But

125

even so, as the door opened, she found herself slinking down in her seat.

Peeking around the arms of the sofa, she watched as a tall, fair-haired woman wrapped in fur embraced Mrs Daley. "Hello, Mother dear."

"Gloria, you're looking too thin."

"Now, mother, don't fuss. Look, Bill has come to see you."

The man who followed Mrs Beaumont in was heavy-set and balding. He spotted Josie at once. "Who's that?"

Gathering her courage, Josie rose. "I'm Josie Morgan." She started to move forward with her right hand extended, but Mr Beaumont drew back. Then he turned to Mrs Daley. "I think we should all have a cup of tea. Perhaps this girl could show me where everything is."

"Would you mind, Josie?" Mrs Daley asked.

Josie realised at once that he wanted to get her alone. As she moved, she felt like she was a condemned prisoner on her final walk. And when she was face-to-face with Mr Beaumont in the kitchen, he looked exactly like an executioner.

He didn't waste any time on small talk. "What are you doing here? I told your mother you were not to see, call, or have any contact with my mother-in-law again."

He kept his voice down, but the anger in it

was apparent. Josie fought the urge to cower.

"I want to know why you told my mother that. And why Mrs Daley thinks I resigned."

His skin darkened. "I told her that to hide the truth from her. Obviously, you had her fooled. She didn't realise that you were trying to use her, to take advantage of her generosity."

"That's not true!" Josie exclaimed. "How can you say that? I'd never do anything to hurt Mrs Daley!"

Could a person's voice be low and thunderous at the same time? Somehow, Mr Beaumont managed it. "I have proof of your intentions, young lady!"

Josie faced him squarely. "Oh yeah?" she challenged him. "What's your proof?" She was amazed to find herself speaking so strongly to a grown-up. But she wasn't going to let this man intimidate her.

"My daughter heard you," Mr Beaumont stated.

Josie stiffened. She should have guessed Heather was behind all this!

He continued. "She heard you asking Mrs Daley for a loan."

As Josie absorbed this, the kitchen door opened. "What's keeping you two?" Mrs Daley asked. Behind her was Mrs Beaumont.

"Nothing, Mother," Mr Beaumont replied smoothly.

"Oh yes, it *is* something," Josie declared. Disregarding the warning look from Mr Beaumont, she said, "Mr Beaumont was just explaining why I was fired."

Mrs Daley was aghast. "Fired! Bill, you fired Josie?"

"He said Heather told him I was trying to get you to give me money."

"But that's ridiculous!" Mrs Daley exclaimed. "Josie never asked me for money."

"Don't defend her, Mother Daley," Mr Beaumont said. "I know you don't like to admit that there's anything bad about a person, but in this case, you have to."

Mrs Daley rapped her cane on the floor so hard Josie could feel the vibrations. "I am telling you that girl never asked me for a dime! In fact, I offered her a loan, several times, and she refused to take it!"

"Bill," Mrs Beaumont murmured, "you know that Mother never lies."

For the first time, Mr Beaumont hesitated. "But, Heather told me—"

"Heather must have misunderstood," Mrs Daley said smoothly. "And I'm quite annoyed with you, Bill, for not telling me all about this in the first place. I could have cleared this up immediately."

Mr Beaumont looked uncertain. "Well, I suppose it's possible that Heather could have misinterpreted what she heard. . . ."

"Precisely," Mrs Daley said. "Now, where's that tea?"

"I'll fix it," Josie said. "Why don't you all go back in the living room and sit down."

She was grateful for a moment alone. She needed it. Although she'd always considered herself a pretty gutsy person, this confrontation had really drained her. And thinking about what Heather had done sent a burning anger through her. But at least the truth was out.

When she brought the tea in, Mrs Daley nudged her son-in-law. Looking slightly abashed, he rose. "Josie, I believe I owe you an apology."

Actually, Josie thought it was Heather who should be offering the apology, but it was highly unlikely she'd ever get one from her. "It's okay."

"Of course, you can have your job back," he added.

Josie considered it. She remembered what Mrs Daley had said about enjoying her daughter's regular visits. And there was something else that had always bothered her. "No, thank you. I never felt right about getting paid for coming here. I'd rather just visit Mrs Daley as a friend."

Mrs Daley seemed pleased, but then she frowned. "Josie, what about your horse?"

Before Josie could respond, Mr Beaumont groaned. "Don't talk about horses." Mrs Beaumont nodded in agreement.

"What do you mean?" Mrs Daley asked.

"Two days ago, out of the blue, Heather asked me to buy her a horse," Mr Beaumont told them.

"Which was very strange," Mrs Beaumont interrupted, "since she's never shown any interest in horses before."

Mr Beaumont went on with his story. "Of course, I wanted to get her a thoroughbred. But for some reason, she insisted on some ten-year-old quarter horse. I don't know what's so special about this animal, but she was adamant."

A cold shiver ran up and down Josie's spine. Strangely, she wasn't at all surprised. "Sunshine."

"Oh, did she tell you about him?" Mrs Beaumont asked.

Mrs Daley's eyebrows shot up. "Josie, was that the horse you wanted to buy?"

Silently, Josie nodded.

"Now, why would Heather suddenly buy the horse you wanted?" Mrs Daley wondered.

If she hadn't been seething with anger, Josie would have smiled. Funny, how family members can know so little about each other.

"Well, anyway," Mr Beaumont continued,

"now that she's got her horse, she's shown no interest in him whatsoever. That horse hasn't received any attention or exercise since he arrived."

"Sometimes I think we spoil Heather," Mrs Beaumont said with a sigh.

It was all Josie could do to keep from asking how you could spoil someone who was already rotten.

"A horse has to have attention and exercise," Mrs Daley declared. "You know, that sounds like the perfect job for Josie."

"That's an idea," Mr Beaumont said. "Would you be interested, Josie?"

Josie's first instinct was to refuse. How could she go work for the Beaumont family, when Heather Beaumont had gone out of her way to be the Morgan girls' sworn enemy?

But there was such a thing as cutting off your nose to spite your face.

"Of course, we'll pay you," Mr Beaumont said. "Just what you've been making here."

"More," Mrs Daley commanded. "Taking care of a horse is a lot more work than sitting around talking to an old lady."

"Okay, okay," Mr Beaumont agreed. "How about it, Josie?"

It would mean time with Sunshine, Josie thought. Then there was the money, too. Maybe the Beaumonts would get fed up with Heather's neglect of the horse. Maybe . . . just maybe, someday, they'd want to sell him.

And of course, there was the satisfaction of seeing Heather's reaction when she found Josie in the stable!

When Josie got home, a strange scene greeted her. Becka sat in the rocking chair, grinning from ear to ear. Ben was scowling, scratching his head, and pacing the room. Annie, looking flustered and confused, sat on the arm of the sofa.

"What's going on?" Josie asked. "Why aren't you at the store?"

"We had to close," Annie told her. "We didn't have anything left to sell."

Josie gaped. "What happened? Were we robbed?"

"No," Ben said. "Your sister here happened to tell a reporter from the *Daily News* about her ad. He thought it was a cute story and wrote about it in his column."

"The customers were *pouring* in," Becka finished smugly.

"That's fantastic!" Josie exclaimed. "But Ben, you don't look very happy about it. What's wrong?"

"I can't help feeling we're getting all those customers under false pretences."

"Nonsense," Annie said. "They're coming

because the article said we had good things to sell."

"But none of this would have happened in the first place if Becka hadn't written that silly ad," Ben argued. "We're benefiting from something she shouldn't have done. The ends don't justify the means."

"Look, you don't have to thank me," Becka said patiently. "And I learned my lesson about false advertising. Why don't we just chalk it up to good fortune?"

Annie laughed. "That sounds like a fine idea to me."

Ben grunted and sank down in a chair. "Doesn't seem right," he muttered. Then he sighed and smiled. "But I guess I'll just have to live with it."

"How do I look?" Cat appeared at the bottom of the stairs, dressed in black velvet. She struck a pose and sauntered across the living room.

"Beautiful, Cat," Annie said. "But what are you wearing it now for?"

"I just wanted to try it on for you." She twirled around. "I still can't believe it's really, truly mine. Of course, I worked hard enough for it."

Josie rolled her eyes.

"Where have you been, by the way?" Annie asked Josie.

"To see Mrs Daley."

Annie was dismayed. "But Josie—"

"Wait," Josie interrupted, then she told them the whole story.

When she finished, Annie shook her head. "Surely Heather couldn't have lied on purpose. I'm sure it was just a misunderstanding, like Mr Beaumont told you."

"Buying the horse, that was probably just a coincidence," Ben added.

Josie, Cat, and Becka exchanged meaningful looks. They knew better.

"Anyway, I've got a new job," she announced. "I'm going to exercise Sunshine."

She was right to try to avoid Cat's eyes. "You can't work for the Beaumonts!" Cat screeched. "Don't you have any pride?"

"I'd trade it in for a horse any day," Josie replied promptly.

Cat opened her mouth to continue her lecture. Then she caught sight of herself in the mirror over the fireplace and forgot all about her sister's disgraceful action.

Ben was staring at his three daughters in bewilderment. "I don't get it. Just this morning, the three of you were miserable. Now you're all happy as clams."

Annie smiled. "Better get used to it, Ben. They're teenagers.

"Can't you just stay like this?" Ben asked hopefully.

"We'll try," Becka said.

"Sure we will," Cat agreed.

Josie just smiled. She knew better. But right this minute, the world seemed bright. The store was back on its feet. Becka had helped get it there. Cat had her dress. As for herself, she didn't have exactly what she'd wanted, but she was closer to it than she'd been before.

Yes, life was good. Not perfect, maybe. But definitely good.

Here's a sneak peek at what's ahead in the
exciting sixth book of THREE OF A KIND:
101 Ways to Win Homecoming Queen

Cat leaned forward. "Guys, we have to think
of some way to cheer Marla up."

Britt and Trisha agreed. "But how?" Trisha
asked.

"Shh," Britt hissed. "Here she comes now."

Cat turned. "Hey, you know, she doesn't look
like she needs cheering up." Marla's expression
had changed dramatically since that morning.
As she carried her tray to their table, she was
greeting people with a bright smile.

"Maybe she's faking it," Britt said.

If so, it was a great performance. Marla was
grinning from ear to ear and her eyes were
sparkling as she joined them. "Wait till you
guys hear this!"

"What happened?" Trisha asked.

Marla sat down. "Guess what I just found
stuck on my locker door?"

Cat took a stab at it. "A note?"

Marla nodded.

"From who?" Britt asked eagerly. "Steve Garner?"

Marla wrinkled her nose and shook her head. "Better than Steve Garner."

"Well, that includes about ninety-five per cent of the male student body," Cat said. "C'mon, tell us. Which guy sent you a note?"

Marla grinned mischievously. She was obviously enjoying the suspense. "I didn't say it was a guy."

"Tell us!" Trisha demanded.

Marla laughed. "I'll let you read it. No, I'll read it to you." She extracted a plain white envelope from her purse and pulled out a sheet of paper. She paused dramatically, then began to read.

"To Marla Eastman. From the Student Council."

Cat smiled, but the opening was a letdown. It must be another committee appointment. What was so thrilling about that?

Marla continued, reading slowly, savouring each and every word. "It is our great pleasure to inform you that you have been selected as a nominee for Winter Carnival Princess."

There was a moment of utter silence. Then Britt let out a shriek, and Trisha clapped her hands. Marla happily accepted their congratulations.

"That's fantastic!" Cat exclaimed. It was great seeing Marla look excited and full of life again. But she had a question. "What's a Winter Carnival Princess?"

"It's part of the whole celebration," Britt explained. "There are three nominees, and the school votes on them. The Princess is crowned at the basketball game. It's supposed to be a secret, but it always leaks out before the game."

Cat beamed at Marla. "This should make up for all those bad things that have been happening."

Marla nodded. "Of course, I'm not the Princess yet. I have to be elected."

"You will be," Trisha said with conviction.

"I guess I have a decent chance," Marla said. "But I wonder who the other nominees are."

Cat's eyes roamed around the cafeteria to see if she could spot any other girls looking particularly excited.

"Gee, I hate to leave this celebration, but I have to go to the library," Britt said. "You do, too, Trisha."

"We'll try to find out who the other nominees are," Trisha said as she rose. "See you guys later."

"It doesn't even matter who they are," Cat

assured Marla. "You're going to win. I feel it in my bones. Besides, you're one of the most popular girls at school."

She realised Marla was looking past her, at Heather Beaumont. "Yeah, but there are other popular girls. And some of them are awfully persuasive."

"You think Heather's one of the nominees?"

"I don't know." A look of uncertainty clouded Marla's face.

"Well, there's one way to find out." Cat rose from her seat. Luckily, Heather's table was right by the water fountain. Cat walked over, took a drink, then smiled brightly at the girls gathered around Heather.

"Congratulations," she said.

Heather's cold green eyes met hers. "Are you speaking to me?"

"Well, no, actually, I was congratulating Blair. I heard she's going to be a cheerleader. Is there some reason I should be congratulating you, too?"

Two of the girls started giggling. Heather smiled smugly. "Oh, you'll find out sooner or later." And then Cat spotted it – a plain white envelope, identical to Marla's, lying by Heather's tray.

Cat went back to her own table and reported what she had seen to Marla. She watched all the happiness evaporate from Marla's face.

"Oh, well," Marla said with a sigh. "I guess it was nice being nominated."

"Cut that out," Cat said firmly. "Stop being so negative! Just because Heather was nominated doesn't mean she's going to win."

"She beat me when we ran against each other for pep club vice-president last year," Marla reminded her. "And she kept me from becoming a cheerleader."

"So what? The whole school is voting, remember? You've got more friends than Heather."

"Yeah, but for some reason Heather always gets her way."

"Not this time," Cat said with determination. "I always get my way, too, you know." She thought for a minute. "I'll get my sisters to help. Josie can pull in the basketball vote. Becka can work on the brains. And *I'll* get everyone else!"

A tiny smile began to form on Marla's face. "You think you've got that much influence?"

Cat didn't have to fake any modesty around Marla. "There isn't anything I've wanted bad enough that I couldn't get if I worked at it. And I've decided I want you to be Winter Carnival Princess."

She was pleased to see the effect her words had on Marla. She wore a real smile now, and a little of that old self-assurance had returned to her eyes. "Gee, Cat, I don't know what I'd do without you. You're a real friend. You're really going to help me get this?"

"I promise." Cat got up. "I have to run by my locker before class. I'll call you tonight and we'll start planning our strategy."

Annie's right, Cat thought as she left the cafeteria. It *did* give her a nice feeling inside, knowing she could help Marla get something she wanted so much. It was almost as nice as getting something for herself. Besides, Marla's grumpy mood was beginning to get on her nerves.

"Cat, wait up!" Becka appeared by her side. "This is so depressing. I've asked a dozen kids if they'd want a little sister. Nobody's showing the least bit of interest."

"That was a dumb promise you made to Michelle. And besides," Cat continued, "you can't expect people to want a kid they've never even seen."

Becka nodded. "Maybe I can ask Ben and Annie if she can visit on Saturday. Then we could take her to the basketball game and show her around."

"There you go, saying 'we' again," Cat said. "This is *your* problem, not mine."

"Come on, Cat, you've got to help me," Becka wheedled. "I'll bet you're going to need *my* help one of these days."

Cat recalled the conversation she'd just had

with Marla. "You know, for once in your life, you're right. There's something I do need your help with." She told Becka about Marla's nomination for Winter Carnival Princess. "I promised her we'd help getting her elected."

"Fine," Becka said promptly. "You help me find a family for Michelle, and I'll help get votes for Marla."

"All right," Cat said. "It's a deal."

"Hey, there's something on your locker," Becka said.

Cat stood very still. Becka was right. Taped to her locker door was a familiar-looking, plain white envelope. She stared at it in disbelief.

"Aren't you going to see what it is?" Becka asked.

Cat could feel her heartbeat speeding up as she ripped the envelope off her locker. She opened it and pulled out a sheet of paper.

Becka read aloud over her shoulder. "To Catherine Morgan. From the Student Council. It is our great pleasure to inform you that you have been selected as a nominee for Winter Carnival Princess."

Reading the words and hearing them at the same time still didn't make them real. Cat read the lines over and over, checking to make sure that it was really her name on top. A tingle started in her toes and shot all the way up through her entire body. She could almost feel the Winter Carnival Princess crown on her head. She was dizzy, she was floating, she was riding on a cloud.

She turned to Becka in ecstasy. But Becka wasn't smiling. Her words brought Cat back down to earth with a thud.

"*Now* who's making dumb promises. Still want me to help get votes for Marla?"

101 Ways to Win
Beauty Queen

For Moira Longino

One

Becka Morgan shivered. The cold wind outside seemed to be coming in through the walls of the old farmhouse.

"Cat! Come on, let's go!" Becka pulled on her parka and fumbled with the zip. When there was no response to her call, she tried again. "Cat!"

A voice drifted out from the kitchen at the other end of the house. "Just a minute!"

Becka glanced at the clock on the mantel over the fireplace and tapped her foot impatiently. "What is she doing, anyway?"

Josie Morgan uttered a snort. "Three guesses, and the first two don't count. Talking on the phone, what else?" Josie grabbed a faded knitted cap from the coat-rack and tugged it down over her short, unruly red hair. Then she flung a scarf around her shoulders.

5

Annie Morgan joined them in the living room. "Ben will be down in a minute," she said. "Are you all ready to go?"

"*We're* ready," Becka said. "But Cat's still on the phone."

"Cat!" Annie called.

"In a second," the voice floated back.

"Becka, put your hood up," Annie said.

Carefully, Becka tucked her long blonde hair under the hood of her coat. At least there was one benefit from the cold weather – her hair didn't frizz like it did in the summer.

Annie took a long woollen scarf from the coatrack and wrapped it around Becka's neck. It wasn't very comfortable, but Becka didn't object to her fussing. There was something nice and cozy about Annie's concern. Even after eight months, Becka still got a special pleasure from having a mother who cared.

"You, too, Josie," Annie ordered. "That scarf won't serve any purpose just hanging there." She beckoned Josie closer and tied it tighter. "I don't want you girls getting the flu."

"I'm never ill," Josie replied. She crooked her arm and flexed a muscle, which wasn't very impressive under her bulky jacket. "I'm an athlete."

Ben Morgan entered the room just in time to catch that announcement. "No one's arguing

6

that. Not after your performance last night on the basketball court."

Josie flushed slightly, but Becka could see the glow of pride in her eyes. "That was pure luck, making that basket in the last second."

"I don't call it luck," Ben replied. "I call it talent. I'll bet those boys are pretty happy they let a girl in the team."

Josie pulled the scarf over her mouth, and her voice was muffled. "Yeah, I guess."

The room was getting warmer, and Becka was beginning to feel stifled by her wrappings. Again, she looked at the clock. "We have to go."

Ben put on his jacket. "Okay, I'm ready." Then he scratched his head and turned to Annie. "Wait a minute. I may be mistaken, but don't we have three daughters?"

"You forget," Annie said. "One of them happens to be permanently attached to a telephone. Cat!"

"Coming!"

"Annie, do something," Becka pleaded. "She's going to make us late."

"Well, it may require surgery to separate her ear from the phone, but I'll see what I can do." Annie headed back towards the kitchen.

Becka started chewing on a fingernail, and Josie eyed her with scorn. "Don't be so jittery. We'll get there."

"But I want us to be there on time," Becka said. She fished the invitation out of her pocket and read aloud: "'On Sunday, February fifth, Willoughby Hall will celebrate its fiftieth year of caring for homeless children. You are cordially invited to join us for a reception and tour at two o'clock.'"

"I think we can pass up the tour," Josie said.

Becka nodded. They knew every nook and cranny of the building — after all, they'd lived there for thirteen years. "But I don't want to miss the reception. I'll bet Mrs. Parker's whipped up all kinds of fabulous goodies."

"Here's the missing daughter," Annie announced, with Cat in tow. Despite her annoyance, Becka couldn't help being impressed with the way Cat looked. Her thick, glossy black hair bounced on the shoulders of her pale green sweater, and her smooth complexion was highlighted by just a touch of make-up.

"Then we're all set," Ben said. He slapped his trouser pocket. "Uh-oh, I left the car keys upstairs. Be right back." He turned and took the stairs two at a time.

"It's about time," Becka told Cat sternly. Cat didn't look the tiniest bit apologetic, but at least she had the courtesy to pretend she was.

8

"He still likes you," Marla murmured.

"Too bad," Cat replied. "There's no way I'd ever be interested in one of Heather Beaumont's rejects."

"You used to like him," Marla said.

Cat didn't need reminding. "That was different." She smiled at the memory. It had been fun, luring Todd away from Heather when Cat had first moved to Green Falls. And for a while, she'd been satisfied with the relationship. Todd was cute, athletic, and popular. Too bad he was also boring.

"Of course, I suppose you don't need Todd," Marla said. "Now that you've got Bailey."

There was a slight note of envy in her voice, and Cat couldn't blame her. With his California-surfer good looks and sense of humour, Bailey was definitely a major improvement over Todd. Cat marvelled at her own good fortune in attracting him. Yes, she was lucky. Not like poor Marla. She felt a surge of sympathy. What could she say to cheer up her friend?

She did know one sure-fire method, and she gave it a shot. "Want to go shopping after school today? I could get out of working at the store, and there's a sale at the Town Shoppe."

"I can't," Marla said with regret. "I'm

on the planning committee for the Winter Carnival, and we've got a meeting today right after school."

"What's this Winter Carnival thing anyway?" Cat asked. "I keep hearing people talk about it."

Marla shrugged. "Oh, just lots of activities. Ice skating, skiing, that sort of thing. There's the big basketball game with Easton High, and a dance."

It all sounded like fun to Cat, but Marla wasn't showing any enthusiasm at all. "That's something to look forward to," Cat said encouragingly.

"I'll be lucky if I even get a date," Marla mumbled.

They entered the noisy locker room, packed with girls changing into shorts for class. Cat's eyes went to a sign on the wall that hadn't been there the day before. It read, CHEERLEADER TRYOUTS, TODAY, 3.30 P.M., GYM.

"Why are they having cheerleader tryouts in the middle of the semester?" Cat asked.

Trisha Heller, sitting on a bench nearby, answered her. "One of the cheerleaders got kicked off because her grade average dropped."

"Heather Beaumont?" Cat asked hopefully.

Trisha grinned. "Unfortunately, no. Some other girl."

"Oh." Cat had always admired the cheerleaders, in their adorable short skirts, kicking and leaping and doing cartwheels, with the eyes of the entire student body on them. And Heather Beaumont, Cat's sworn enemy, was captain.

Well, Cat could kick and leap and turn a cartwheel. And she'd look great in one of those short skirts. She could just imagine Heather's reaction – she'd have a fit if Cat became a cheerleader. What a pleasant thought. Cat studied the sign again and made a mental note of the time and place.

"I think I'll try out," Marla said.

Cat looked at her in surprise. Marla had never shown any interest in cheerleading before, although Cat knew that she had run for pep club vice-president last year. "Why?"

"I don't know. It might cheer me up. If I get chosen, that is." She pulled a pencil from her bag and jotted down the time and place on her notebook. "I hope there's not too much competition."

Cat smiled thinly. She mentally erased the time and place from her mind.

*   *   *

Josie stood with her knees slightly bent, her hands on her knees, and her eyes on the basketball in Alex Hayes's hands. She tried to block out the sound of the girls jumping up and down and cheering on the other side of the gym. This was an important play that they were practicing for the first time, and she had to concentrate.

According to the strategy Coach Meadows had laid out for them, Alex would pretend he was about to throw the ball to the player on his left, then quickly turn and toss it right, to Todd. Todd was supposed to aim toward the basketball hoop, then shoot the ball to Josie, who was closer to the hoop. Hopefully, the guy from the other team who was blocking Josie would be looking at the hoop instead of at the ball, and Josie would have a clear shot at the basket.

Alex faked his throw and got the ball to Todd. Todd pretended he was about to try for the hoop, then threw the ball toward Josie. Josie ran forward to get it. But suddenly, Gary Cole darted in front of her and grabbed it.

The shrill sound of Coach Meadows's whistle filled the air. Everyone froze and waited while the large man stalked out onto the floor. His expression was fierce.

"What was that about?" he barked. "Murphy, can't you remember a simple instruction? That ball was supposed to go to Morgan."

Todd scratched his head. "Yeah, Coach, I know. But – "

Gary Cole spoke up. "She wasn't paying attention, Coach. She didn't even see it coming. I figured if that's what she does during a real game, I'd better be prepared to catch it myself, since I'm closest to her."

Josie glared at him. "What are you talking about? I saw it coming! I was heading straight for it when you – "

A short blast from the coach's whistle silenced her. "Cut it out!" he bellowed. "I don't want any arguments. Now, we've got a big game coming up on Saturday. We haven't been able to beat Sweetwater in two years, and I want that record broken. So let's see a little teamwork here. You got that?" He gave them his standard threatening look.

There was a general bobbing of heads among the players. The coach turned to Josie. "That was a nice shot you made earlier. Keep it up."

Josie beamed and murmured, "Thanks, Coach."

"Okay, hit the showers! Murphy, I want to talk to you." Todd, the captain of the team, scooped up the ball, tucked it under his arm, and followed Coach Meadows to the benches. The other boys, laughing and talking and slapping each other on the back, headed towards the door leading to their locker room. As Gary Cole passed Josie, she called out to him, but he hurried by as if he hadn't heard her.

What was that all about? she wondered. She'd never paid much attention to Gary before, except to notice that he was probably the weakest member of the team. When they practised hoops, he hardly ever got the ball in. He had short arms and short legs, and the coach never put him in crucial positions. Luckily, the other guys liked Gary and didn't make fun of his lack of talent. Josie didn't understand why Gary had snatched that ball away from her. What was he trying to prove?

She started toward the girls' locker room, but then she noticed that Todd had finished his conversation with the coach. She backtracked and hurried over to him before he could enter the boys' locker room.

"Listen, Todd, I wasn't daydreaming or anything on the court. Gary jumped right in front of me. You must have seen him do that."

Todd looked distinctly uncomfortable. He bounced the ball a couple of times. "I wasn't really watching."

Josie stared at him in bewilderment. Of course he'd been watching! He'd been the one throwing the ball! Todd started edging backward, as if he was trying to get away from her. Josie tried to remember what Mrs. Parker had told her. *Just play the best possible game you can play, and the guys will love you.* She didn't want their love. A little acceptance would be enough. And it looked like she wasn't even going to get that. "Wait a second, Todd."

With a show of reluctance, Todd stopped moving, but his eyes didn't meet hers. "Yeah?"

"How am I doing?"

He shrugged. "Okay. You heard what the coach said."

Why couldn't he grin and slap her on the back, like the guys did with each other? Josie gave up. "Thanks." She turned to go to her locker room.

"Hey, Josie . . . "

Eagerly, she whirled around. "Yeah?"

"Um . . . how's Cat doing?"

Josie didn't let her disappointment show. "She's fine."

"Still going out with that Hudson guy?"

"I guess. I don't keep her social calendar."

Just then, Gary Cole stuck his head out the door. "Hey, Murphy, hurry up. We're all going to the bowling alley."

Todd brightened. "Right, I'm coming." He disappeared into the locker room. Josie waited a minute, hoping that the invitation to the bowling alley might be extended to her. She smiled brightly at Gary, trying to show him that she didn't hold a grudge about his move on the court.

His only response was a sneer. Then he pointed to the sign by the door. "Boys only," he stated, as if she couldn't read. As if she was about to walk in there!

Or maybe he was referring to their bowling plans. With as much dignity as she could muster, Josie turned and walked away.

At Morgan's Country Foods, there was a momentary lull between customers. Annie pushed a wisp of hair out of her eyes. "What an afternoon! I don't know how we would have managed without you girls here."

Becka could believe that. Ever since she and Cat had arrived from school, they'd been waiting on customers while Annie handled the cash register and Ben unpacked some crates. They had Becka to thank for the recent upswing in business. Because Becka had miss-stated an ad about the store, then had to retract it, the store had got some publicity. Now they were busy almost every day.

"You two must be beat," Ben said. "As soon as Josie gets back, you can take a break."

"Here she comes now," Cat announced,

peering out of the window. She immediately reached under the counter and started putting on her gloves. *So typical*, Becka thought. Cat wouldn't stay a minute more than necessary.

"How was practice?" Ben asked as Josie pulled off her jacket.

"Okay," Josie replied. "But we couldn't use the whole court because of the dumb cheerleaders."

"Did you see Marla with them?" Cat asked.

Josie shook her head. "I had more important things to do than watch girls acting goofy."

"I didn't know Marla was a cheerleader," Annie remarked.

"She's not, yet," Cat told her. "But there's an opening on the squad, so she's trying out."

"Good grief, why?" Josie asked. "I thought Marla had some brains. Cheerleading is so stupid."

"Are you crazy?" Cat screeched. "Cheerleading's only about the coolest thing you can do."

Becka eyed her curiously. "If you feel that way about it, how come you're not trying out?"

"I was going to," Cat admitted. "But when Marla said *she* wanted to try out, I decided I'd better not. She's been pretty down lately. I'd hate for her to have another disappointment."

"Honestly, Cat, you're so conceited," Josie said. "You act like you're positively sure you would have beaten her for the place."

"Well, excuse me," Cat said in an offended voice. She turned to Annie. "Honestly, you try to do something nice for a person and some people can't deal with it."

Annie spoke soothingly. "I think what you did was very noble. Making a sacrifice for a friend isn't easy, but I'll bet you feel good about it."

Cat preened. Josie started coughing loudly, like she was trying to cover up a laugh. Becka had a hard time choking back a giggle, too. Making *any* kind of sacrifice for *any*one wasn't exactly Cat's style.

Cat shot them both a dirty look. "I guess you guys don't understand what it's like to be unselfish for a change."

It was getting impossible for Becka to hold back the laughter that was rising in her throat. Cat, a noble and unselfish person. Accepting that would take a major mental readjustment!

A jingle over the door ended the conversation. "Customers," Annie said unnecessarily. They all turned towards the front of the store with their fixed welcoming smiles. But those forced expressions dissolved when they saw who the customers were.

"Mrs. Parker!" Josie shrieked. "What are *you* doing here?"

The cook embraced Josie, Becka, and Cat, and shook hands with Annie and Ben.

"It's lovely to see you," Annie exclaimed. In the general chorus of greetings, no one seemed to notice the girl huddling at Mrs. Parker's side. Except Becka.

"Michelle, hi! Remember me?"

Michelle smiled shyly, nodded, and looked around the store. "Do you work here?"

"We all do," Becka said. "It's a family business." She turned to the others. "Hey, everyone, this is Michelle." She introduced the girl to Annie and Ben.

"This isn't just a social visit," Mrs. Parker told them. "Word has it you folks have the best jams and jellies around. How would you like Willoughby Hall's business?"

"We'd be delighted," Ben replied, beaming.

Mrs. Parker continued. "Since I'll be buying in quantity, perhaps we can negotiate on prices."

"Plus a discount for being a friend of the family," Josie added.

Ben pretended to be offended. "Hey, whose side are you on?" He grinned at Mrs. Parker. "I'm sure we can figure out something. Let me show you what we carry, and then we can sit down and make arrangements."

Cat was pulling on her coat. "Can I go? I want to call Marla." When Annie nodded, she yelled, "Nice seeing you, Mrs. Parker," and ran out of the door.

"Becka, why don't you take Michelle out and show her around," Annie suggested. "Josie and I can take care of customers while Ben's with Mrs. Parker."

Michelle looked up at Becka eagerly. "Sure," Becka said. "Come on, Michelle." She put on her coat and led Michelle outside. "That's our house across the street."

"It's beautiful," Michelle breathed.

Becka looked at it. Of course, in *her* opinion, it was beautiful because it was home. But objectively, she knew it was a run-down old farmhouse that needed a lot of work. "Want to see inside?"

Michelle's head bobbed happily. Her enthusiasm couldn't have been greater if she'd been invited to Disney World. And as Becka took her through the house, Michelle responded to each room with oohs and aahs.

When they entered the kitchen, Cat was just hanging up the phone. "Did Marla get picked to be a cheerleader?" Becka asked her.

"She won't find out till tomorrow morning," Cat replied. "What are you two doing?"

"I'm showing Michelle around."

38

"Better not take her into my room," Cat warned. "It's a disaster." She sailed out of the kitchen.

"What does she mean, 'a disaster'?" Michelle asked Becka.

"She means it looks the way it always does, like it's just been hit by a tornado. She hardly ever makes her bed and she leaves her clothes all over the place."

Michelle was shocked. "But doesn't she get into trouble for that?"

Becka shrugged. "Annie says if Cat wants to live like that, she can. It was awful when we were all sharing a room, because Josie and I aren't anywhere near as messy. We're all a lot happier now that we've got our own rooms."

If Michelle's eyes had been wide before, now they were saucers. "You each have your own room?"

Suddenly, Becka felt uncomfortable. Was she showing off, making Michelle even more aware of being an orphan? But Michelle was so eager for information. As Becka continued her tour of the house, she asked question after question. "When's your bedtime?" "Do you get an allowance?" "What happens if you get in trouble?" "Do you and your sisters ever fight?"

Becka answered patiently. She didn't mind,

really. They were the same things she'd wondered about when she was an orphan.

As they went into Becka's bedroom, Michelle noticed the ring on Becka's finger. "That's pretty."

Becka fingered the tiny ruby. "Our parents gave one to each of us when we were adopted. See, we met Annie and Ben in July, and the ruby is July's birthstone. Annie says this ring symbolizes our birth as a family."

To her horror, Michelle's eyes welled up with tears.

"Oh, Michelle, I'm sorry!" Becka grabbed a tissue from the box by her bed.

"That's okay," Michelle mumbled, wiping her eyes. "It's just that, well, this is like my dream. Having a family and a real home . . . "

Becka put her arms around the younger girl and hugged her. "I know. It was my dream, too."

"And your dream came true," Michelle said, hope springing into her eyes.

Becka smiled and nodded, but she was feeling more and more uneasy, like she was leading Michelle on. What had happened to her and Cat and Josie had been pretty unusual. Despite what Becka had told Michelle back at Willoughby Hall, the stories the orphans told were true. Older kids hardly ever got adopted.

Of course, Michelle was only nine, not that old. But most parents wanted babies. Which was too bad. It seemed to Becka that a sweet, polite girl like Michelle would make a perfect daughter.

Michelle was studying a framed photo of the Morgan family on Becka's dresser, and her face was taking on a wistful look again. Becka decided she'd better get her out of the house. "Let's take a walk."

It was cold outside, but the snow was gone. Becka took Michelle around to the back of the house, pointing out the garden and the barn.

"Wow, a real horse!"

"That's old Maybelline, our mare. Would you like to ride her?"

"Gee, I've always wanted to ride a horse. I've never been on one before."

"Maybe you'd better not, then," Becka said. "I wouldn't want you falling off and hurting yourself. Maybelline's very gentle, but – "

"*That* horse doesn't look gentle," Michelle said.

Becka looked in the direction she was pointing. "Oh, that's Red MacPherson on his horse, Belinda. Red lives next door." She waved to him, and Red steered his horse in their direction.

"Hi, Becka, what's up?"

41

"Hi, Red. This is Michelle. She's from Willoughby Hall, where Cat and Josie and I lived."

Michelle reached out and stroked the horse's nose.

"Hi, Michelle. Want to take a ride?" Red hopped off Belinda.

"She's never been on a horse before," Becka told him.

"I'll ride with her," Red said.

Michelle's eyes lit up and she looked at Becka. "Go ahead," Becka encouraged her.

Michelle giggled nervously. "Okay." Red hoisted her up so she could get her foot in the stirrup and pull herself onto the horse. Then he mounted up behind her.

Keeping one arm around Michelle's waist, Red guided the horse slowly. Becka walked along beside them.

"This is fun!" Michelle squealed.

They went all the way over to the Mac-Pherson property. Red's mother was outside, sweeping the path.

"Hi, Mum," Red called. Becka said hello, too, and introduced Michelle.

"Would you kids like to come in for some cocoa?" Mrs. MacPherson asked.

A few minutes later, they were sitting around the table in the MacPhersons' cozy kitchen. Becka and Red started talking about school.

After a while, Becka was afraid they were ignoring Michelle, but she realized that Mrs. MacPherson and the younger girl were talking happily.

"How about another cup?" Mrs. Mac-Pherson offered.

It was a tempting offer, but Becka couldn't take her up on it. There was a knock on the back door, and it opened.

"*There* you are," Annie said. "Becka, I've been looking all over for you two! Mrs. Parker's ready to leave."

"Oh, I'm sorry," Becka said. "I forgot the time. I'll take her back to the store right now."

"Goodbye," Michelle said. "Thanks for the ride, Red. And thanks for the cocoa, Mrs. MacPherson."

"You're very welcome, dear. Come see us again."

Annie remained behind to chat with Mrs. MacPherson. Becka and Michelle left and headed back across the street. "I like them," Michelle said. "Is Red's father nice, too?"

"Red doesn't have a father. He died when Red was a baby."

"Oh." Michelle considered this. "Then I'll bet he half understands what it's like to be an orphan. Oh, Becka, this has been so much fun today!"

"Maybe you can come back for a real visit soon," Becka said.

"I'd like that." Before they walked into the store, Michelle turned and looked back at the house. "Becka, do you believe someday I'll have a real home and a family, like you?"

Becka looked down into her shining eyes. She couldn't bear to tell her that it wasn't likely. Maybe she should be more optimistic. After all, surely there was somebody in this world who would want this girl.

The words spilled out before she'd even formed them in her mind. "You'll have a home, Michelle. *I'll* find you a home."

Three

"Do you know anyone who wants a nine-year-old sister?" Becka asked Cat and Josie as they walked up the steps to school. Snow had started to fall, and they hurried into the lobby.

"Oh, sure," Josie replied. "Why, just the other day, I heard someone say, 'What I really want for my birthday is a nine-year-old sister.'"

"I'm serious," Becka said. "I have to find a family for Michelle."

"Why do *you* have to find a family for Michelle?" Cat asked.

"Because I promised her I would."

"Very smart, Becka," Josie said. "How do you plan to go about doing that? Take out an ad in the newspaper?"

Becka ignored Josie's sarcastic reference to the mistake she had made not long ago. "I

45

don't know. But Michelle needs a home. We've got to help her."

"Why?" Cat asked. "No one helped us find a home."

Josie hooted. "There goes the noble, unselfish Cat." Then she looked directly at Becka. "Hey, what's this 'we' business? You told Michelle *you* would find her a family."

"But you guys will help me, won't you?" Becka pleaded. "Please?"

Josie groaned. Cat smiled, which gave Becka hope, until she realized the smile wasn't aimed at her. Turning, she saw Bailey, Cat's new boyfriend, coming in the door and towards them. He greeted them all cheerfully, brushing the flakes of snow off his jacket.

"Boy, I love this weather!" he announced.

"Must be a big change for you after living in California," Josie said. Bailey had moved to Green Falls only a month or so earlier.

"No kidding. Back there we had one season all year."

"Is this school different from the one you went to?" Becka asked.

"Oh, Becka," Cat said. "A school is a school. They're all alike." She tossed her hair and gave Bailey her famous sidelong glance. "Of course, maybe Bailey has a special reason for liking this school more than his old one . . ."

Bailey gave her a meaningful look. "Yeah, maybe I do."

"Oh, *please*," Josie muttered.

Bailey grinned at her. "You know, I started appreciating school when I had to be out for a week while my parents moved. Not going to classes," he added hastily. "Just being with people. It's lonely when you're an only child. You guys are lucky to have each other."

At that, Josie made her usual gagging sound, but Becka eyed him with interest. "Do you wish you had brothers or sisters?"

"Sure," Bailey said. "It might take some of my parents' attention off me."

Cat caught on to what Becka was getting at. "Becka, you're not about to ask what I think you're going to ask, are you?"

"Why not? Bailey, how would you like to have a nine-year-old sister?"

Bailey blinked. "Huh?"

"We know the sweetest girl who happens to be an orphan," Becka told him. "I know you'd love her."

"Becka!" Josie exclaimed. "You can't just walk up to people and ask them to adopt a kid!"

Bailey was taken aback. When he recovered, he smiled apologetically. "I'm sure she's terrific. But if my parents had wanted another child, they would have had one."

47

"But you could ask them, couldn't you?" Becka persisted.

"Becka!" Then Cat was distracted. "Look, there's Marla. I want to find out if she made the cheerleading squad."

"Wait," Becka said. "I don't think you need to ask." They watched Marla walk across the lobby. One look at her slumped shoulders and woebegone face told them the answer.

Cat put her lunch tray down at her regular table in the cafeteria. Britt and Trisha were eating at an unusually rapid rate. "Where's the fire?" Cat asked her lunchmates.

Trisha spoke with her mouth full. "We've got an assignment due next period that we both forgot about. We have to get to the library."

"Where's Marla?"

"She had to stop by her locker," Britt said.

"I can't believe she didn't make the cheerleading squad," Cat said, sitting down. "Who did, anyway?"

Trisha made a face. "Blair Chase."

Cat's mouth fell open. "Blair? That's impossible! She can barely walk in a straight line!"

"Yeah, but the cheerleaders were making the decision," Britt told her. "And they got a little pressure from their captain."

Cat should have known. Blair was Heather

48

Beaumont's best friend. Cat's eyes drifted over to the table where Heather was sitting with her usual group of admirers. Blair was one of them. "That's disgusting. Why do people always do what she tells them to? Nobody *really* likes her."

"I've been trying to figure that out since third grade," Trisha said. "I think she puts spells on people. Maybe she's a witch."

"I can think of a rhyming word that would describe her better," Britt said with a wicked glint in her eyes.

Cat laughed half-heartedly. "Guys, we have to think of some way to cheer Marla up."

Britt and Trisha agreed. "But how?" Trisha asked.

"Shh," Britt hissed. "Here she comes now."

Cat turned. "Hey, you know, she doesn't look like she needs cheering up." Marla's expression had changed dramatically since that morning. As she carried her tray to their table, she was greeting people with a bright smile.

"Maybe she's faking it," Britt said.

If so, it was a great performance. Marla was grinning from ear to ear and her eyes were sparkling as she joined them. "Wait till you guys hear this!"

"What happened?" Trisha asked.

Marla sat down. "Guess what I just found stuck on my locker door?"

49

Cat took a stab at it. "A note?"

Marla nodded.

"From who?" Britt asked eagerly. "Steve Garner?"

Marla wrinkled her nose and shook her head. "Better than Steve Garner."

"Well, that includes about ninety-five percent of the male student body," Cat said. "Come on, tell us. Which guy sent you a note?"

Marla grinned mischievously. She was obviously enjoying the suspense. "I didn't say it was a guy."

"Tell us!" Trisha demanded.

Marla laughed. "I'll let you read it. No, I'll read it to you." She extracted a plain white envelope from her purse and pulled out a sheet of paper. She paused dramatically, then began to read.

"'To Marla Eastman. From the Student Council.'"

Cat smiled, but the opening was a letdown. It must be another committee appointment. What was so thrilling about that?

Marla continued, reading slowly, savouring each and every word. "'It is our great pleasure to inform you that you have been selected as a nominee for Winter Carnival Princess.'"

There was a moment of utter silence. Then Britt let out a shriek, and Trisha clapped her hands. Marla happily accepted their congratulations.

"That's fantastic!" Cat exclaimed. It was great seeing Marla look excited and full of life again. But she had a question. "What's a Winter Carnival Princess?"

"It's part of the whole celebration," Britt explained. "There are three nominees, and the school votes on them. The Princess is crowned at the basketball game. It's supposed to be a secret, but it always leaks out before the game."

Cat beamed at Marla. "This should make up for all those bad things that have been happening."

Marla nodded. "Of course, I'm not the Princess yet. I have to be elected."

"You will be," Trisha said with conviction.

"I guess I have a decent chance," Marla said. "But I wonder who the other nominees are."

Cat's eyes roamed around the cafeteria to see if she could spot any other girls looking particularly excited.

"Gee, I hate to leave this celebration, but I have to go to the library," Britt said. "You do, too, Trisha."

"We'll try to find out who the other nominees are," Trisha said as she rose. "See you guys later."

"It doesn't even matter who they are," Cat

assured Marla. "You're going to win. I feel it in my bones. Besides, you're one of the most popular girls at school."

She realized Marla was looking past her at Heather Beaumont. "Yeah, but there are other popular girls. And some of them are awfully persuasive."

"You think Heather's one of the nominees?"

"I don't know." A look of uncertainty clouded Marla's face.

"Well, there's one way to find out." Cat rose from her seat. Luckily, Heather's table was right by the water fountain. Cat walked over, took a drink, then smiled brightly at the girls gathered around Heather.

"Congratulations," she said.

Heather's cold green eyes met hers. "Are you speaking to me?"

"Well, no, actually, I was congratulating Blair. I heard she's going to be a cheerleader. Is there some reason I should be congratulating you, too?"

Two of the girls started giggling. Heather smiled smugly. "Oh, you'll find out sooner or later." And then Cat spotted it – a plain white envelope, identical to Marla's, lying by Heather's tray.

Cat went back to her own table and reported what she had seen to Marla. She watched all the happiness evaporate from Marla's face.

"Oh, well," Marla sighed. "I guess it was nice being nominated."

"Cut that out," Cat said firmly. "Stop being so negative! That's not like you. Just because Heather was nominated doesn't mean she's going to win."

"She beat me when we ran against each other for pep club vice-president last year," Marla reminded her. "And she kept me from becoming a cheerleader."

"So what? The whole school is voting, remember? You've got more friends than Heather."

"Yeah, but for some reason Heather always gets her way."

"Not this time," Cat said with determination. "I always get my way, too, you know." She thought for a minute. "I'll get my sisters to help. Josie can pull in the basketball vote. Becka can work on the brains. And *I'll* get everyone else!"

A tiny smile began to form on Marla's face. "You think you've got that much influence?"

Cat didn't have to fake any modesty around Marla. "There isn't anything I've wanted badly enough that I haven't got if I've worked at it. And I've decided I want you to be Winter Carnival Princess."

She was pleased to see the effect her words had on Marla. She wore a real smile now, and a little of that old self-assurance had returned to her eyes. "Gee, Cat, I don't know what I'd do without you. You're a real friend. You're really going to help me get this?"

"I promise." Cat got up. "I have to run by my locker before class. I'll call you tonight and we'll start planning our strategy."

Annie was right, Cat thought as she left the cafeteria. It *did* give her a nice feeling inside, knowing she could help Marla get something she wanted so much. It was almost as nice as getting something for herself. Besides, Marla's grumpy mood was beginning to get on her nerves.

"Cat, wait up!" Becka appeared by her side. "This is so depressing. I've asked a dozen kids if they want a little sister. Nobody's showing the least bit of interest."

"That was a dumb promise you made to Michelle."

"Yeah, maybe, but I can't do anything about that now."

Personally, Cat thought Becka was being ridiculous, but she was in such a good mood she could afford to be kind. "You're going about this the wrong way," she advised. "Don't ask kids. They don't make those kinds of decisions. You need to be talking to grown-ups."

"I guess you're right," Becka said.

"And besides," Cat continued, "you can't expect people to want a kid they've never even seen."

Becka nodded. "Maybe I can ask Ben and Annie if she can visit us on Saturday. Then we could take her to the basketball game and show her around."

"There you go, saying 'we' again," Cat said. "This is *your* problem, not mine."

"Come on, Cat, you've got to help me," Becka wheedled. "I'll bet you're going to need *my* help one of these days."

Cat recalled the conversation she'd just had with Marla. "You know, for once in your life, you're right. There's something I do need your help with." She told Becka about Marla's nomination for Winter Carnival Princess. "I promised her we'd help get her elected."

"Fine," Becka said promptly. "You help me find a family for Michelle, and I'll help get votes for Marla."

"All right," Cat said. "It's a deal."

"Hey, there's something on your locker," Becka said.

Cat stood very still. Becka was right. Taped to her locker door was a familiar-looking plain white envelope. She stared at it in disbelief.

"Aren't you going to see what it is?" Becka asked.

Cat could feel her heartbeat speeding up as

she ripped the envelope off her locker. She opened it and pulled out a sheet of paper.

Becka read aloud over her shoulder. "'To Catherine Morgan. From the Student Council. It is our great pleasure to inform you that you have been selected as a nominee for Winter Carnival Princess.'"

Reading the words and hearing them at the same time still didn't make them real. Cat read the line over and over, checking to make sure that it was really her name on top. A tingle started in her toes and shot all the way up through her entire body. She could almost feel the Winter Carnival Princess crown on her head. She was dizzy, she was floating, she was riding on a cloud.

She turned to Becka in ecstasy. But Becka wasn't smiling. Her words brought Cat back down to earth with a thud.

"*Now* who's making dumb promises. Still want me to help get votes for Marla?"

Four

The benches in the gym were packed on Saturday afternoon. To Becka, it seemed like half the town had turned out to watch the Green Falls Junior High basketball team play Sweetwater. The action on the court had been non-stop, but Becka was more interested in the audience. For her purposes, the bigger the crowd, the better.

"I've never been to a real basketball game before," Michelle said. "This is so exciting!"

Becka could barely hear her over the noisy and enthusiastic fans. And responding was impossible, because just then a roar went up from the crowd.

Behind Becka, her father bellowed, "That's my girl!" Michelle was hopping up and down. "Wow, I can't believe Josie got that basket!"

Becka smiled, clapped her hands, and nodded, but she hadn't really been paying attention. She was too busy scanning the crowd for prospective parents for Michelle.

At the end of the first quarter, Mrs. MacPherson turned around. "Are you enjoying this, Michelle?"

"It's great! Josie's scoring more points than anyone!"

While they talked about the game, Becka studied a figure sitting a few rows below them. It was Mr. Davison, one of her teachers. Becka considered Mr. Davison's qualities. He was handsome, funny, and he handled their rambunctious class easily. She figured the woman by his side must be his wife. She wished she could get a good look at her face.

In the same row, Becka saw her friend Louise Nolan, with her parents. Louise was always telling Becka how lucky she was to have sisters. Louise only had one older brother, who was constantly teasing her.

"Josie got the rebound!" Michelle squealed.

"That's nice," Becka said vaguely. She was making a mental note of where Mr. Davison and Louise were sitting. Then she started to examine the occupants of the other benches.

"Becka, are you looking for somebody?"

Becka turned to Red, who was sitting on her other side. "Sort of." She glanced back at Michelle, who was completely engrossed in

58

the game. Even so, she lowered her voice and spoke directly into Red's ear. "I'm looking for people who might want to adopt Michelle."

Red's eyebrows went up. Then Becka felt a hand on her shoulder. "Becka, watch," Annie said excitedly. "Josie's got a foul shot."

Becka wasn't even sure she knew what a foul shot was, but she directed her attention to the court. The audience became quiet, and all eyes were on Josie. She stood there, clutching the ball. For a moment, Becka forgot her mission and shivered, imagining how nervous Josie must be. Even though she couldn't really see Josie's face from where she was sitting, she could imagine the tense determination of her expression.

Josie aimed the ball and tossed it. The ball sailed up through the air and fell through the basket, barely ruffling the net. An ear-shattering cheer filled the gym. Relieved, Becka returned to studying faces.

Finally, the second quarter was over and the players left the court. In the stand, people stood up and stretched, or began milling around. Becka took Michelle's hand. "Come on, let's walk around."

"Where are we going?"

"I want you to meet some people." She gave Michelle a once-over, adjusted her hair clip, and examined her face. "Let's see a nice big smile."

Michelle obliged, baring her teeth. Becka thought about instructing her on charming behaviour, but she didn't want to make Michelle nervous. Clutching Michelle's hand tightly, Becka pushed through the crowd down to where Mr. Davison was sitting.

"Hello, Mr. Davison."

He smiled. "Hello, Becka." He turned to the woman next to him. "Honey, this is one of my students, Becka Morgan. Becka, this is my wife, June Davison."

Becka liked the way he called his wife "honey". That meant they had a good relationship. And she was pleased with Mrs. Davison. She was attractive, but not glamorous – sort of motherly looking.

Becka nudged Michelle forward. "This is Michelle. She's visiting us from Willoughby Hall. That's where I used to live, before I was adopted." For special emphasis, she added, "When I was an orphan. Like Michelle."

Unfortunately, the Davisons didn't catch that. Their attention was diverted to a small girl sitting in front of them, tugging at Mrs. Davison's sweater. "Mum, can I have another cookie?"

While Mrs. Davison reached for her purse, Becka spoke to her teacher. "Is that your daughter?"

"One of them," Mr. Davison replied. "I've got five in all."

Becka gulped. "Five daughters?"

He grinned. "And on a teacher's salary."

Becka smiled thinly and nodded. There was no point in pursuing this. "Nice seeing you, Mr. Davison. Come on, Michelle." She pulled her across the row, towards Louise. Then she spotted someone else – Mademoiselle Casalls, her French teacher, with her new husband. They were holding hands.

Becka greeted them and introduced Michelle. Mademoiselle Casalls responded with her usual cool elegance. "Bonjour, Becka, Michelle." Becka loved the way she said the name "Michelle". It dawned on her that Michelle must be a French name. That was a good sign.

Her husband spoke pleasantly to them, too. "Michelle's visiting us from Willoughby Hall," Becka began. But before she could use words like *orphan* or *adopted*, Mademoiselle's husband began whispering in her ear. Mademoiselle ducked her head and began giggling softly. It was like Becka and Michelle weren't even there.

Lovebirds, Becka thought. They seemed more like teenagers than possible parents. She could see there was no point in wasting time on them.

Still holding Michelle's hand, Becka led her over to Louise. "This is Michelle," she

61

announced. "Michelle, this is my friend Louise Nolan and her parents."

"Hello, girls," Mrs. Nolan said in a friendly voice. "Are you visiting, Michelle?"

"I'm from Willoughby Hall," Michelle said. It was apparent that the Nolans knew what Willoughby Hall was. Becka was pleased to see the appropriate looks of sympathy on their faces.

"Your sister's playing a great game," Louise noted.

"Yeah, I'm real proud of her," Becka replied. "It's great having sisters."

She couldn't blame Louise for looking at her oddly. Becka was much more likely to complain about her sisters to Louise than praise them.

"Did you see Mr. Davison over there?" Louise asked.

Becka had an inspiration. "Yes. Did you know he has five kids?"

"Five!" Mrs. Nolan exclaimed. "My goodness. I wonder how they manage. I've got my hands full with two. If I had any more, I would just give up."

Becka's smile drooped. "Well, nice seeing you. Come on, Michelle."

"Congratulations, Cat!"
Cat glanced at the passing classmate. "Huh?"

"I heard you've been nominated for Winter Carnival Princess."

"Oh, yeah," Cat said. "Thanks."

After the classmate moved on, Bailey turned to her. "You're going to have to be friendlier than that if you want votes," he said in a teasing voice.

Cat nodded. He was right, of course. Normally in a situation like this, she wouldn't need reminding. She'd be out there talking to everyone, flirting with the boys, gushing compliments to the girls. If there was one thing she knew how to do well, it was how to be popular.

She tried to concentrate on the image of herself as Princess. But every time she conjured up a mental picture of herself with a crown on her head, another picture took its place. Marla.

She gave Bailey a bright smile. "Maybe I'd better go do a little campaigning. I'll be right back."

She went up a few rows, to where she'd seen Marla sitting with Britt and Trisha. But Britt and Trisha were alone.

"Where's Marla?"

"She's around somewhere," Britt said. Both of the girls looked at her uneasily, and Cat couldn't blame them. Ever since the day the nominations had come up, things had been strange. They all still sat together at lunch, but it wasn't the same. They talked about everything but the Winter Carnival. Marla avoided speaking directly to Cat. There were no more daily telephone conversations. When they ran into each other at school, they were polite. But each time they met, Cat could see the hurt in Marla's eyes.

"Here comes Marla now," Trisha said. Cat turned and saw her making her way up the stand. She paused at each row, to smile and chat. *Campaigning*, Cat thought.

When Marla saw Cat, her smile seemed to fade.

"Hi, Marla," Cat said. To her own ears, her words sounded falsely bright.

"Hello, Cat," Marla replied coolly.

"Great game, huh?" Trisha said loudly. "Looks like we just might beat Sweetwater this year."

"Yeah, great game," Britt echoed. "I think Josie's scored more points than any boy on the team."

Marla nodded. To Cat, she said, "You Morgan girls certainly know how to take over, don't you?"

Cat choked back a gasp. How could her best friend speak to her like that?

Luckily, there was a distraction.

"Don't look now, but guess who's coming

this way," Britt muttered. It was Heather, looking particularly cute in her little cheerleading outfit.

Cat tried giving Marla that special look they always shared when Heather was around. If nothing else, surely they were still united in their dislike of her. But Marla wouldn't even meet her eyes.

"Hi, girls," Heather drawled. She focused her attention on Marla and Cat. "I don't think I've congratulated you two on being nominated for Winter Carnival Princess."

"Why, thank you, Heather," Cat said sweetly. "I'm sure you're just as happy about that as we are."

"Actually, I am." Heather tossed her head. "You two have the same friends. That means you'll split the vote." She laughed, as if it were a joke, but Cat knew it wasn't.

Having made her point, Heather moved on. Cat glared after her. "Honestly, she makes me so sick. One of these days, she's going to be sorry."

"Is that a promise or a threat?" Trisha asked.

"Both," Cat replied.

Marla spoke in a quiet, even tone. "And we all know how much a promise means to you."

"Uh, the game's starting again," Britt announced quickly.

Cat returned to her seat.

★ ★ ★

Josie could feel the perspiration dripping down the side of her face. She understood now why Green Falls hadn't won a game against Sweetwater in two years. Sweetwater was *good*.

Which wasn't to say Green Falls was playing badly. Every member of the team was doing his – and in Josie's case, her – very best. They followed the plays that Coach Meadows had made them practise, and it was a good policy. The coach obviously knew what Sweetwater could do, and all his instructions to the team had been designed around Sweetwater's strengths and weaknesses.

Unfortunately, Sweetwater didn't appear to have many weaknesses. What they did have were three players who were pretty tall for junior high students. And the tallest one could do a real dunk shot, something Josie had only seen in professional basketball on television.

Somehow, though, Green Falls managed to hold its own, and the score was very close. Over on the Sweetwater side, the boy dribbling the ball was surrounded by Green Falls players. Josie could see that the dribbler was trying to get into a position where he could throw the ball to that unbelievably tall guy on their team, so he could make another one of his amazing dunk shots.

But the Green Falls boys were doing their

best to prevent this. Every few seconds, one of them got the ball away, but a Sweetwater player kept getting it back.

Josie blocked out the noise of the crowd and the cheers of the cheerleaders, and put all her mental energy on Alex, who was closest to the dribbling Sweetwater boy. *Come on, Alex, get in there*, she ordered silently.

And then, Alex did. He was immediately surrounded by Sweetwater boys, and he was in no position to get the ball to Josie. He threw the ball to Gary Cole. Josie darted within Gary's range of vision and threw up her arms. She was in a good tossing position.

Gary had to have seen her. But he didn't throw the ball. He started dribbling. Josie realized in dismay that he was going to try for a basket. *What an idiot*, she fumed. There was no way he could get close enough to shoot, not with those Sweetwater guards already heading in his direction. Even if he did get close enough, Josie doubted that he could clear the net. If he couldn't do it in practice, what made him think he could do it now?

Josie moved faster than she ever had in her life. Luckily, no one was paying attention to her. She dashed forward and snatched the ball away from Gary. Her action took the Sweetwater players by surprise, and she actually was able to get a few feet closer to the basket before taking careful aim.

The ball went through the net, and now the score was tied. With only a few seconds remaining, Sweetwater got the ball and started towards the other end of the court. But Todd swept in, grabbed the ball, and took a wild shot. It was in!

The crowd went wild. For the first time in two years, Green Falls had beaten Sweetwater. For a second, Josie just stood there, trying to catch her breath. Then she turned to her teammates.

They were gathered in a group, shrieking and cheering, slapping one another on the back, and giving one another high fives. Josie hurried over to join them. But just as she reached the group, they all took off, running towards the boys' locker room.

She paused a moment, watching after them, then started off in the opposite direction. Passing the stand, she saw Annie and Ben waving and making victory signs with their hands. Josie waved back. Several kids called out to her, yelling stuff like "Congratulations" and "Great game". That was nice. But she really wanted to be exchanging comments like that with her teammates.

It was lonely in the girls' locker room. Josie hurriedly showered and changed, not even bothering to dry her hair. Annie would have a fit if she knew Josie was going out in the cold with a wet head, but Josie didn't want to keep her teammates waiting. Surely they'd want to go out and celebrate their victory.

Emerging from the locker room, she saw the boys gathered at the end of the hall by the school exit. She walked towards them, pulling on her coat, and didn't see Gary Cole by her side till he spoke.

"Thanks a lot, Josie." They were words she'd expected to hear but definitely not spoken in that tone. There was no mistaking the resentment and sarcasm in his voice.

"What do you mean?"

"That was my big chance," Gary said. "You stole that ball right from under me."

"Gary, I just wanted us to win! Look, we're all in this together, right?"

"Oh, give me a break," he muttered. He ran over to the others, and in a loud voice, said, "Party's at my place, guys! Let's go!"

Josie just stood there and watched as the boys headed out of the door without her. A second later, she was surrounded by her parents, her sisters, and assorted friends. She could feel their hugs, hear their congratulations, Becka yelling, "Yay, Josie!"

But all she was really aware of was a great big lump in her throat.

Slowly, Becka replaced the telephone receiver. Then she scratched a name off her list.

Annie came into the kitchen, took the lid off the pot on the stove, and breathed deeply. "Mmm, Josie really has a talent with stew." She dipped a spoon in and tasted. "Becka, try this and see if you think it needs to simmer a little longer."

Becka obliged. The stew tasted perfect to her, but she wanted to make some more phone calls. "I think it should sit a few more minutes," she said.

"All right," Annie said, but she didn't leave the kitchen. "I'll put the noodles on to boil."

Becka looked down at her list. She still wanted to try Lisa Simon and Patty Jackson. Lisa was an only child, and Patty only had one brother, away at college. Either of them might like the idea of a kid sister.

"You've been on the phone quite a bit this evening," Annie noted. "Some big project going on?"

"I guess you could call it a project," Becka said. Annie glanced at her curiously, but she didn't ask any questions. She was always good about not prying into the girls' lives, waiting instead for them to come to her with problems. And they usually did. But Becka had an uneasy feeling Annie might not give her wholehearted

70

approval to Becka's promise to Michelle. More than once, Becka had been admonished for biting off more than she could chew.

"I'm sorry if I was tying up the phone," she said. "Did you want to make a call?"

"It's not urgent," Annie said. "I just want to thank Helen MacPherson for driving Michelle back to Willoughby Hall. I think Michelle enjoyed herself today, don't you?"

That was a good opening. "I wish I could find parents for Michelle," Becka began tentatively. "She really wants a family."

Annie nodded. "I wish there were homes for all the orphans in the world. And Michelle is such a darling child."

Those were encouraging words. Becka was just about to blurt out what she was up to when the phone rang. She picked it up. "Hello?"

"Uh, could I speak to Cat, please?"

The voice was familiar. "Just a minute." She covered the mouthpiece and yelled, "Cat!"

A second later, Cat appeared. "Is it Marla?" she whispered.

Becka shook her head. "It's a boy." She wasn't surprised to see Cat's face fall slightly. But Annie's eyebrows went up, and now her curious look was directed at Cat.

Cat took the phone. "Hello? Oh, hi, Todd."

Annie busied herself pouring noodles into the boiling water, but Becka didn't bother to

71

disguise her interest. It had been a long time since Todd had called.

"No, I'm busy tonight," Cat said. There was a pause. "No, I can't get out of it. I don't *want* to get out of it. Goodbye, Todd." She hung up.

"*Honestly*," she mumbled.

"I thought you said you weren't going out tonight," Annie said.

"I'm not," Cat replied. "Bailey has to do something with his parents. But I still don't want to go out with Todd. I don't know why he called. He knows about Bailey and me."

"Can't blame a guy for trying," Annie said lightly. "Todd's a nice boy, Cat."

"You think I should have gone out with him?" Cat asked. She cocked her head thoughtfully. "I guess it wouldn't hurt to make Bailey feel like he's got some competition."

"Oh, no, Cat," Annie said. "I'm not suggesting you go out with Todd. Not if you don't have any feelings for him. That would just be using him."

Cat looked at her blankly, and Becka suppressed a giggle. Cat had never had a problem with using people to get what she wanted.

Just as they were all sitting down to dinner, the phone rang again. Cat jumped up from her seat. "I'll get it!" A moment later she was back. "That was Mrs. MacPherson," she told Annie. "She said not to disturb you, just call her back after dinner." She kept looking back at the kitchen, as if she was waiting for the phone to ring again.

"Expecting an important call?" Ben asked as he served the stew.

Cat shrugged. "I just thought that might have been Marla."

"Have you guys had a fight or something?" Josie asked.

Cat gave her an aggravated look. "Josie, you *know* we were both nominated for Winter Carnival Princess."

"Oh, *that*." Josie made it clear how totally unimportant that was to her.

Annie looked more sympathetic. "Is that causing a strain on your friendship?"

Cat nodded. "See, I promised Marla I'd help her win the election. But that was before I knew *I* was going to be nominated, too."

"Making promises like that can be dangerous," Ben said.

"I know that *now*," Cat said.

Annie reached over and patted her hand. "I'm sure that once the election's over and done with, you and Marla can go right back to being friends again."

"I don't know," Cat said. "She really wants

73

to be Princess. She's going to hate me when, I mean if, I win."

"Well, at least you've learned something," Ben said, smiling. "Be careful before you make promises you might not be able to keep. Becka, don't you like the stew?"

Becka looked down at her barely touched plate. "Oh, I like it," she said quickly, and started eating. But Ben's words were ringing in her ears. *Be careful before you make promises* . . .

"The stew's delicious," Annie said. "I was just thinking that we might make this for Tuesday night."

"What's happening on Tuesday night?" Ben asked.

"Don't you remember? We've invited the Laytons for dinner," Annie told him.

Becka's head jerked up.

"We could ask Helen MacPherson, too," Annie said. "Do you girls want to invite anyone? Cat, what about Marla?"

Cat brightened. "Yeah, that's a great idea."

"Josie, how about you?" Ben asked. "One of the kids from the basketball team?"

Josie shook her head. "No, I don't think any of them would be interested."

"Oh, come on," Ben urged. "I'll bet any one of those boys would like to have dinner with the team star!"

Becka spoke up. "Can I invite Michelle?"

"Of course," Annie said. "But it's a school night. I'm not sure she'd be able to get permission from Mrs. Scanlon."

"Maybe you could call Mrs. Scanlon and ask her," Becka said. "She wouldn't say no to you. And it would mean so much to Michelle. She loves being here. *Please?*"

Annie seemed a little puzzled by the urgency in Becka's voice, but she nodded. "All right, I'll call tomorrow."

Satisfied, Becka began eating her stew with gusto. The Laytons! She hadn't even considered them. They were good friends of her parents, and they'd just moved to Vermont a few months ago to open an inn. They didn't have any children, and they were always saying how much they admired Annie and Ben's decision to adopt. Why hadn't she thought of them sooner? They were the absolutely perfect parents for Michelle!

Five

On Tuesday afternoon, Cat strode briskly down the hall and stopped at the open door to the *Green Gazette* office. She looked in at the students milling around inside, but she didn't see Becka. Folding her arms, she tapped her foot impatiently.

"Hi, Cat," a skinny boy with glasses greeted her.

"Hi, Jason. I was looking for Becka."

The newspaper editor nodded. "I just saw her. She's on her way. I guess you must be getting excited about the election for Winter Carnival Princess on Friday."

Cat hesitated. Now was the perfect time to turn on the charm full force. After all, Jason was a pretty influential person. Oh, if only this were just a battle between herself and Heather. And if only she could erase the image of Marla's disappointed face from her head.

76

She compromised and offered a modest smile. "Oh, sure. Jason, could you give Becka a message for me? Oh wait, never mind." She spotted Becka coming towards the room.

"Tell Annie and Ben I'm going to Brownies with some friends, okay?" Cat asked her.

"I can't," Becka said. She cocked her head towards the *Green Gazette* office. "I've got a newspaper meeting."

"Darn," Cat muttered. "I guess I'd better call them."

"Don't forget, we've got company coming for dinner," Becka reminded her. "Cat, what do you think of the Laytons? Don't you think they'd be perfect parents for Michelle?"

"How should I know?" Then Cat saw Josie heading towards her locker. "Hey, Josie! Tell Annie and Ben I went to Brownies, okay?"

Josie gave a nod to indicate she'd heard and kept on moving.

"Come on, Cat," Becka pressed. "You promised you'd help me find parents for Michelle."

"Yeah, but that was only because you promised to help Marla be Winter Carnival Princess. And you're off the hook on that one. So I don't have to keep my promise to you, either."

Becka put her hands on her hips. "Are

you saying sometimes promises count and sometimes they don't?"

"I'm saying – I'm saying . . . " Cat stopped and rubbed her head. She didn't know what she was saying. It was all getting too complicated. If she heard one more word about promises, she was going to scream.

"Excuse me."

Cat turned. It was the last person in the world she wanted to see. "What do you want, Heather?" she asked testily.

"I'd like to get into this room, but you're blocking the door."

"This is the *Green Gazette* meeting," Becka said.

"I know what it is," Heather replied. "I'm interested in joining the staff." With that, she breezed by them into the room.

Cat watched her, incredulous. "Heather Beaumont on the newspaper staff? That's crazy! It's not even one of the cool activities."

Becka disregarded the insult. "I don't think that's why she's really here. I bet she just wants to hang around and get votes for Winter Carnival Princess. She was at the French club meeting this morning, and she's not even taking French! And Louise Nolan told me she showed up at the science club meeting yesterday, acting like she wanted to join."

That was enough evidence to convince Cat

78

that Becka's suspicions were correct. Only brains and geeks belonged to the science club. "What a sneaky scheme," Cat said.

"Yeah," Becka agreed. "I'm surprised you didn't think of it first."

"Mmm," Cat murmured. "Of course, then Marla would really hate me. See ya later."

But how much more could Marla hate her? Cat pondered as she went off to join her friends. Marla was still shooting Cat odd looks and barely speaking to her. She'd turned down Cat's invitation to dinner that evening without even making up a good excuse.

Britt and Trisha were waiting for her by the school exit. "What took you so long?" Britt asked.

Cat told them about seeing Heather in the newspaper meeting. "She's just faking an interest to kiss up to those kids. You know how she can turn on the charm when she wants to. The kids who don't really know her always fall for it. Ooh, she gets me so mad."

"You always find ways to get back at her," Trisha offered as comfort.

"But what can I do?" Cat complained. "I can't start really campaigning to win, or Marla will *never* speak to me again. Everything's bad enough as it is."

"I asked Marla to come to Brownies with

us," Britt said. "She said she'd meet us there if she finished some work she has to do in the library."

Cat brightened. "That's good. Oh, I hope she comes."

"Well, I didn't tell her you were coming, too."

"Oh." Cat stamped her foot in frustration. "What's the matter with her, anyway? I didn't *ask* to be nominated!"

"She just keeps saying you promised to help her win," Britt said.

"It'll all be over soon," Trisha said. "The election for Winter Carnival Princess is on Friday. And I've got a connection with a guy on the Student Council. He's going to let me know the results as soon as the votes are counted."

"Personally, I don't care who wins," Britt said. "As long as it's not Heather."

"Right," Trisha agreed. "I'll be happy if either you or Marla wins."

"Oh, sure," Cat said. "That's how I feel, too." She hoped her words rang true. She wasn't convinced that they were. Winning would make Marla awfully happy. But in the back of her mind, she could hear the words *Princess Cat*. They had such a nice sound.

★   ★   ★

Josie fumbled around in her locker for her books. Thank goodness there was no basketball practice that day. She was in no mood for Gary Cole's dirty looks.

Todd Murphy approached her. "Josie, do you know where Cat is?"

"She went to Brownies."

"Okay." He started to walk away.

"Todd, wait. I want to talk to you about the team."

"What about it?"

She ignored the look of discomfort on his face. "Do you think I'm any good?"

He shrugged. "Yeah, sure."

"Do the other guys think I'm good?"

He shifted his weight from one foot to the other, making it clear that he wanted to escape this inquisition. But Josie wanted some answers. "Do the guys think I'm a good basketball player?"

"Well, yeah, I guess so. Hey, you scored more than half the points in the last game."

"Then why do you guys act different around me than you act with each other?"

He struggled to find the right words. "Because, you know, it's like, well . . . " Finally he blurted it out. "You're a girl!"

Josie clutched her head. "What's that got to do with anything?"

Todd looked at her as if she were unbelievably stupid. "The guys aren't used to having a girl in the team. Boys act different around girls than they act around other boys."

"Then stop thinking of me as a girl," Josie demanded. "Consider me just another team member."

Todd's eyes swept over her jeans and unruly short hair. He actually seemed to be considering the possibility. Then he shook his head. "Nah. Wouldn't work."

"But this is ridiculous!" Josie exclaimed. "They should appreciate me! I'm one of the best players in the team!"

"Yeah, you're right," Todd admitted. "But I guess that's the problem."

"Huh? What does *that* mean?"

"Well, you score a lot of points. The coach is always telling you how good you are. And he's always yelling at the rest of us. Maybe some of the guys don't like that he never finds anything wrong with you."

"Some of the guys," Josie repeated. "You mean, like Gary Cole?"

Todd nodded. "Yeah. You can't blame him, really. The way you play, it makes him look bad."

"But practically every guy on the team is better than he is," Josie protested. "Why doesn't he hate them?"

"I guess he doesn't care if the guys are better. But you're a – "

"I know," Josie interrupted. "I'm a girl." She slammed her locker door shut with unusual force. "Well, thanks for the information, Todd."

"No problem," Todd said, and he took off.

Josie leaned against her locker and sighed. Her thoughts went back to the conversation she'd had at Willoughby Hall with Mrs. Parker. What had she said? *Play the best game you can, and the boys will love you?* Hah! It seemed to her that the opposite was true.

It's hopeless, Josie thought dismally as she walked towards the exit. As long as she was a girl playing a good game, the boys would never accept her.

Then she stopped. Okay, there was nothing she could do about being a girl. But maybe there was something she could do about her game.

There was the usual after-school crowd in Brownies. Britt, Trisha, and Cat slid into a booth and tried unsuccessfully to flag down a harried-looking waitress.

Karen Hall and Sharon Cohen stopped by their table. Karen spoke to Cat. "We've been trying to decide who to vote for on Friday, you or Marla."

"And we finally came up with a solution," Sharon chirped.

"Tell us," Britt demanded.

Karen beamed proudly. "One of us will vote for Cat and one of us will vote for Marla!" With that, the two sailed away.

Britt turned to Trisha. "I guess that's what we'll have to do, too."

"Great," Cat said glumly. "You see what's happening? It's just like Heather said. Marla and I will split the votes of the people who like us. So Heather's going to win."

"There's only one way Heather can lose," Trisha said. "If we get all the kids we know to vote for Marla. Or for you," she added hastily. "What do you think?"

Cat didn't know what to say. She was almost glad to see Todd approaching their table. At least he'd save her from replying.

"Uh, Cat, could I talk to you for a minute?"

"It's a free country," Cat replied.

"Alone?"

Britt and Trisha were watching with interest. Making a show of reluctance, Cat rose. "All right." She followed him to a booth at the back.

"Okay, we're alone," she said. "Now, what do you want?"

Todd reddened. First he scratched his head. Then he coughed. Then he drummed his fingers on the table.

"See, the thing is, well . . . Cat, I've been thinking."

That's a change, Cat thought. But aloud, she asked, "Thinking about what?"

"About us. Maybe we shouldn't have broken up. We had some good times, remember?"

"I'll tell you what I remember," Cat responded coldly. "I remember that you dumped me and went running back to Heather Beaumount."

"Well, you were grounded," Todd said. "I had to go out with somebody."

Cat didn't know whether to laugh at him or yell at him. What Todd was basically saying was that he needed a girlfriend, and any pretty girl would do. It wasn't very flattering.

"Anyway, Heather and I are through," Todd continued. "So I think you and I should get back together."

Cat almost felt sorry for him. How could he be so dense? She tried to be kind. "Now, Todd, you know that Bailey and I – "

Todd interrupted. "Come on, Cat, it would be great. We could go to all the Winter Carnival activities together. You'll be the Princess and – "

Now it was Cat's turn to break in. "What makes you think I'm going to be the Princess?"

"Well, if we were going together, all the guys on the basketball team would vote for you. Football team, too. With those votes, you're bound to win."

Cat was so startled she was momentarily speechless. When she found her voice, she sputtered, "Todd! Are you trying to bribe me?"

Todd looked at her blankly. "Huh?"

With scepticism, Cat examined his face. But Todd's expression was totally innocent. She had to admit that Todd just wasn't smart enough to come up with a scheme that devious. He was just putting two and two together. If the guys knew that Cat was his girlfriend, he figured she'd be elected Winter Carnival Princess. Knowing how popular Todd was with his teammates, Cat had a feeling he was probably right.

Her head was spinning. She knew exactly what she *should* say. "No, thank you, Todd. You're a nice boy, but I've got another boyfriend now. We weren't all that good together anyway. Let's just be friends."

But the words wouldn't come. All five senses were going in her head and they blocked her power of speech. She could almost hear those words – *Princess Cat*. She could feel the crown being placed on her head, hear the cheers, see her photograph in the newspaper. Up to now, it seemed like a remote possibility. But Todd could help make it all happen.

"Well?" Todd asked impatiently. "How about it?"

"I – I don't know," Cat managed to say. "I have to think about it."

Todd groaned. "Jeez, Cat . . ." But just that minute, a bunch of guys walked into Brownies and spotted him.

"Todd! Over here!"

Todd got up. "See ya later," he told Cat.

She nodded and watched as he joined his friends. Then she glanced back at her own table.

Marla was there now, with Britt and Trisha. But Cat didn't go back to them. Luckily, Brownies was so crowded by now she could probably slip out unnoticed.

She could still feel that crown on her head. And she was afraid Marla might be able to see it.

Upstairs in her bedroom, Becka tied a ribbon around Michelle's hair. "There are some nice people coming to dinner tonight," she told the younger girl. "George and Sally Layton. They own an inn right here in Green Falls."

"Are the MacPhersons coming?" Michelle asked.

"Why, do you have a crush on Red?" Becka teased. "No, I don't think he'll be here, but his mother will. Now, when you meet Mrs. Layton, tell her about that A you got on your book report. And tell Mr. Layton how you climbed the ropes all the way to the top in gym."

"Why?" Michelle asked.

Becka hesitated. Should she tell Michelle she had to impress them, that the Laytons were a real possibility for parents? No, she decided, it was better not to get the orphan's hopes up, just in case things didn't work out. *But it has to work out*, Becka thought anxiously.

Michelle was still waiting for an answer. "Why should I tell them about my essay and climbing the ropes?"

"Oh, just to make conversation," Becka said. "They're nice people, so . . . so you want to be nice to them."

Michelle looked up at her solemnly. "I try to be nice to everyone."

Becka hugged her. "Of course you do. Just be especially nice to the Laytons, okay?"

Michelle still looked puzzled. Maybe she'd forgotten Becka's promise to her. But Becka hadn't. "Come on, let's go."

Downstairs, Becka checked out the living

room. Mr. Layton and Ben were sitting on the sofa, and Josie was sprawled on the floor in front of them. A peal of laughter from the kitchen told her Mrs. Layton was in there with Annie. She could see Cat in the dining room, putting candles on the table.

"There's Mr. Layton," she whispered to Michelle. "Doesn't he look like a nice man?"

Michelle followed Becka to the sofa. "This is Michelle Jones," Becka said. "Michelle, this is Mr. Layton."

"How do you do?" Michelle said, and put out her right hand to shake his. *She looks adorable*, Becka thought. *And definitely adoptable*.

Mr. Layton gave her a jovial grin and took her hand. "I'm very pleased to meet you, Michelle."

"Michelle was just telling me about a spelling test her class had at school," Becka said. "How did you do in that spelling test, Michelle?"

She pretended not to see the puzzled look Ben gave her. Michelle had already told them all about the spelling test when she arrived.

Michelle looked at her in confusion. "I told you before. I won."

"Isn't that terrific?" Becka asked, beaming. "Michelle's an excellent student."

"Congratulations," Mr. Layton said. "You must be quite a speller."

"Well, the words were pretty easy," Michelle replied.

"And she's so modest!" Becka continued. "Not at all conceited."

Michelle squirmed slightly, but Becka wasn't finished. "You're good in all your subjects, aren't you, Michelle?"

"Becka, you're embarrassing her," Josie stated.

"George, did you catch the Celtics game last weekend?" Ben asked.

"Yeah! Wasn't it a great one? That's what I call serious basketball."

"We took Michelle to see Josie play last Saturday," Becka said. "Michelle absolutely *loves* basketball. Don't you, Michelle?"

"I guess. That was the first game I've ever seen."

"But you like sports, right?" She mouthed the word *ropes* at Michelle.

"Becka or Josie!" Annie's voice rang out. "Could one of you come in here?"

"We'll go," Becka said to Josie. Grabbing Michelle's hand, she led her back to the kitchen.

"Hi, Mrs. Layton." She propelled Michelle forward. "This is Michelle."

"Hi, Michelle," Mrs. Layton said.

"Becka, would you put these napkins on the table?" Annie asked.

"I can do it," Michelle said. She took the stack of napkins from the table.

"Isn't she super," Becka gushed. "Offering to help like that! She's so cooperative!"

"She's a very sweet child," Annie murmured. Becka smiled at her gratefully and turned back to Mrs. Layton.

"Michelle lives at Willoughby Hall. Where Cat and Josie and I used to live. Before we were adopted."

"I still can't get over you and Ben having three daughters," Mrs. Layton said to Annie. "And it's worked out so well!"

Annie nodded. "We're very happy. But you wouldn't believe the reaction of some people when we told them we were adopting three!"

"I can just imagine," Mrs. Layton said with a laugh. "Adopting three children at once must be pretty unusual."

"But it's not so unusual to adopt just one," Becka said quickly. "Lots of people do it."

"Let's go into the living room," Annie suggested. "Becka, would you bring in that tray of cider, please?"

Passing through the dining room with the tray, Becka pulled Michelle away from where she was talking to Cat. "Come with me."

"Cat might be a princess!" Michelle said.

"I know, I know. Let's talk to Mrs. Layton."

91

But just as they entered the living room, Ben opened the front door to another guest.

"Mrs. MacPherson!" Michelle exclaimed, and hurried over to greet the Morgan's neighbour.

Becka frowned. It looked like she was going to have to continue to sing Michelle's praises for her. Michelle wasn't catching on to what she needed to be doing. Becka went around the room offering cider and finally got back to Mrs. Layton.

"Mmm, this cider is delicious," Mrs. Layton said.

"Josie made it," Annie told her. "And she taught me how to make the stew we're having tonight."

"You're lucky to have such a talented daughter," Mrs. Layton said with a smile.

Annie put an arm around Becka. "They're all pretty special. I don't know how we'd manage in the store without them."

"I'll bet you wish you had kids who could help you at the inn," Becka said.

Mrs. Layton misunderstood. "Why, thank you, Becka, but we've got a full staff now." She wisely didn't look at Cat when she said it, though Cat blushed anyway. A few weeks before, Cat had worked part-time at the inn – and it had been a disaster.

"I'm going to check on dinner," Annie

said, returning to the kitchen. Becka looked for Michelle. She was still in the midst of an animated conversation with Mrs. MacPherson.

"Did I tell you that Michelle is an orphan?" Becka asked Mrs. Layton.

"Yes, you did mention that. It's nice of you to take such an interest in her."

"She's very special," Becka said. "Don't you think so?"

"Well, I don't really know her," Mrs. Layton replied. "You should bring her over to the inn sometime for tea."

"When?" Becka asked eagerly.

"Oh, anytime you like." Her response was too vague to satisfy Becka.

Annie reappeared. "Dinner's ready, folks." As everyone headed towards the dining room, Becka began to feel desperate. Once they were all at the table, there would be lots of conversation and it would be harder to point out Michelle's virtues to the Laytons. This called for drastic measures.

"Mrs. Layton," Becka said urgently. "Wouldn't you like to have a child?"

Becka could have sworn Mrs. Layton's face became a little pink, and she smiled oddly. Becka understood the reason when they all gathered around the table.

"Sally and I have an announcement to make," Mr. Layton said. He put an arm around his wife. "We're going to have a baby."

Becka managed to keep a fixed smile on her face as a chorus of congratulations rose from the table. But a sickening disappointment filled her. She couldn't bring herself even to look at Michelle.

Six

The shriek from Coach Meadows's whistle pierced the gym. "Okay, that's enough. Over here."

The players gathered on the steps below Coach Meadows for the traditional after-practice assessment of their performance. Expectant faces searched his for some indication of his opinion, but Josie knew from experience there was no point in this. His expression never revealed what he thought of them. They had to wait for him to speak.

As the coach studied his notes, Josie pulled off her sweaty headband. As far as she could tell, this practice session had been pretty decent, but Coach Meadows had keener eyes than she had.

Finally, the coach spoke. "Johnson, you went out of bounds twice. Hayes, your dribble's getting sloppy. A baby could have taken that ball away from you." He continued making individual criticisms as his eyes surveyed the group. Eventually, he got to Josie. "Nice shooting."

Josie winced. Funny, in the past his praise had made her glow inside. Now, it only served to set her apart from the others. She could understand now what Todd had been talking about the day before. And if she needed any more confirmation of how the boys felt, Gary's hostile glance at her provided it.

Having completed his evaluation, Coach Meadows went on. "Now, about the game tomorrow. We all know Henderson Junior High is having a crummy season. Every school in the state has rolled over them. They've become the laughingstock of junior high basketball." He spoke in a quiet, even tone, his penetrating eyes moving from player to player.

"No one's expecting much of a match tomorrow. The fact that the game's at three-thirty on a weekday doesn't help. There won't be a big turn-out in the stands like there was last Saturday." He paused, and added with a hint of a smile, "We'll be lucky if the cheerleaders show up."

The group tittered.

"But don't get cocky!" Coach Meadows roared. The sudden change in tone made

Josie jump, even though she was used to this tactic. "A team can be a breeze one day and a hurricane the next. Henderson wants to win. Any team that wants to win can turn their record around overnight. So don't think you can play sloppy ball and still beat Henderson. You get out there tomorrow and play like you did on Saturday! Okay, hit the showers."

The boys leapt up and ran as a group to their locker room entrance. Alone, Josie went in the opposite direction to hers. But she didn't take her shower immediately. Instead she plunked her elbows down on the counter under the mirror and rested her chin in the palms of her hands.

Her thoughts went back to her first days at Green Falls Junior High. She recalled her disappointment at discovering there was no girls' basketball team, and her determination to get on the boys' team. She remembered how thrilled she had been when the boys agreed with the coach to let her join.

Now, here she was, a fully-fledged member of the basketball team. But she didn't *feel* like a fully-fledged member. No matter how well she played, the boys didn't consider her one of them.

Looking into her reflection, Josie realized something was missing. She clapped a hand to her forehead. Her headband – she'd left it on the court. She shuffled back out to the gym to retrieve it.

She thought the room would be empty, but it wasn't. Gary Cole was on the court, alone, shooting baskets. Or at least, trying to. Over and over he tossed the ball, and it went in every direction but into the basket.

Finally, he got one in. "Good shot!" Josie called.

It took less than a split second for the look of surprise on Gary's face to be replaced with a hostile look. "What's that supposed to mean?"

"Just what I said," Josie replied. "That was a good shot."

Now Gary's expression was a combination of hostility and suspicion. "I suppose you could do better."

Josie had no doubt of that, but she denied it. "I've just been lucky. I think we had a good practice today, don't you?"

Gary sneered. "Good for you, maybe. At least, according to Coach Meadows."

It was a major effort to keep smiling, but Josie was determined not to let him get to her. "I think he just tries to be nice to me because I'm new to the team. Hey, what do you think of that new play we worked on? The one where Todd fakes a throw, gets the ball to Alex, and he sends it to me?"

"I think it's another chance for you to show off," Gary replied shortly.

"If you don't like the plays, why don't you tell him?" Josie asked.

Gary snorted. "He doesn't listen to me."

"You want me to ask him?" It was the wrong question. Gary glared at her.

"Why? You think you've got more influence with the coach than I do?" He uttered a harsh laugh. "Yeah, you probably do. You're Coach's little pet. He doesn't even know what I can do because he never gives me a chance. If it wasn't for you . . . " His voice trailed off.

Josie was pretty sure the coach knew very well how little Gary could do. But as Gary began to stalk off the court, she called out, "Wait!"

Frowning, Gary paused. "What do you want?"

"Why did you say if it wasn't for me? What do I have to do with anything?"

"If it wasn't for you, maybe I'd have a bigger part in that play. Like, Alex could be sending that ball to me instead of you. Then I'd get the credit for the basket."

What basket? Josie wondered. If Gary had the ball, there was no way they could score.

Gary couldn't shoot from that distance. Her expression must have reflected her thoughts, because Gary turned away.

"Wait!" Josie called again.

Now Gary looked positively annoyed. He paused, but he didn't turn completely around.

What she was about to suggest was crazy, totally insane. But if she could win Gary over, the other guys would follow. It was worth the risk.

"Maybe . . . maybe you could take my part in that play."

He turned to face her. *"What?"*

"Like you said: Alex could send the ball to you instead of me."

Gary stared at her in disbelief. "The coach would never go for it. Once he sets a play, that's it."

Josie gulped. "Well, we wouldn't tell him. We'd just do it. We don't even have to tell Alex. Just stay close to me, and once I've got the ball I'll pass it to you."

Gary was speechless for a few seconds. "You – you're going to pass it to me?"

"Yeah."

He cocked his head to one side and eyed her thoughtfully, as if he was seeing her for the first time. "Really?"

"I promise."

Gary nodded. "Okay." And he took off.

Josie went over to the benches and picked up her headband. She clutched it tightly. What had she just promised?

It'll be okay, she assured herself. Like Coach Meadows said, Henderson had a weak team. Green Falls could afford to lose a couple of points.

It was worth it, to win some friends.

Sitting in a booth at Luigi's, Cat drummed her fingers on the tabletop and ignored the soda sitting in front of her. She glanced up at the clock on the wall. *Basketball practice should be over by now*, she thought. *Todd will be here any minute.*

That was assuming he got the note she had left on his locker. But it was a pretty safe bet. He always went by his locker before he left school.

Her eyes swept the restaurant. Thank goodness no one she knew was there. She wouldn't want this meeting to get back to Bailey. Of course, maybe it wouldn't hurt to let Bailey think he had a little competition. On the other hand . . .

She rubbed her head, wanting to erase thoughts of Bailey. His image dissolved, but it was immediately replaced by Marla's.

Hurry up, Todd, she thought. Cat didn't want to be alone with her thoughts. She wanted to stop remembering. But the memories kept flooding back.

Cat had met Marla here, at Luigi's, just a few weeks after she, Josie, and Becka had come to live with the Morgans. From the very beginning, she and Marla had hit it off. They had the same interests, they liked the same clothes, and they both hated Heather Beaumont. That last similarity had sealed their friendship. Throughout all of Cat's conflicts with Heather, Marla had been on Cat's side, giving her support, helping her battle Heather's nasty little schemes, and aiding her with her retaliations.

Marla had introduced Cat to all the right people at Green Falls Junior High. She had steered Cat in the right direction when it came to clubs and activities. They'd shared clothes, makeup, and lots of secrets.

Cat had never had a best friend before. Already, she missed Marla so much.

Cat took a sip of her soda and swallowed hard, trying to get rid of the lump in her throat. Why should she be feeling guilty? It was all Marla's fault, anyway. She shouldn't have tried to hold Cat to that stupid promise. There was no way Cat could keep it, not after being nominated herself.

So Cat might as well go all out and try to win.

She saw Todd coming in the door. How her heartbeat used to quicken when she saw him back in the early days of their romance! Now she felt absolutely nothing. But she knew how to act like she did.

"Hi," she said as he slid into the booth. Cat automatically cocked her head and gave him her sidelong look. The grin he returned assured her that she hadn't lost her touch with him.

"Hiya, babe."

Cat tried not to shudder. She hated to be called "babe." Bailey never called her that. "Were you surprised to get my note?"

"Not really," he said. "I had a feeling you'd come around." He looked satisfied, very pleased with himself. It was incredibly annoying.

"How was your basketball practice?"

That set him off on one of his long, dreary descriptions. Back when they went out together, during football season, Cat had learned to block out these descriptions mentally and use the time to plan her wardrobe for the next week. This time, she tried to pay attention but it was hopeless. Basketball was even more boring than football.

When he paused for breath, she broke in. "Think you'll have a good game tomorrow?"

"Oh yeah, we'll slaughter them," he replied.

"That's nice."

"You want to go out after the game?"

Cat was prepared for this. She lowered her eyelids, then raised them to reveal a look of sincere regret. "I can't, Todd. It's a school night. Annie and Ben have laid down the law about going out on school nights."

"But it doesn't have to be at night," Todd argued. "The game should be over by five-thirty. We could just go for a soda."

Cat had an excuse all ready for that, too. "I have to work in the store after school tomorrow. I won't even be able to come to the game."

Todd's forehead furrowed. "You were always able to get out of working at the store before."

"Well, Annie and Ben have become stricter. You know, making rules, giving advice . . . " It wasn't a total lie. Annie and Ben did give advice, when they were asked for it. In fact, she could remember a bit of advice Annie had offered recently, right after a call from Todd. *Don't go out with him if you don't care about him. That would be using him.*

Well, she wasn't actually planning to go out with him, just to let him think she would. Any date she made, she'd break – after the election.

At least Todd was buying her excuses. "I

guess we'll have to wait till this weekened," he said. "We'll go out on Friday night and celebrate."

"Celebrate?"

"Yeah. By then we'll know that you're going to be the next Winter Carnival Princess."

Cat gave him a wide-eyed look of innocence. "Oh, Todd, do you really think I can win?"

"Sure," he said with total confidence. "I'll tell the guys at the basketball game that we're back together. Word gets around fast, and it'll be all over school by Friday morning. Everyone will know."

Cat's stomach began to jump. Everyone. Including Bailey. She quickly began devising a plan. She'd have to convince Bailey that it was all in Todd's head. Or maybe a rumour Heather was spreading to split them up. Then she could get Marla to—

No. She couldn't ask Marla to do her any favours.

"What's the matter?" Todd asked. "You look like you've got a headache."

"Yeah, I do. I think I'd better go home. I'll talk to you tomorrow, Todd."

"You bet."

Cat rose from the table and made her way to the door. Why did she have the feeling she was getting into a web that was becoming more and more tangled? After all this planning and scheming, she deserved to be Princess.

Once outside, it dawned on her that she really was getting a headache. Maybe it was her imaginary crown. It was beginning to get heavy.

Becka couldn't sleep. She turned from one side to the other, squeezed her eyes shut, counted sheep, but nothing helped.

When she was little, sometimes she couldn't go to sleep because she was afraid she'd have nightmares. Tonight, even a nightmare would be preferable to being awake and thinking about Michelle.

Becka had racked her brain, but she still hadn't been able to come up with any potential parents for the little orphan. She had to face facts. She wasn't going to get Michelle adopted.

Of course, Willoughby Hall wasn't the worst place in the world to live. As orphanages went, Becka thought it was probably okay. But Michelle wanted a family. And Becka had promised her one.

Thank goodness she hadn't told Michelle her hopes for the Laytons. Michelle couldn't have suspected, because she didn't look at all disappointed when the Laytons made their announcement at dinner.

But one of these days, Michelle would remember Becka's promise. She'd want to know where her family was. Becka would have to admit she'd failed her and witness the little girl's heartbreak.

These awful thoughts were making sleep impossible. *Maybe a rummage in the refrigerator will help,* Becka thought. She got out of bed and tiptoed out into the hall.

There was a light coming out from under Josie's door. Becka rapped lightly and went in.

Josie was sitting up in bed, her arms wrapped around her knees. She gave Becka a half-hearted smile. "Can't you sleep either?"

"No," Becka said. "It must be something in the air." She sat down on the edge of Josie's bed. "I just can't stop thinking."

"About what?" Josie asked.

"Keeping promises."

"Yeah." Josie grimaced. "It's really stupid, isn't it? Promising something without thinking about it first. And then you get stuck."

Becka agreed. "I shouldn't give up. But I can't think of anyone."

"What are you talking about?"

"A family for Michelle, of course. Isn't that what you're talking about?"

Josie shook her head. "I'm talking about *my* promise."

The door to her room opened again. Cat

107

was standing there. "What are you guys doing up?"

"We could ask you the same question," Josie replied.

"We can't sleep," Becka told Cat. "I guess you can't either."

"I could sleep if I wanted to," Cat said. "I'm just not tired." She plunked herself down on Josie's bed. "What's going on?"

"We were talking about promises," Becka said. "Josie made a promise she can't keep."

Cat groaned. "I don't want to hear that word." But she didn't leave.

Josie corrected Becka. "I didn't say I *can't* keep it. I'm just not sure I want to."

"What kind of promise?" Becka asked. She listened with interest as Josie told her about Gary Cole.

"Why did you tell him you'd pass the ball to him if he can't get it through the basket?" she asked.

"So the others would accept me," Josie explained. "So they'd treat me like one of the guys."

Cat wrinkled her nose. "Who wants to be treated like one of the guys?"

"*I* do," Josie replied. "But I shouldn't have to do something stupid like this. When you're on a team, you're supposed to do whatever you can do to help your team win. If I give

108

this ball to Gary like I promised . . . well, we probably won't lose. But it certainly won't help us win."

"Then don't do it," Cat said.

"And break my promise to Gary?"

Cat shrugged. "Sure."

Becka was shocked. "Cat! Breaking promises is wrong!"

"You broke your promise to Michelle," Cat pointed out.

"But not on purpose!" Becka exclaimed. "At least I've tried to keep it. And I still might find a family for her."

"Oh yeah?" Cat challenged her. "Like who?"

Becka sat very still. An idea, something she'd never considered before, had suddenly sprung up in the back of her mind. Was it crazy? Totally unrealistic? Maybe not.

She spoke slowly. "How would you guys feel about having a little sister?"

Josie's mouth dropped open. "Becka!"

"Are you nuts?" Cat asked.

"Just listen," Becka said eagerly. "You both like Michelle. Annie and Ben do, too. They've got three daughters. What difference would one more make?"

This was probably the first time she'd ever seen Josie and Cat wearing the same expression – total, utter disbelief.

"It's not so crazy," Becka insisted. "Just think about it for a minute. Can you come up with one good reason why we shouldn't adopt Michelle?"

"*I* can," Cat said. "We've each finally got our own bedroom. And there aren't any more in this house."

"I'd share mine with her," Becka said. But even as she spoke, a little uncertainty crept into her voice. She loved having her own room.

"There's no point in even discussing this," Josie stated firmly. "It's not our decision to make. You have to ask Annie and Ben. But don't get your hopes up. Adopting three daughters was a pretty outrageous thing for them to do. No matter how much they like Michelle, I don't think they're up for a fourth."

Becka knew there was logic in what she said. "But it's the only way I can keep my promise to her!"

"Oh, Becka," Cat said in disgust. "You're making such a big deal out of this."

"Promises *are* a big deal," Becka shot back. "Maybe not to you, but – "

"Yeah," Josie interrupted. "I don't get it, Cat. Isn't Marla your best friend?"

Cat stiffened. "She was."

"I guess being Winter Carnival Princess must mean an awful lot to you," Becka said.

Cat was quiet for a minute. "Of course it does. Getting something like that . . . well, it means you're special."

Becka considered that. "I guess it's pretty exciting. But you'd only be special for one night."

Josie agreed. "I'll bet nobody even remembers who last year's Winter Carnival Princess was."

"The Princess gets her picture in the newspaper," Cat pointed out.

"And you know what people do with newspapers after they read them?" Josie asked. "Throw 'em in the garbage."

Becka spoke up quickly. "Or recycle them, if they care about the environment."

Josie shrugged. "Either way, they're gone."

"That's true," Becka said. "Being Winter Carnival Princess is a one-night deal. Friendships last forever." She could have gone on talking about the meaning of friendship, but the look on Cat's face stopped her. In fact, she was completely taken aback by the expression. Cat was as close to tears as Becka had ever seen her.

But when Cat spoke, her voice was harsh. "Okay, I made Marla a promise. But then I was nominated. There's nothing I can do about it now."

"Maybe there is . . . " Josie said slowly.

111

"What are you saying?" Cat's eyes darkened. Then she clapped a hand to her mouth. "You're not suggesting I withdraw my name from the candidates, are you?"

The horror in her voice made Becka feel really, truly sorry for Cat. But Josie was making a good point. "It's a way to keep your promise. Like I'm going to keep mine. And Josie . . ." She paused and turned to her.

"Yeah," Josie said in a tired voice. "I'll keep mine."

Becka turned back to Cat. "What are you going to do?"

Cat tossed her head, but the gesture didn't have the confidence it normally did. She rose from the bed and went to the door. "I'm going to sleep."

Seven

Becka was waiting for the right moment.

Breakfast in the Morgan household tended to be a cozy time. Annie always insisted that everyone needed a good, unrushed breakfast to get them all going. She made sure that they were all at the table on time and together, and she wouldn't tolerate any dawdling, not even from Cat. She didn't allow Ben to read his newspaper at the table, either. Breakfast was a family time, and it was usually a noisy time, with all of them talking about their plans for the day.

But not this morning. Silence reigned at the table. Josie ate her porridge methodically, like a robot who wasn't even aware of what was being eaten. Cat stirred hers listlessly with one hand, using the other hand to twist a lock of hair, a sure sign that she was preoccupied with her thoughts.

Becka was eating, but without giving much attention to her breakfast. She was too busy examining her parents' faces, trying to assess their moods. Her eyes darted back and forth between them.

"Mmm, this porridge is delicious," Ben remarked. "What did you put in it?"

"Cinnamon," Annie told him. "And nutmeg. It's a trick Josie taught me."

"It certainly doesn't taste like the bland porridge I used to get when I was a kid," Ben said. "Josie, did you learn this at Willoughby Hall?"

Josie blinked. "Huh?"

"Did Mrs. Parker at Willoughby Hall teach you to make this porridge?"

"Yeah."

Becka didn't miss the puzzled looks Ben and Annie exchanged. This might not be the perfect time, but at least Ben's words had given her an opening.

"Speaking of Willoughby Hall, don't you think Michelle is sweet?"

"Of course, dear," Annie said. But her attention was now on Cat. "Cat, you haven't touched your porridge."

"What?"

"Don't you like the porridge?"

Cat looked down at the bowl as if she was seeing it for the first time. "Oh yeah, it's terrific." But her tone was flat.

Annie glanced at Ben, and then bit her lip. Becka knew what that meant. She was dying to ask the girls what was bothering them, but she didn't want to pry.

She finally gave in. "Is there something you girls want to talk about? Or ask us?"

Ben picked up on that. "You know there's nothing you should ever be afraid of saying to us."

The right time had come. "Yes, there's something I want to ask," Becka announced. "It's about Michelle."

"What about her?" Ben asked.

Becka chose her words carefully. "Well, it's like this. We were talking last night, Cat and Josie and I . . . " She faltered. Her eyes beseeched Cat and Josie for help, but they were both lost in their own thoughts.

"Yes?" Annie said encouragingly.

"We were talking about Michelle." The next words came out in a rush. "She's so sweet and we really like her and we wondered if you and Ben might want to adopt her."

Their immediate reaction didn't surprise her. In her private fantasies, she'd imagined gasps of joy, applause, cries of "Why didn't we think of that first?". But in reality, she suspected the response would be pretty much what she was now seeing. Total astonishment.

Ben spoke as if he wasn't sure he had heard correctly. "Adopt Michelle?"

"She wants a family so much," Becka said. "She loves being with us, and she's comfortable here."

"Oh, Becka," Annie sighed. "Oh, dear." *That* wasn't very encouraging.

"Don't you like Michelle?" Becka asked.

"Of course we like her," Ben said. "She's a very nice little girl."

"I'm sure we'd like every orphan at Willoughby Hall if we knew them," Annie added. "And I'm sure every one of them would like a home. But honey, that doesn't mean we can adopt them all."

"We don't have to adopt them all," Becka said. "Just Michelle."

Annie gave her a sad, apologetic smile. "I'm sorry, Becka. But we just can't adopt another child. We're happy we've got you three – "

"But three daughters are about all I can handle," Ben teased. Then he caught himself. "I shouldn't joke. This must mean a lot to you."

"I knew you liked Michelle," Annie said. "But I didn't realize you'd become that attached to her. Cat, what about you?"

"Huh?"

"Do you feel that strongly about Michelle?"

"Michelle who?"

116

"Cat!" Becka exclaimed.

"Oh yeah, sure," Cat said hastily.

The slightest hint of doubt crossed Annie's face. "Josie? Did you want us to adopt Michelle?"

"It would have been okay with me," Josie said. But her voice definitely lacked any real conviction.

Annie and Ben exchanged looks.

"Becka, tell the truth," Ben said. "Why do you want us to adopt Michelle?"

Becka squirmed. Both her parents were waiting for an answer. She'd never been able to sweet-talk them like Cat. It was confession time. She gave them a weak smile. "Well, I sort of promised her I'd find her a family. And I can't think of anyone else."

Ben looked like he was about to explode. "Becka! You've got no business making promises like that!"

"Darling, we know you meant well," Annie added hastily. "But you can't make promises you're not capable of keeping!"

Becka hung her head. "I know that. *Now*."

Ben groaned. "I thought I had made myself perfectly clear on that subject before." He glanced at Cat. Now she began to squirm.

"But what am I going to say to Michelle?" Becka asked plaintively.

"Tell her the truth," Annie said. "Tell her

117

you wish you could help her, but you made a mistake in promising her a family, and that you're sorry."

"I just feel so awful about this," Becka moaned.

Ben reached over and stroked her head. "Well, we all make mistakes. Just chalk it up to experience." He turned to Josie. "At least you can learn from your sisters' mistakes and avoid getting yourself into a predicament like this."

Josie squirmed.

Well, it certainly didn't look like Becka was going to be able to keep her promise, Cat thought as she walked into school. She still didn't know about her own.

It was fairly quiet in the building. Becka had had to get to school early for a newspaper meeting, and if they wanted a ride, the other two had to come along, or else walk almost a mile through the slush of melting snow.

Cat ran into Bailey in the entrance hall. A smile spread across his face when he spotted her. "Hi," she said. "What are you doing here so early?"

"I have to use the library before school starts. But I wanted to see you first."

Fear closed her throat. Despite his smile,

she wondered if he'd found out about her meeting with Todd yesterday. "Why?"

"Just wanted to see you. No particular reason." His smile broadened. "I like looking at you."

Cat smiled back. He was really so sweet.

"Especially when you smile," he added. After a second, he asked, "What's wrong?

Cat was looking beyond him. "Check that out."

Bailey turned. Heather was at the other end of the lobby, surrounded by a bunch of boys. What made that unusual was the fact that they were all seventh-graders, and Heather never spoke to seventh-graders.

"They must be members of some club," Cat murmured. The boys were gazing at Heather in awe. They were obviously thrilled to have this pretty, popular eighth-grade girl paying attention to them. And they'd remember her name when it was time to vote for Winter Carnival Princess tomorrow.

Bailey read her mind and shook his head ruefully. "She's just using those poor guys. After tomorrow she won't even know them." He looked at Cat seriously. "I'm glad you're not like that, out campaigning for this thing. I mean, it would be nice if you win, but it's no big deal, really – why are you looking at me like that?"

She could have said something cute and flip and flirty. But she didn't. All she could do was repeat what he'd said to her. "Because I like looking at you."

He grinned. "I wish we could spend all day looking at each other, but I'd better get to the library. See you later."

She nodded and didn't try to make him linger. She had somewhere to go, too.

She'd already written out the note. It lay neatly folded between the covers of one of her books. She'd even remembered to put some tape in her purse so she could stick the note to the locker door.

But as she rounded the corner to the hallway, she saw that the note wouldn't be necessary. Todd was standing there, twirling the combination on his locker.

"You're here early," she said.

"Yeah, I've got detention for being late yesterday. Look, are you sure you can't get out of working at the store? We're going to mutilate Henderson this afternoon, and I'm going to feel like celebrating."

"No, I can't go out with you this afternoon," Cat said. She took a deep breath. "Or this weekend. Or ever."

Todd scratched his head. "What do you mean?"

"I mean . . . I mean, I've had some time

to think it over. And I don't want to get back together with you."

He still looked puzzled. "Why not?"

She recited the words on her note from memory. "Because I don't care about you, not that way. You're a nice person and I hope we can be friends, but that's all." She marvelled at how adult she sounded.

Maybe too adult for Todd. Confusion remained on his face. "I don't get it."

Cat sighed. She reached into her book and pulled out the note. "Here. Read it over a few times. It's got to sink in eventually."

She turned away and went back down the hall. The first part of her mission was accomplished. Now came the hardest part.

The main office was empty. Cat waited a minute, then called, "Hello?"

Ms. Sanders, the secretary, emerged from the principal's office. "Hello, Catherine. What can I do for you?"

Cat took a deep breath. "It's about the election for Winter Carnival Princess."

Ms. Sanders looked at her reprovingly. "The election's tomorrow, Catherine. And you know the results are kept confidential until Winter Carnival week."

That's what you think, Cat thought. From what she'd heard, the entire student body knew who won within hours of the vote. But aloud, she said, "Oh, I'm not interested in the results, Ms. Sanders. It's about the ballot."

Ms. Sanders pursed her lips. "The names are listed alphabetically, Catherine. Your name cannot come first on the ballot."

Cat was getting annoyed. It was bad enough having to do what she was about to do, without Ms. Sanders misinterpreting her intentions. "I don't *want* my name to come first. In fact, what I want you to do is . . . is . . . " Why was she having such a hard time saying it? Maybe because it was such an out-of-character thing for her to be doing.

It took every ounce of willpower she had to finally get the words out. "I want you to take my name off the ballot."

Ms. Sanders looked dumbfounded. "*What?*"

Cat held her head high. "I wish to withdraw my candidacy."

The secretary's eyebrows rose. "You don't want to be the Winter Carnival Princess?"

Odd, how some lies came easily to her while others were caught in her throat. "No . . . "

"I find that difficult to believe," Ms. Sanders stated.

Cat forced herself to look directly into the secretary's eyes. They were bright with interest. Cat felt a sudden, urgent need to confide. This mature, impartial, down-to-earth woman might be just the right person.

Plus, Cat wanted to prove to Ms. Sanders that she really wasn't the kind of girl the secretary seemed to think she was – someone who was just out for herself. Or maybe she just wanted to prove that to herself.

She leaned across the desk and said softly: "See, Marla Eastman is one of the candidates, and she's my best friend. I want her to win."

The secretary's lips twitched. "And you think she can't win if *you* are on the ballot?"

Why did this woman have to make her sound like she was so conceited? But she didn't want to go into the whole complicated story, so she just nodded.

"Marla Eastman is a very popular and well-liked student," Ms. Sanders said. "I believe she has as good a chance as you have to be selected."

"I just want to help her – " Cat began, but the secretary wouldn't let her finish.

"It's too late anyway," the woman said briskly. "The ballots are already prepared."

Slowly, Cat let out her breath. She just stood there deflated for a minute. Then she murmured, "Thanks anyway," and left the office.

Becka and Josie were waiting outside. "I saw you go in there," Becka said, her eyes wide. "You really did it! You took your name off the ballot!"

"I never thought you had it in you," Josie said with grudging respect.

Cat didn't even allow herself a moment to bask in their admiration. "I tried, but it was too late. The ballots are already made."

"Oh." Becka's shoulders slumped. "Then I guess you won't be keeping your promise either."

"Boy, we *are* a bunch of idiots," Josie mumbled.

Cat wasn't about to lump her serious situation in the same category as their silly promises. "Speak for yourself." She started to walk away, but then she stopped and turned back. "Hey, Josie, when you have your game this afternoon . . . "

"What about it?"

Cat drew herself up proudly. "Tell the guys to vote for Marla."

As if the guys would listen to her, Josie thought, remembering Cat's request. Well, she had to give Cat some credit. At least she was making a stab at keeping her promise. Sometime in the next few minutes, Josie would have to make a decision about hers.

So far, Coach Meadows had been right about this game. There weren't many people in the stands, just some classmates who didn't have anything better to do after school. The few cheers she heard were pretty weak. Even the cheerleaders didn't seem to be leaping as high as they normally did.

She could understand why every school in the state had rolled over Henderson. These guys were pathetic. They were into the fourth quarter, and the score was fifty to twelve. Green Falls could afford to do without her points today, Josie thought. It would be easy to pass a ball to Gary. If the coach questioned her about her action later, she could always say she got confused, or she forgot the play, or something.

Josie was suddenly aware of the ball coming in her direction. She made a dash for it, but it was too late, and one of the Henderson guards caught it.

It was so hard to keep her mind on the game! Over and over, she saw herself sending that ball to Gary, which amounted to sending it directly to the opposition. Okay, Coach Meadows wouldn't like it, but only she'd know she'd done it on purpose. Well, Gary would know, but he'd never tell. Everyone would forget about it. Except her. She would know that she'd deliberately done something that was not in the best interests of the team. It would be sitting on her conscience.

"Morgan!" someone yelled.

Josie realized a Henderson player was about

to go past her, dribbling the ball. She darted forward, and easily slipped the ball away from him. Dribbling, she headed down towards their basket. Then she caught Gary's eye.

Would this be a good time to send the ball to him? She could get it over with. But as she was debating, some pipsqueak from Henderson moved in front of her. Suddenly her ball was gone.

There were only a few minutes remaining. Josie began to hope that maybe she wouldn't have to make a decision about Gary. The play where she'd promised to pass the ball to Gary couldn't go into effect unless Todd got the ball from Alex. And Todd hadn't been playing as well as usual. He seemed to be having a hard time concentrating, too. He might miss the ball completely. If the play never went into motion, it would cancel her promise.

But her hopes were dashed when a Henderson forward, in a feeble attempt to throw the ball to one of his teammates, sent it almost directly into Alex's hands. Alex moved as if he was about to throw the ball to the player on his left, then quickly turned and tossed it to Todd.

Todd woke up. He pretended to aim toward the hoop. Then he threw the ball towards Josie.

Josie grabbed it. Frantically, her eyes searched the court for Gary. But he was so far away! Why hadn't he come closer to her, like she'd told him to? Even if by some miracle he could catch her ball, there was no way, absolutely no way he could get it in the basket.

There were only seconds left. Everyone's eyes were on her. Gary was waiting for her to keep her promise.

But Josie couldn't. It was wrong. She'd made a very stupid promise. Just like Becka and Cat, she couldn't keep it.

She threw the ball at the hoop. For what seemed like an eternity, the ball teetered on the rim of the basket. Then it fell off the side.

Of course, it didn't really matter. They'd still win. At least she'd blown the points honestly.

Josie couldn't even hear the buzzer that signalled the end of the game. She was thinking about facing Gary.

But first, she had to face Coach Meadows. They all did. And despite their win, the coach did not look happy.

"You guys were lucky!" he thundered. "You sure didn't win that game with skill! I've never seen such sloppy playing in my life! Murphy, you were a space cadet! Benson, I don't think you moved twelve inches out there!" He whirled around. "Morgan! You weren't even watching the ball! You didn't even aim for that last basket!"

"I'm sorry," Josie mumbled, but the coach had gone on to reprimand someone else.

"You make me sick, all of you!" he yelled. "If you don't shape up, I'm going to be looking for a new team!" With that and a final look of disgust, he marched out of the gym.

No one seemed very upset by his comments. They were all used to the way Coach Meadows yelled and criticized and threatened.

"Hey, we weren't *that* bad," Todd said.

"Yeah, Henderson wasn't worth too much effort anyway," another boy commented.

"Look, we won, didn't we?" Alex slapped a player on the back. Now that the coach was out of sight, they all went into their usual post-victory performance – back slapping, high fives, rustling each other's hair.

So far, Josie had managed to avoid Gary. But any minute now he'd confront her. She started to slink away.

Then she felt it. A slap. On her back. She turned in disbelief. Gary stood there. "So Miss Perfect wasn't so hot today, huh?" He was grinning.

There was another slap on her back. She wasn't even sure who it came from. Alex ruffled her hair. It dawned on her that there were other guys around her. She wasn't on the outside of the circle.

"Come on, let's go to Luigi's," one guy yelled. There was a general chorus of agreement. For the first time, Josie knew the invitation included her.

Eight

"Was that the phone?" Cat asked anxiously, pulling herself up to a sitting position.

"No, honey, it's the tea kettle," Annie replied. She rose from the rocking chair and went back to the kitchen. Cat let out a deep, heart-wrenching sigh and lay back down on the couch. It was already seven o'clock on Friday evening. How long did it take to count ballots, anyway?

Ben was moving logs in the fireplace with a poker, sending the flames higher. "For a city fellow, I think I've become pretty darn good at this. Isn't this a beautiful fire, girls?"

"Beautiful," Cat muttered.

"Yeah, it's beautiful," Becka echoed, in the same dismal tone.

"Boy, you guys are a couple of deadbeats," Josie announced. "Ben, this has got to be the most gorgeous fire in the state of Vermont. Maybe in the universe."

"Thank you, Josie," Ben said.

Annie returned with her tea and sat down by Cat. "Ah, this is nice. A quiet, cozy family evening at home, just us."

Ben agreed. "But it would be even nicer if we could see happy faces on all our daughters."

Josie faced her sisters with her hands on her hips. "Cheer up, you guys. Look, we all tried. We did our best. Like you said, Ben, we all make mistakes, right?"

"Right," he replied. "Though I must say, Josie, I'm still amazed that all three of you got yourselves into these predicaments."

"Oh well, that's life," Josie said. "It's all over and done with. We can't mope forever."

"That's easy for you to say," Becka murmured. "You didn't keep your promise, but everything worked out for you."

"Yeah, weird, isn't it," Josie responded cheerfully.

"Do you think Gary forgot about your promise?" Annie asked.

"No," Josie said. "He told me he couldn't get close enough for me to throw it to him. But he thinks I would have thrown it to him if he'd been in the right position. As long as he thinks that, he'll believe I kept my promise! Personally, even though he'd never admit it, I

131

think Gary stayed away from me on purpose. He must know what a bad player he is."

"Then why did he agree to go along with you in the first place?" Becka asked.

"He just wanted to see if I *would* do it. It was like a test. He thought I always wanted to show off and be the team star. I'm sure he was really happy when I didn't make that last basket."

Ben stopped poking at the fire and eyed her quizzically. "Did you miss that basket on purpose?"

"No," Josie said. "I was just having a bad game. It happens." She gave them a cocky grin. "Even to me."

"It all worked out for the best," Annie said.

Josie nodded happily. "Now that the coach has yelled at me like he yells at them, they can accept me."

"I don't understand," Becka said. "You play badly, and the guys like you better. It doesn't make sense."

"Sure it does," Josie argued. "Look, I've been playing really well so far this season. The guys were jealous."

"Boys can be so immature," Cat said.

"Exactly," Josie said. "But as soon as I messed up, they saw that I'm not perfect." She snapped her fingers. "Poof! Now I'm one of them."

Listening to Josie chatter was making Cat feel even more disgruntled. There was something very annoying about Josie's happiness, when she herself was so tense and irritable. She looked at Josie through narrowed eyes. "I don't suppose you remembered to do what I asked you to."

Josie went blank. "What did you ask me to do?"

"Tell your teammates to vote for Marla."

"Oh. No, I forgot."

"Figures," Cat grumbled.

"When do you find out who won?" Annie asked Cat.

"We're not supposed to find out until the Princess is announced at the Winter Carnival. But Trisha has a connection on the Student Council who's going to call her tonight as soon as they've counted the votes. Then she's going to call me."

"Who did you vote for?" Josie asked Becka.

"Don't ask her that," Ben admonished. "This is America. Voting is a private matter."

"For crying out loud," Josie said. "We're not exactly talking about President of the United States."

Cat stirred restlessly. The phone hadn't rung in ages. "Do you think the phone might be out of order?"

A shrill ring provided an immediate answer

133

to her question. Cat leaped up. "I'll get it."
She flew out of the room.

"Hello?"

"Hello, Cat, this is Helen MacPherson. Is your mother there?"

Cat heaved another sigh. "Just a minute, I'll get her."

She went back to the living room. "Annie, it's Mrs. MacPherson." Annie got up and left the room. Cat flung herself back down on the sofa.

"I wonder if I should call her," Becka mumbled.

"Call who?" Josie asked.

"Michelle."

"Oh, quit worrying about her," Cat ordered. "I'll bet she's forgotten all about your promise."

"Sure she has," Becka retorted. "Just like Marla's forgotten yours."

Annie returned. "Helen and Red are going to drop by in a bit. She says they have a surprise for us."

She'd barely finished speaking when there was a knock on the door. "Good grief, that was fast," Ben said.

But it wasn't Helen MacPherson. Cat jerked up at the sound of the familiar voice.

"Hello, Mrs. Morgan. Is Cat home?"

"Yes, Marla, come in."

Cat rose from the couch, turned, and faced her. "Hi, Marla."

"Hi, Cat."

For a few seconds, they both just stood there, their eyes not really meeting. From the floor, Becka and Josie stared at Marla with undisguised curiosity.

"Um, I wanted to talk to you," Marla finally said. The word *alone* was unspoken, but Cat knew Marla well enough to hear it.

"Come on up to my room."

Marla followed Cat up the stairs. Once they were in Cat's room, Cat sat down on her bed, while Marla kept standing. "Why don't you take your coat off?"

"I can't stay long."

"Oh."

There was a moment of silence. Then, as casually as she could, Cat asked, "Have you heard from Trisha yet?"

Marla shook her head. "Have you?"

"No."

Marla went over to Cat's dresser and began to examine her perfume bottles. "It's going to be weird for someone, finding out she's going to be Princess. And then having to pretend she's surprised when it's officially announced."

"Yeah," Cat replied.

There was another moment of silence. "I came to tell you I'm sorry," Marla said.

"Sorry?"

Marla smiled sheepishly. "I've been a real jerk. I should have known you'd keep your promise."

Cat looked at her in total confusion. Dimly, she heard a phone ringing downstairs. A second later, she heard Josie's voice bellow, "Cat! It's for you!"

Cat went to the door. "I'll get it up here," she yelled back. She went into her parents' bedroom and picked up the receiver.

"Hello?"

"Cat, it's Trisha."

Cat listened very carefully as Trisha relayed her message. Then she went back to her room.

"What were you saying about my promise?"

"I didn't find out till this afternoon. One of the guys on the basketball team told me."

"Told you what?"

"Oh, come on, Cat, you know what you did."

Cat looked at her uncertainly. "Tell me what you heard."

"I heard that Todd Murphy told all his buddies to vote for me."

For a moment, Cat didn't comprehend what she was saying. "Todd did what?"

Marla rolled her eyes. "Quit acting like you

don't know anything about it. It's common knowledge that he still has a major passion for you. I know you must have gotten him to do it."

Suddenly, it all made sense. It must have finally penetrated Todd's thick skull that Cat wasn't going to start seeing him again. He got angry, and wanted to get back at her. He certainly wouldn't tell the guys to vote for Heather, after she'd dumped him. The only way he could ensure that Cat wouldn't win was to make the guys vote for Marla."

"I know it couldn't have been easy for you," Marla continued. "Playing up to him when you don't really care about him anymore. But you did it for me." Her eyes were shining. "Oh, Cat, I've been so awful. You really are a friend."

Now that she'd recovered from her confusion, Cat could smile modestly. "Well, after all, I did promise to help you."

"And you kept your promise. That's what really matters. Win or lose, I don't really care anymore." She unbuttoned her coat. "Maybe I will stay a while. Who was that on the phone? Bailey?"

"No, it was Trisha."

Marla looked almost comical, frozen with her coat dangling off one arm. "What – what did you say?"

Cat fingered a lock of hair. Should she enjoy the drama of the moment for a while? No, that would be too cruel. For days, she'd felt like she was wearing a crown on her head. Magically, it had turned into a halo.

She cocked her head and eyed Marla thoughtfully.

"How good are you at acting surprised?"

Becka couldn't believe her ears when she heard peals of laughter coming from upstairs. A moment later, Cat and Marla came running down.

"May I have everyone's attention?" Cat asked. "I'd like to present to you the next Green Falls Junior High Winter Carnival Princess!"

Becka gasped. While Annie, Ben, and Josie congratulated Marla, she examined Cat's face. She didn't even look upset.

"I owe it all to Cat," Marla told them. "I know she must have wanted to be Princess, but she sacrificed that for me. She promised me she'd help, and she did!"

Josie gaped. Ben and Annie were staring at Cat as if they were trying to figure out who had taken over their daughter's body. Becka was incredulous. "She did? How?"

Cat shot her a fierce look. Then she smiled at Marla. "Let's keep that to ourselves."

138

Ben and Annie still wore identical expressions of disbelief. But they didn't press the question.

Annie got up. "This calls for a celebration. Josie, want to give me a hand in the kitchen?"

Ben went to the stereo and put some music on. Cat started quizzing Marla on what she would wear for the crowning and who she would ask to be her escort. A few moments later, Annie and Josie reappeared with a cake and a pitcher of cider.

Becka curled up closer to the fire and observed the celebration through dull eyes. It wasn't fair. She and Cat and Josie had all made the same stupid mistake. But she was the only one who was still suffering.

When the doorbell rang, she didn't stir, even though she was the closest to the door.

"That must be the MacPhersons," Annie said.

She was right. The door opened to Helen and Red MacPherson. But they weren't alone.

Becka stood up. "Michelle!"

The little orphan ran across the room and threw her arms around Becka. "Oh, Becka," she said. "Thank you!"

"For what?" Becka asked stupidly.

"What's going on?" Annie asked in bewilderment.

"I wanted you all to meet someone very

special," Helen said, her warm eyes resting on Michelle.

"We already know Michelle," Josie said.

"You know Michelle *Jones*," Mrs. MacPherson corrected her. "This is Michelle MacPherson. Or at least, she *will* be. As soon as the final adoption papers are signed."

Annie squealed and clapped her hands while Ben embraced Mrs. MacPherson. Josie let out a whoop. Red swooped Michelle up in the air.

Becka was in a state of shock. When the full impact of Mrs. MacPherson's announcement finally hit her, she felt almost dizzy. Then Mrs. MacPherson came over and embraced her. "We owe this to you, Becka. Why, if you hadn't brought Michelle to visit, we might never have met."

"I didn't even know you were considering adoption," Annie said.

"Neither did my mother," Red said laughing. "But every time she saw Michelle, she'd go on and on talking about her. And when I reminded her that I'd always wanted a kid sister – "

"That clinched it," Mrs. MacPherson finished.

Michelle was hopping up and down. "I'm going to have a mother and a brother and my own room and a horse – golly, Becka, when you promised you'd find me a family, I didn't really believe you could. But you did it!"

"I did it," Becka repeated in wonderment. "I don't know how. But I did it!"

Bailey arrived a few minutes later. Then a couple of guys from Josie's basketball team dropped by. The quiet family evening turned into a real party.

The MacPhersons were the last to leave. A sleepy-eyed Michelle clung to Red's hand as Becka accepted more thanks from Mrs. MacPherson.

"This is amazing," Josie remarked when the family was finally alone. "None of us could really keep our promises. But everyone *thinks* we did. And everything worked out the way we wanted it to!"

Ben looked sceptical. "It seems to me that you're all taking a lot of credit for things you haven't really done."

"Actually, in a way, I *did* keep my promise," Cat said. "If I hadn't told Todd I wouldn't go out with him, he wouldn't have told the guys to vote for Marla."

"Me, too," Becka said. "I mean, I never considered the MacPhersons as a family for Michelle. But I *did* introduce her to them. So I guess I kept my promise, too."

Ben's forehead puckered. He shook his head wearily, frowned, and sat down.

"Now, Ben, don't worry about it," Annie said. "The girls know what they did."

"But have they learned anything from this?" Ben asked. He turned to his daughters. "Look, I'm glad everything's worked out for the best. But let's not have any more foolish promises. Try not to get yourselves into these kinds of situations again. Don't take on things you can't handle, or bite off more than you can chew. Okay?"

Becka, Josie, and Cat exchanged looks. Becka could tell they were all thinking the same thing. It was irresistible. With solemn faces, they all raised their right hands and spoke in unison.

"We promise." Then they dissolved in laughter at the look on Ben's face.